This Mess We Made

Bronwyn Stuart

For the survivors.

CW: This book is based on the lives of two people. One is
a war hero in hiding and the other is an actress taken down
first by fear, and then by vice. The subject matter bleeds into
the pages and includes but isn't limited to personal attack,
personal loss, post-traumatic stress and battle violence. If you
go on this journey with Callum and Audrey, I can guarantee
you a satisfying ending that is all the more beautiful for how
hard the fight is...

One

♥

Callum West had zero problems with self-medicating. He was still a doctor with a prescription pad after all, but when a high-powered engine sped past his houseboat at the crack of dawn, the sound broke through his sleeping pill haze and he came to with a start.

He waited for the inevitable rocking to begin, sitting bolt upright in bed, the sheets bunched around his hips, and then swore. "Fucking moron." What was it about losers and their pleasure crafts who thought it was okay to wake people before- He swore again. Half past ten?

Rubbing the sleep from his eyes, he stood and stretched. Then he performed his only homage to the OCD gods, tapping his left arm, then his right. His left leg and then the right. He flexed his fingers and curled his toes, rolled his head and cracked his neck. Yep. All of his limbs were still there, still working, still whole.

What had started as a joke between he and his buddies in Afghanistan had become a religious practice for Callum all these years later. He'd seen too many men wake up after the crude anaesthesia had worn off and reach for something only to remember the IED that wiped out half their patrol had also taken their hand, their arm, their legs. They were the unlucky ones. To Callum, the lucky ones never woke up to reach for anything.

This is usually how he woke up after a week of insomnia and then giving into the sleeping tablets in the early hours. Cranky. Wound up. Glad he lived alone and didn't have to face a smiling, bouncy bundle of female over the breakfast table talking about happily ever afters and squealing about her plans for the day.

Damn. He needed coffee and a shower. In that order. Padding around his ancient houseboat in nothing but a worn pair of board shorts, he turned on the percolator and then went outside in an attempt to greet the day. It was going to be a hot one which was probably why the moron from earlier thought it was okay to speed around on the river and make a nuisance of himself. Ten years ago that would have been Callum and his mates, blowing off steam in their down-time. Summer didn't last long so hot weekends were at a premium and packed with water skiing and tubing from sunup to sundown.

How nice it would be to return to that state of naivety. No more worry than what to have for breakfast to cure the hangover. Before he knew the realities of war. Back when he'd been a stupid intern with stupid ideals. Before he knew more than he wanted to about meatball surgery in the middle of the desert. The stuff he'd seen in his years in the Australian Army made M*A*S*H look like a friggin' Hawaiian vacation.

Callum barely tasted the coffee but he knew it was strong and bitter, a lot like him. Maybe his godmother had been right when she'd warned him he'd need a hobby if he wanted to be *so* alone. He'd laughed then but as the months rolled by after her death, he'd come to realise she was right. That bloody woman was always right. Drunker than two skunks most of the time but she always knew what was going on with the people around her.

He missed Mavis and wondered for the billionth time in his life if there was a heaven for the special ones.

"Jesus," he cursed, the sound echoing across the still-as-glass water and bouncing back off the towering red cliff face on the other side of the Murray River. He was in bad shape and possibly even in need of some human company.

He looked through his cupboard searching for something appropriate to wear to town, or what passed for a town in Jupiter Creek, and decided he had to shop for food anyway. He might even make a day of it and head into Mannum or Murray Bridge. He hated crowds but sometimes he had to test the edges of his self-imposed limits just to make sure he hadn't died and was living in stunning purgatory for his half-sins.

When he had all he needed, he jumped from the back of the houseboat to the landing, his bare feet sinking into the thick carpet of cool grass before he walked up to the house.

Mavis's house.

Sure, he had a shower on the boat but it only dripped water on the back of his neck. He liked the hard spray of her shower. Before her death, she'd liked him to come inside so she knew he was okay. That's what she said anyway. He knew she craved the company and he liked to make sure she'd survived the night and her own personal demons.

When he stepped through the back door, he inhaled the earthy scent of Mavis's kitchen. Even though she was gone, the house still smelled like her. Not like ten-day old gin but like cloves and spices and home. It's why he'd stayed after the funeral. No one had come to kick him out and when the bills arrived at Jupiter Creek's post office, Nancy gave them to him and he just paid them and kept going on.

He had the words on a bumper sticker on his ute, *Just Keep On Keeping On*. Not his motto but when he'd bought the workhorse, he hadn't wanted to take it off just in case it left a mark.

Ignoring the sad memories and the calls of a dead woman, he headed for the bathroom. He left the door open like he always did now. He didn't mind his houseboat with its walls of windows and open plan but he didn't like to be shut in small dark spaces. It reminded him of army tents and hastily hung shelters, heavy camo covers blocking out the intensity of the sun but not the sand or the fear.

Both antique copper taps turned on full blast to the sounds of groaning pipes. Callum didn't care if the water was scalding hot or freezing cold as he stripped off his shorts and stepped under the spray, letting it wash away the residues of the demon sleeping tablets.

When he felt a little more human and a little less walking dead, he shut off the water and turned to reach for his towel. But that's as far as he got.

In the open doorway stood...someone. An almost naked someone. She was yawning, one hand in the air, the other near her ear, her elbow bent. Her blonde hair was everywhere that was up and matted like she hadn't brushed it this year. She looked like a hobo in designer undies. No fear, no fury, just a little brow raise when her eyes lowered to his package which was followed by a bored shrug.

She moaned something, swayed a little, and then ran for the toilet, heaving what had to be half her guts up into the porcelain bowl.

"What. The. Fuck?" was about all he could muster.

Audrey Hobson didn't remember much about the last few hours, or days. In her mind she saw loads of little clear bottles of vodka. She remembered a shiny black stretch limo with twinkling stars reflected off the roof and doors. She hoped she tipped the driver after she'd thrown up in the back. She remembered sleeping after the rocking car had stopped spinning around her. What she didn't know was where she was. That information was grainy at best, like the reception on the old-style televisions as a kid when a plane flew over or the day was windy.

The hot naked guy in the shower said something but she had only enough energy to get rid of whatever was left in her stomach. She couldn't even raise her arms to get her hair out of the way. Had she gone on a date? Blacked out again? She groaned. Had she had sex with hot naked guy and couldn't remember? God, it was all so blurry.

"Are you okay?" Hot naked guy asked from somewhere behind her.

More retching was about all she had. A cool flannel hit the back of her neck as her hair was pulled gently back.

"Are you sick?" he asked.

Are you a rocket scientist? she wanted to come back with but only more retching. She didn't think there was anything left to come up but her stomach just wouldn't stop heaving. She tried to take a deep breath, anything to calm her body, but a chunky hiccup left her coughing and shaking. She was used to the hangovers and the morning chuck, but this was different. Through the haze of unpleasantness she suddenly felt cold and just could not stop the shivers.

There was a rustle of plastic and the stranger who might not have been a stranger pulled her back from the rim and handed her a small bin to hold. "How long have you been sick like this?"

That was a good question. "About three months. I think," she managed to whisper. As she spoke, she actually felt her dry lips stretch and then split, tasting blood on her tongue. Where was her gloss? Where was her handbag? Where was *she*?

He snatched something from the top of the vanity and held her wrist while he looked at it. A watch. He had nice hands, she noticed. They were big and warm. Like a hug but not.

"Who are you?" she mumbled. He looked familiar so she must know him. *Please don't just be a random.*

"I live here. Did you get lost? Break in?"

Little glimpses flashed in her hurting brain. She didn't break in. She'd had a key. The limo driver had carried her to the front door but it wasn't locked. He'd put her on the couch and then she'd lost consciousness. She woke up in the dark, her jeans riding up and her ridiculous disguise hat still on her head. She kind of remembered throwing off her clothes and pulling a blanket from the back of the sofa but then it all went black again once she'd warmed up.

"Where are we?" Panic edged in and for a moment she felt too close to the looming stranger.

"Jupiter Creek," he said, giving her a kind of strange look mingled with wariness.

Her stomach started up again but there really was nothing left. Nothing left of Audrey Hobson. Nothing left of her career or her life. She tried to open her eyes again to tell the stranger she couldn't be back in Jupiter Creek. She lived a world away in Los Angeles. She was a star. Or at least she had been.

Jupiter Creek? "Are you sure?" she managed to murmur but she didn't hear his answer. Darkness swamped her and for a moment the pain and panic just...went away.

Two

♥

Just when Callum thought his four-letter word limit was done for the day, he swore again. And again. To top off the list of weirdness, he'd never had a woman look at his body and then run for the loo before. His scars were bad but they weren't gross enough to make someone sick. Were they? Alison had said they made him seem more dangerous, '*in a hot way*'. But then again, she was a lying bitch.

The real damage wasn't to his body anyway. What was a few bullet holes compared to the memories? He'd rather be shot again and again than see their faces when he closed his eyes.

Damn it.

Placing the filthy woman gently down on the bathmat, he pulled his shorts on in record time and banished the memories from his mind. Now was not the time. He kept an eye on the woman's chest while he moved, making sure she was breathing and not going to choke on anything that hadn't come up yet. He almost didn't bother with a shirt as he rolled her into the recovery position while he ran outside to start the ute. He hadn't driven the car in over a week and as he turned the key in the ignition where it stayed when parked in the carport, he prayed it would start right away.

After a splutter and a shudder, the engine purred to life and he ran back for the girl. There were no ambulances this far out and even if he did call one, he'd still have to drive to meet them. He snatched the blanket from the couch, finally noticing two suitcases near the front door and a handbag on the table, purse next to it on the scarred wood. Damn it, where had she come from?

He pushed aside all the questions as he hauled her to her feet and over his shoulder. Her skin was clammy and cold but he hoped it was more the fact that she was in her bra and undies than near death. She smelled like vomit but she was cleaner than he'd initially thought, her little feet perfect to look at as they dangled before him. He'd ask questions, like who the hell she was and where did she come from, after he got her to the hospital.

Her blood pressure was low and even though she took one breath after the next, he worried how long she'd been so sick for. She could have done herself some permanent damage and would have been stuck in the middle of nowhere on her own.

Not that he cared. Once he found out her story, she was on her bike.

Callum half dropped her into the passenger seat, lifting her legs in and folding the blanket over her. He did not take in strays. He did not take care of people anymore. He did take an extra second to pull the seatbelt tight and then tried to close the door without giving her a head injury. As he backed out of the driveway, he hoped like hell she didn't wake up and chuck again. He liked his car vomit smell free.

As he raced towards Mannum, he looked in the rear-view mirror but didn't see a car on the road in front of Mavis's house. What the hell?

As the speedo picked up towards a hundred kilometres an hour, Callum reached into his pocket for his phone but swore again. That friendly little four letter one starting with f. He didn't grab his phone. He had no way of warning the hospital he was on his way in.

The thirty-minute drive was torture as he kept one eye on Miss Out-of-it and another on the dirt road. He breathed a little easier when the loose gravel gave way to asphalt and pressed down harder with his right foot. Only about ten minutes between him and a doctor who wasn't him. Callum knew by the way she was sick that it could be anything from food poisoning to drugs to Ebola. The on-call doc would have to do a blood test, maybe even send her down to Adelaide for specialist care. God, he hoped it was only something minor. He'd have to stay long enough to know she wasn't dying but he hated hospitals. Well, not so much hospitals. It was the death and despair that happened in hospitals he'd grown allergic to.

He flew past the caravan park and campgrounds, the ferry dock, the supermarket and lunchtime cafe goers, but didn't slow unless he absolutely had to. Surprise barely registered when blue and red lights lit him up after the main drag. He was shocked not to have already gained the attention of the local police. He didn't stop. When the siren sounded and the cop gestured for him to pull over in the rear-view mirror, he only pressed down harder on the accelerator. A couple of hundred metres later he screeched to a stop in front of the hospital doors.

Callum left the car running, pressed the latch for both seatbelts and then jumped out of his seat, rounded the front end of the car, the furthest from the cop, and opened her door, catching the girl before she fell. She was still out as he ignored demands to stop and only moaned a little while he juggled her in his arms, heading for the entrance to the nursing home wing.

"Jesus, Callum, what did you do to her?" the constable asked as he rushed to get the door open.

Callum hadn't even noticed Daniel was the officer who'd chased him. They'd met a few years before at a fatal car crash in Jupiter Creek. Callum had heard the two cars twisting into one and his instincts had kicked in as he'd run on foot to the scene. It was another instance where his medical training just hadn't been enough. Both drivers had died on the side of the road, covered in blood and broken beyond fixing.

A little breathless, Callum growled, "I didn't do anything to her."

"Who is she?"

"Don't know." He strode down the corridor to where the hospital took in ski boat injuries and tourists with mosquito bites and rashes.

He wasn't even particularly gentle as he laid the girl on one of the beds so he could push a red button on the wall intended for emergencies. A clicking sounded down the halls and Callum started rifling drawers for supplies as nurses came running.

Anita was first there. "What the hell happened?" she asked throwing a glare at Daniel and then giving the same chilly treatment to Callum.

He ignored the tension and the cranky nurse's attitude. She hated when he rocked up to go through the cupboards for this or that. "Her BP's low and she's been vomiting for an extended period of time."

"What did she take?" Anita asked as she snapped to, pushing Callum aside as she went for a saline bag and a drip kit.

"I don't know. I don't know who she is or what she took or anything. She was there when I got out of the shower."

This time it was Daniel who glared as he removed a notepad and pen from his top pocket. "On your boat?"

"No, she was in Mavis's house. I think she broke in." A niggling started at his nape while another three nurses joined them and Daniel stared like he didn't believe a word of any of it.

"I know who she is," Anita told them, lifting the matted blond hair from the girl's face and tucking it back out of the way.

"Who?" both he and Daniel asked at the same time.

"I think it's Audrey Hobson."

Callum nearly bit the end of his tongue off. "It is not." He'd have known if this person was Audrey. He would have known straight away, anywhere, anytime.

"It is," Anita argued. "She died her hair for her last movie. She played a woman who lost her baby and then nearly drank herself to death before being saved by the widowed hero and his six kids. B grade but it worked okay."

He shut the words out, the noise, and turned to brace his hands on the cool aluminium sink. He thought maybe it was his go to have a chuck. One of the last times he'd seen Audrey had been at Mavis's fortieth birthday celebration. She'd been sixteen going on a hundred and twenty with her seriousness and killjoy attitude. She'd sat by the beer fridge and scowled at everyone. He'd tried to cheer her up but she'd shut him down. That was the summer he'd nearly graduated university, the year before he'd joined the army and thrown his life to the wolves.

Callum barely took in anything else as Anita talked and talked. Alcoholic caught his attention again though. *Binge drinking just like her mother* had him turning to defend Mavis but then he closed his mouth and just stared at Audrey. It couldn't be her. He wouldn't watch the same thing happen to the daughter as had happened to the mother. The Audrey he'd known hated alcohol. Hated it to the point of tipping whole bottles down the sink while her mother cried that she would change, she'd stop drinking and be a better role model to her only daughter.

Audrey wasn't a drinker. She couldn't be.

His hand shot out and he tipped the tray of sterile instruments on the floor with another four-letter word then he left the room, left the hospital, left the death and despair and hopelessness.

The next time Audrey came to, she was not much more in the know than she had been that morning. At least this time she knew what room she was in. A tube of oxygen weighed down her ears and felt foreign against her cheeks while a stabbing in the back of her hand when she tried to sit told her they'd put in a cannula. A heart monitor beeped away next to her head and a nurse in blue stood at the end of the bed making notes on a clipboard.

The nurse smiled when she saw Audrey was awake. "Well, good afternoon, Audrey. Nice to see you back in the land of the conscious."

Did they know each other? "Where am I?" She knew the answer to that question straight away as she lifted her head and took in the rest of the room. She'd been there often enough with her mother when they'd first moved to the middle of nowhere. "Never mind," she finished with a sigh. "How did I get here?"

"Callum brought you in this morning. Just between you and me, I think he's a little ticked off so be careful when he comes back in. If he comes back in."

"What did you say?" There was no way hot shower guy was Callum West. No way.

"I'm not sure if you scared him or what happened but he's not hap-py." The nurse ended the sentence in a sing-song voice and it grated on Audrey's nerves like nails on a chalkboard.

"Do I know you?"

At the end of the bed, the other woman feigned hurt with a fake pout. "Anita Cauld. We went to school together for a year or so. I've been following your journey to the top and I have to say, you go girl."

The top, yeah right. Is that where'd she'd been all these years? Audrey hadn't been at the top of anything for a long time and everyone knew it. Now that she was no longer blind drunk, a few facts floated back. She'd returned to Jupiter Creek because her agent, her manager and the producer of her latest movie had told her to get away from it all for a bit. They'd also told her to re-evaluate where she wanted to be in five or ten years. Tinka had asked where her favourite place was in the world. Fabien had told her to get as far away as she could. *Asshole.*

This was it.

The one place she hated about as much as she loved it.

It reminded her of her mum and the downward spiral they'd been stuck in all those years before but it was also the most peaceful, serene place on the face of the planet. Then add in the fact that she had nowhere else to go that was kind of off the map where she'd be left alone by the media, her fans, Fabien's wife.

But Callum West? Why was her mother's godson there? The last she'd heard, he was off fighting insurgents and patching up wounded men somewhere in the Middle East. Mavis had written it in one of her many letters. Audrey hadn't kept up the best contact with her mum after she'd left for America with her biological father (husband number two for Mavis). She'd been angry for a long time, but then the letters had started. Mavis didn't like to call the USA on her landline, it was too expensive, she always claimed. So her mother had written her a letter every three months from the first year Audrey had left all the way up to her death. Never once had she mentioned Callum coming for visits.

Audrey had paid for her mother's funeral over the phone but hadn't come back for it. Her schedule was crammed and they'd threatened her with legal action if she left the country while shooting a movie. By that stage she hadn't seen her mother in years. There were a few phone calls after Audrey's dad passed from cancer. Mavis had asked if she was going to come home but Audrey had a life in the states. She had her career, her stepmother and younger half-siblings. Once upon a time she'd been happy.

After Mavis died, Audrey was pretty sure she'd cried more tears for the fact she hadn't had one of her mum's hugs in a decade. She felt like crying now as well. Mourning her career and her mother and both their messy lives. After Audrey's most recent behaviour, she would be surprised if America ever let her come back, let alone find work and start fresh. *If that's what she wanted.*

Of course it's what she wanted. She was an actress. She didn't have anything else. And she was damned good at what she did. If you took away the alcohol. If you took away the fear that came when she took away the alcohol...

She knew she had a problem, she just didn't know how to fix it.

"Audrey?" came a gruff voice from the corridor.

Tears burned her eyelids when she saw him standing there, looking lost and uncomfortable and...angry? Was Callum mad with her? "Hi," was all she managed.

"What are you doing out here, Audrey?"

It took all of the rest of her tiny bit of energy not to openly bristle. "Welcome back to you too."

"No, seriously, what are you doing here?"

It was too embarrassing to tell him the truth. That she was on her way to being a washed up drunk just like her mum had been. That her colleagues were losing faith in her. That she got so blind sometimes she didn't know where she was or who she'd been with. He didn't want to know any of that.

An image of Callum getting out of the shower at her mum's house flashed in her mind. Dripping wet, his mouth open in shock, his body right there on display, tattoos on his chest and scars on his abdomen. There was a much more important question than what had happened that morning. "What are *you* doing here?"

Three

♥

Sixteen-year-old Audrey Hobson had never looked at him with these eyes before. They'd been friends even though he was seven years older than her. His mum and Mavis had been best friends, almost like sisters and Callum had tagged along on visits and weekends away. Mavis had been the only person to truly understand his grief after he'd lost her. His own brother and his father kind of just took her death in their strides but he'd been devastated. A part of him still was all these years later. Being close to Mavis was like being close to his own mum.

He couldn't look at Audrey now with her messy hair, cracked lips and unnatural skinniness, and see the innocent child who hated the fact her mother drank so much all the time. He wanted to ask what happened to her, the Audrey who'd punched him the nose when he'd asked if her boobs were on the way or lost in transit. He'd taught her to swim the currents of the river and saved her arse when she'd gone out with friends and found herself stranded and alone in a bad part of Adelaide.

Where was the gap-toothed smile and matching dimples? Where were her glasses and wild blonde curls? Even her eyes looked different now, not the honey gold he remembered.

Callum turned to Anita and asked, "Are you sure this is Audrey? I just don't see it."

Anita grinned. "It's her all right. You want me to google an image for you?"

"I am right here," the object of his confusion pointed out from the hospital bed with a wave of a hand and a curl of her American accent on the r's.

Callum flicked his gaze back to her. "I just don't understand."

She appeared hesitant and for a second he almost thought he saw her in there but then the woman in the bed lifted her chin and glared right on back. "Can we talk about this some other time? I feel better now and I want to get back to the house."

Anita huffed. "You're not going anywhere. The doctor is on his way and has to examine you first."

Audrey shook her head. "No need. I just had a long and awful flight. Too much booze and not enough food is all. I'll be fine after an antacid, a sandwich or three and a good sleep."

This time Anita got pissy and Callum nearly smiled. At least he wasn't the only one the surly nurse gave attitude to. "Listen here, Audrey Hobson, it's hospital policy. If you check in, you have to be checked out."

He watched some more as Audrey disconnected the oxygen from her nose and began peeling the thick white tape back from the cannula on her hand. "I didn't actually check in," she pointed out.

Callum went to her side and swatted her free hand out of the way. "Leave that in," he snapped, pressing the tape back to her translucent skin. She was still as stubborn as she had been at sixteen. She also clearly hadn't remembered she wasn't wearing much. The sheet dropped lower as she straightened and she wasn't doing anything to cover up.

Callum then did something he was probably going to regret later. "If she says it's alcohol then that's okay. I can discharge her and take her home, keep an eye on her." His gaze lifted to Audrey's. "But you have to stay on the drip for at least another bag. You're dehydrated and," he dropped his eyes to where her flesh pushed against a lacy black bra, right above ribs poking through skin. "Malnourished," he finished.

Her cheeks went all pink when she looked down and snatched the blanket up in her skinny little fingers. He nearly smiled. Instead he said to Anita, "Get her something to wear please, I'll sign the papers."

"You aren't officially a doctor here, Callum West. You can't be taking over like you own the place."

He also technically wasn't a doctor in Afghanistan yet he'd patched them up and sent them back to fight. His medical training went everywhere he did, as did his actual qualifications. "Put me down as her private physician. Then I can sign her out and into my care. Doc Lawson won't mind and if he does, get him to call me in a bit and I'll take the blame."

"What about her Medicare? Who's going to pay the bill?"

Callum snorted and looked back to Audrey, her perfectly coloured hair and manicured nails. "Send it to Mavis's. I'm sure Miss Movie Star can pay her own bills."

He expected an argument from one of the women but Anita just stomped off to find clothes and Audrey stared at him with big, round eyes. "Thank you," she whispered. She rubbed her hands over her face and sighed, not lifting her head again until Anita came back.

Callum gave the women his back as the nurse grumbled about helping Audrey into a set of theatre greens. They were old and faded and must have been sitting in a cupboard since the dawn of time but at least she was covered. He didn't want to see the hollows of her collarbone or the ridges of her ribs. He wondered how long it had been since she ate something nutritious. Something that wasn't in liquid form with a number and percentage on the bottle or a solid the size of a tic tac.

She was pale and skinny and quiet. Teenage Audrey had never shut up long enough for anyone else to have a say or argue with her. Helping her with the seatbelt took him back to the times he'd brought Mavis to the hospital. But Audrey's was a different story. She would never get hooked on the booze. Not after what her mum had been through.

He showed her how she'd have to hold her drip bag and then padded barefoot across the hot asphalt and jumped into the driver's seat. He gave a two fingered salute to Anita and she replied with a one finger gesture and a flash of her tongue. Callum grinned. She may pretend to hate everyone but he was sure there was a heart of gold in that woman somewhere.

As he and Audrey silently drove back along the Mannum main street, Callum lifted a hand to wave to Daniel where he sat in his patrol car watching a group of kids heading down to the playground. He was lucky his friend hadn't had a radar gun when he'd sped past him earlier. Callum would have lost his licence. He was lucky his friend let him off with a warning to call an ambulance next time and not be a hero.

Callum was no hero. Despite what the media reported, despite the medals he'd been awarded and despite the lives he'd actually managed to save. He was no hero.

Once they'd cleared town and the woman next to him stopped shielding her face and sat up a little more in the bucket seat, he asked, "Are you going to tell me what this is all about? You just turn up out of the blue after twelve years? Is everything okay with you?" The last bit was redundant since she still had the drip in the back of her hand. Everything was definitely not okay with her.

Her gaze seemed trapped on the passing scenery and he wondered if she would answer when finally, she sighed. "It's been five years since I had a holiday, twelve since I moved away. I just needed some time out."

Moved away? Ran away more like. "Time out? You expect me to believe that bullshit?"

"You don't have to believe it," she said with another sigh. "But here I am and I'm going to stay for a bit."

His grip tightened on the steering wheel. "How long's a bit?"

In the corner of his eye, she shook her head. "I really don't know."

"It's a long way to come for a holiday."

"I needed to be far away from it all."

"Did someone or something drive you away? Are you in trouble?" His heart kicked up a notch as he waited for her answer. She was a big girl with loads of cash who could handle her own problems but if she was running from someone, Callum wanted to know. They may not be friends anymore but he had to watch out for her. Mavis would haunt him if he didn't.

"The truth is I was losing it a bit. Call it exhaustion or burn out or whatever. My agent thought a break might be all I need to kick start my career again."

She wasn't telling him the truth. It didn't take a brain surgeon to know there was something else going on. He might not know her anymore but he knew when someone had the weight of the world dragging them down. The real question was did he want to get involved in whatever it was that had Audrey Hobson running back to Jupiter Creek? Thousands of miles from her home and her friends and her career?

The short answer probably started with hell and ended with no.

She was an idiot. She should never have come back. She could have rented a house in the Hamptons or a chalet in France or even an apartment in Hawaii. She only needed a chill out space, a bed to sleep in. But. If she were to tell the truth, she'd missed this place. In her hearts of hearts, she missed her mum. She'd spent years telling herself she didn't really need Mavis. Didn't really need her sad attempts at being a mother. They'd never been close but things felt different now she wasn't just a phone call away. As Callum pulled his ute into the carport, she took it all in, the changes around the house, the lush greens and vibrant colours of the front garden.

At twenty-eight, Audrey was independent and had been on her own for a while, but every now and then she missed her mother's hugs. The one's where she would wrap her arms around her daughter and rock her a little, tell her it would all be okay one day. But that was before their lives went to shit, before they moved to Jupiter Creek and Mavis drank more and more and more. Nothing was ever okay after that.

The tension was thick as Callum helped her from the car with gentle words to be careful of the step and was she okay while he got the door. She murmured her thanks and nodded when she had to, holding the liquid bag in her hand the way he'd shown her. What was she supposed to say to him? He'd been there her whole life, in the background, but on her fifteenth birthday she'd half fallen in love with him when he'd let her drive his Supra around town even though she didn't have a licence. She'd done her country best to flirt with him but he'd laughed away her attempts.

She was a kid. He'd pointed it out often enough. But then, at sixteen, she'd kissed him, determined to make him see her as a woman and not a child. It was meant to be a goodbye kiss one night after he'd come to have dinner with Mavis, quick and then done. But he'd kissed her back, on the lips. With tongue! Before practically throwing her across the room when Mavis had turned the porch light on.

Her cheeks heated. She hoped he didn't remember that incident.

Why wasn't he off with the army, saving the world? That had been his dream back then. Mavis had written that he was high up and really good at what he did.

"Can I get you anything?" the object of her thoughts asked from a good distance away.

Vodka tonic? "No thanks. You don't have to stay here with me. I'll be fine now."

He shook his head and leaned over the tiled kitchen bench, his unkempt dark hair falling over his eyes before he pushed it back with one hand. "I don't have anywhere else to be and I did say I'd keep an eye on you."

"I know that's what you told the nurse but you don't have to babysit me. I'm fine on my own." *Another lie.*

He narrowed his eyes and Audrey almost took a step back as he let her have it. "Do you realise how close you came to being dead this morning? If you'd passed out and hit your head, or fallen face first in the toilet, you'd be really dead right now. Why aren't you taking it more seriously?"

She had passed out once and hit her head. On the back of her scalp there was a bit of hair missing where she'd had five stitches. Her hair people always had to make sure it didn't show in any shots when they were filming. The media had reported it as exhaustion. The bottle of gin didn't get a mention and she was fine with that.

"You're exaggerating a bit don't you think? I was just tired and running on empty. Like I said, I really hate to fly and had a few too many drinks."

"I'm going to watch you for a few hours and when and if I'm satisfied you're okay, then I'll leave you in peace."

No argument came to mind so she just nodded and turned her back on his penetrating stare.

Not much had changed in the little cottage. Mavis's trinkets sat on the shelves collecting dust, her old timber-grain box television in the corner of the room, the comfy couch right in front with crocheted pillows resting in the middle.

She'd expected cobwebs and musty smells. "Do you know who cleans this place?"

There was a shifting behind her and she turned back to find Callum looking anywhere but at her while he filled the kettle. "I do. I look after the place for Mav- Well, I guess for you since you own it now."

"Do you drive up from Adelaide or are you at the army base at Woodside?"

"I'm not in the army anymore."

"Why not?"

He shrugged but Audrey didn't miss the rigid line of his back as he straightened or the way he almost seemed to brace himself before answering. "I got out a few years ago."

She didn't press him. He obviously didn't want to talk about it. "So what do you do now?"

"I don't really do anything. Not much anyway."

Audrey rolled her eyes at his great conversational skills and walked around a bit more, taking it all in. She wandered down the hallway and looked into the rooms. What had been her bedroom when they'd moved in had been converted to a sewing room. Mavis had once loved to sew and had taught Audrey how to hem and repair missing buttons. She'd had the crafty touch, her mum. Audrey didn't have it at all. If she tore a hole or lost a button, she threw it out and bought a new one.

Next she drifted to the threshold of what had been her mother's room. There was a bit more dust here but it still smelled like her. Like the earth and the river and Mavis.

"You can sleep in here if you want."

She jumped and dropped the bag with the fluids in it on the worn beige hall runner.

"Sorry," Callum apologised, bending down and scooping it up, handing it back to her. "I didn't mean to scare you."

"You didn't. I was just thinking about her. Ghosts of the past, I guess you could say."

"She was quite a woman," Callum said with a soft sigh.

"Did you visit her often?" It'd be nice to know she wasn't completely alone out here. Even the most beautiful locations could be lonely when you were on your own.

He walked into the bedroom and started stripping the covers off the bed, knocking dust off the pillows and opening the window for fresh air. "When's the last time you spoke to Mavis?" he asked.

Actually spoke to her mother? It had been a long time. Mavis's letters had come like clockwork and sometimes Audrey had ten minutes to write a quick one back. Mostly she called and Mavis told her it was too expensive to waffle on the phone. She smiled and leaned against the door frame. "Mum wasn't much of a talker."

Callum moved around like he owned the house instead of her but he stopped what he was doing suddenly and looked at her like she'd sprouted two heads. "Mavis talked plenty."

Audrey gaped like a fish out of water as he opened a cupboard door and took out a clean set of linen, setting to making up the bed. Something was off here, she decided. It wasn't the fact there was a six-foot-something man looking all domestic in her mum's house. Actually, that was exactly the problem. "How much time did you spend with Mavis, Callum?"

He shrugged and she got a little more annoyed. "Did she ask you to visit her? Did your dad?"

"No one *asked* me to stop and spend time with a lonely, discarded woman."

Ouch. "Then why are you here?" He was skating around it now well and truly. She'd asked him what he was doing there a few times and he hadn't given her a straight answer.

"Not that it's any of your business, Princess, but I happen to live here."

Not any of her business? "You live here? In the house? With my mother?"

He gave her a look that clearly said she was an idiot. "Of course not in here. I have a boat out back. I paid rent, kind of, and Mavis let me moor and use the bathroom and kitchen sometimes."

"But she's been gone a while." Audrey didn't need to point it out but confusion gripped her and she couldn't think like a normal functioning person.

"Only fourteen months. No one came to ask me to leave. I've been keeping Mavis company for years."

"Don't you have a life? A job? A girlfriend or wife?"

"Long story," he said abruptly and turned back to making the bed.

"It's a bit weird."

"Weirder than coming home after more than a decade to have a," he lifted two fingers on each hand and bent them at the knuckles, "'rest'?"

He had her there. "I guess you have your reasons and I have mine."

Callum threw the pillows back on the bed. "I guess so."

Four

♥

Over the next hour or so, they didn't talk much more. Callum gave her a pack of dry crackers and Audrey tried to eat a few but her stomach rolled at the first bite. She needed something greasy. She always needed bad food after a bad night.

She checked her watch but she hadn't changed the time over after landing.

"You got somewhere else to be?" Callum asked from the other couch where he pretended to read a magazine. Audrey knew he hadn't turned a page for at least fifteen minutes.

"Do you think we could order a pizza? Maybe get some Chinese?"

"No one delivers out here. They never have."

That had been the case twelve years ago but she'd assumed they'd moved up with the times a bit more than that. Mannum looked like a bustling town when they'd driven back from the hospital. "Still a backwater," she muttered under her breath.

"That's what I don't understand," Callum said putting the book down and glaring at her, his elbows on his thighs, hands between his knees. "You hated this place back then, you couldn't wait to leave, but *now* you come back? Don't tell me it's for a rest, Audrey, you never were a good liar."

He couldn't have been more wrong. She was an actress. Lying is what she did for a living and Jupiter Creek itself wasn't why she'd left. "I needed obscurity. No paparazzi, no cameras or journalists. No ex-boyfriends or fans. You don't know how hard it is to find the middle of nowhere to put your head down for a bit."

He looked like he'd argue that fact but then he stood and walked around her to the kitchen. "Well, with no fan club at your heels, and no pizza coming, the best I can do is beans on toast if you didn't like the crackers. I haven't been shopping for a while."

Mavis had considered baked beans on toast dinner fare. Maybe at ten years old Audrey had too. Dinner out of a can was something she didn't have to do anymore. "Thanks that would be nice."

"I'll have to go out to the boat for the bread. I'll be back in a minute."

"Do you think you could take this out of my hand first?" She held her arm up where the needle was still stabbing into her. She'd had the two bags of hydration and was feeling okay now. She needed a shower and her own clothes to feel more like herself again.

He hesitated but then grabbed a box of tissues from the counter and came back to sit next to her on the couch. He took her hand in his, warm and huge, familiar yet not. As he leaned over the needle, being so gentle and sure, she just stared at the top of his head. He needed a haircut, she decided. And a shave.

She'd never seen him at ease like this. So casual and at home. "You've changed a lot," she commented, not really thinking about what she was saying before she said it. From his whiskered cheeks to his bare feet, he was worlds away from the Callum she remembered. Back then he'd always worn slacks and collared shirts and was neat and trimmed. A good boy, Mavis had called him. Sensible and with his head screwed on straight. Audrey had always drooled and told her friends he looked as if he'd stepped off the cover of a magazine.

How she'd wanted to ruffle his feathers back then.

She felt his sigh against her arm as he said, "It's been a long time. Everyone changes."

She knew she had changed in some ways but in others, she had to wonder. She still felt like a stranger in her mother's home just the same as she always had. She still felt like a kid next to Callum but there'd always been this sense of...something. He'd always been able to make her smile and feel like whatever teenage drama she had going on, it wouldn't be the end of the world. He'd always talked about closing doors and opening new ones. He'd always listened to her, really listened. She wondered if she told him about her present problems, if he'd hear her and help, offer some sage advice?

Blinking a few times, she held back. She couldn't tell him. She couldn't tell anyone. Her agent had warned her not to tell anyone anything. Well, unless of course she wanted it all over social media within the hour and tabloid media the next day.

It was the hardest part of her career, holding back. Never really sharing any authentic pieces of herself. But this was Callum. He'd held her hair back as she'd spewed only that morning. It wasn't the first time he'd performed that duty for her either. Before her mother had moved them from the city to the Riverland, she'd had friends, a great school, an easy life. All that had changed when things had gone pear-shaped, as they always did with Mavis, her mum had fallen apart again and shipped them off to the middle of nowhere. No schools. No friends. No pizza.

"How is your dad?" she asked him. She hadn't thought about Mick in forever.

"He's good. Still has his law practice in Unley. He runs it with Stephen."

"Stephen is a lawyer too?"

Callum chuckled and looked up to meet her gaze. Audrey was shocked. Back in the day, Stephen had smoked pot and skipped weeks of university at a time. He was nothing like his older brother at all. Callum studied hard and kept on the right side of the law, achieving his medical degree a year earlier than he should have, he was so conscientious and stable. Stephen hadn't been any of those things.

"It took him a few extra years but he made it out the other side. Dad takes the serious hi-profile cases while Stephen chases ambulances and hot reporters."

Mavis had always liked Callum more so it was no surprise she hadn't included any of Stephen's antics in her letters. Seeing Callum at ease around the house, it was no wonder Mavis always made it sound like they kept in touch.

"Why do you think mum didn't tell me you were living here with her?"

He shrugged but there was something else there. A flash of hurt? Pain? Maybe he'd had a bad break-up? He bent his head one more time, there was a pinch and then pressure on the back of her hand.

"Hold this nice and tight for a few minutes. I'll go get the bread."

Mavis hadn't told anyone he was living with her because he'd asked her not to. If the world knew where he was, then he wouldn't be hiding. He'd be outed.

Callum's heart thumped uncomfortably against his ribs for a few minutes at the concept of facing the world, his old friends, his family. Tripping lightly across the bouncy length of timber leading from the grass to his houseboat, he didn't go straight to his kitchen. Instead he sat on the bed and let his head fall into his hands.

For months he'd lived out there all alone. Only the waves from other water users and pleasure crafts let him know he wasn't as isolated as he liked to think. He took the occasional journey into the bigger towns around, and only ever for the essentials, but he liked being alone. After his few years in the army, bunking with other guys in dorms and tents, and university living before that, he'd really appreciated his own space and the silence. It really was golden. Audrey was going to ruin his peace and his slice of heaven. He could feel it already.

He grabbed a few cans of beans and a box of bread mix and headed back into the house to see what he could rustle up to pass for a late lunch, early dinner. Audrey wasn't on the couch when he walked through the door and into the darkening house. He had to keep telling himself she was a big girl, she could sort her own shit out. He turned on a few lights, breathing a bit of a sigh of relief when he heard the shower running. God, he hoped she wasn't staying long. Then again he couldn't kick her out if she did hang around.

Panic gripped him when he realised she could sell up once she did leave. She didn't need this place. Not in the way he needed it. Maybe he could talk to the bank and see if he could buy it off her. But did he want those kind of roots? A full-time job to pay for it since his pension wouldn't come close? When he'd used his discharge payout to buy his houseboat, he'd loved the idea of just reversing out onto the river and going wherever he wanted for however long he wanted. He took occasional day trips but the water had been low for a while and it stopped him cruising very far. In fact, when he put his mind to it, he hadn't been very far in a long time. There had to be somewhere peaceful where the fish bit and people were a distant memory.

Maybe he'd leave Miss Movie Star to her own devices and shove off for a while.

Just as he started to form a plan which involved zero conversation and lots of being one with nature (except for the boat) Miss Movie Star emerged from the bathroom, the scent of soap drifting in with the steam to tease his nostrils.

She was dressed in impossibly short shorts and a dark tank top that hugged her bones. Vulnerability still hung like a storm cloud around her but she was clean and the heat had given her cheeks a glow that hadn't been there a few hours earlier.

She'd always been slim, her waist so tiny. He used to imagine the way his hands would span the distance. He'd wondered would his fingers touch on her lower back while his thumbs covered her belly button. Thoughts that would have landed him in a lot of trouble then. More trouble now despite the fact they were older.

"I had to use your towel, I hope that's okay," she said, flicking her long blond hair over her shoulder and using said towel to wring the moisture from the ends.

Callum was a little dazed at the transformation one little steaming fountain of water could provoke. He swallowed hard and with a nod said, "Next time, turn the fan on."

She rolled her eyes but a ghost of a smile lit her lips. "Mum used to nag me so much about that bloody fan."

Callum sort of knew that. Mavis had lectured him a few times too. Mostly in the dead of winter when he came in for a shower to defrost his hands and feet. He never wanted to use the fan and have the cold air chill him all over before he had the chance to get dressed.

Looking anywhere but at Audrey, Callum measured some bread flour into a bowl and then added water. He moved around the kitchen, grabbing what he needed, deliberately ignoring her when she pulled out a bar stool and sat at the breakfast bar.

The silence didn't last long.

First she yawned and then she gestured to his handiwork, leaning her elbows on the bench until he could nearly see down her top. "I thought it was beans on toast." Her voice dropped low and he assumed she was mimicking him.

"No fresh bread left. I'll make a focaccia base so it's not just beans."

"I didn't know you could cook."

Again, he wanted to point out that she didn't know anything about anything anymore but he bit his tongue. She was only trying to make small talk and he should let her. It would save him his breath. "Why don't you tell me a bit about America? Where do you live?"

She hesitated. Interesting. "I live in an apartment complex in LA, close to work."

"I thought all you celebs owned million dollar mansions in the burbs."

Audrey smiled but shook her head. "According to the magazines we do. It's just me though, what would I do with twenty-six rooms, a pool and a tennis court?"

"For all the wild parties?"

It took her a long time to smile again as if she didn't get that he was joking. Eventually she said, "You shouldn't believe everything you Google."

"You don't like it much, do you?" Whoa? Where did that come from? He nearly groaned. He did not want a deep and meaningful right before dinner. He got busy with kneading the dough and kind of hoped she wouldn't answer.

"I used to really love it," she said softly. "Now it's endless days of shooting with pissed off directors and highly-strung actresses."

"So you're not a highly-strung actress?"

This time she did have a chuckle. He was kind of glad there was still a slight sense of humour in there somewhere. Her seriousness was a worry but then she'd had that at sixteen too.

"Maybe I am," she conceded with a nod.

"So, you used to love it. What changed exactly? What brought about this need for a rest?" Perhaps if he could talk her through it, she'd go back and forget about Jupiter Creek for a bit longer.

"Enough about me," she said, sitting up straighter on the stool and plastering a faux smile on her lips as he spread the dough on a baking tray. "Tell me more about you. The last time we were together, you were all about saving the world's war torn."

The way he remembered it, the last time they'd been together, she'd been underage and he'd been more attracted to her than he should have been. "There's nothing to tell. I did my four years, went to Afghanistan for a tour and then I got out."

"You always struck me as career army. Mavis made it sound as though you were on your way to a general or something."

The *or something* would be the only correct part of his military career. But he didn't talk about what had happened over there. Not with anyone.

He threw the tray into the oven and washed his hands. "I have to turn on the sprinklers." And then he left. This was the one thing he did and did well. There wasn't a conversation he couldn't or wouldn't walk out on if it meant he had to think about the men who didn't come home with him. The dads who didn't come back to their kids. The half-shells who still called themselves men even though they quaked inside like mice.

Not the dozen psychiatrists or men with epaulettes on their shoulders had been able to get him talking. Audrey would learn quickly to not even try.

Small talk was all he had left now. And it was all she was going to get.

Five

♥

A wkward didn't even come close to dinner that night. Audrey kept her mouth shut unless she was shovelling another spoonful of beans in. She'd tried the television but the old thing wasn't working and neither was the radio since mice had made a lunch out of the internal workings sometime in the last decade. Her phone had gone flat and she hadn't tried to find the charger yet so no music, only a tense and awkward silence. She hated silence.

Being left to her own thoughts was dangerous. Why had she told Callum she *used* to love being an actress? She still did. It was her whole life. Or it had been before it all went so horribly so wrong.

Every now and then she felt the sharp edges of Callum's stare but she kept her head down.

She couldn't have known asking him about the army would draw such a response. Clearly they both had their reasons for being out there in the middle of nowhere seeking peace and solitude. She was almost sorry that she'd destroyed his so spectacularly but then again, this house was hers. The spot was hers too and she needed it. They might be in the same place at the same time but their reasons sat worlds apart.

He was so strong and in control. As he'd kneaded the dough for the bread thingie he'd made for the beans, she'd watched the play of muscles on his forearms, the stretch of his knuckles and the power of his hands. He probably wasn't scared of anything. She wondered if he was running from a girlfriend but then shot the thought down. There was no way someone like Callum ran. Something must have happened to him. It wasn't like he was a hippy with dreads and growing his own vegies to be self-sustaining. Just because he could make a slice of bread heaven out of virtually nothing just meant he'd picked up a thing or two over the years.

She startled when he dropped his plate on the table with a clang, breaking the silence.

"I'm going to hit the hay," he said. "You all right doing the dishes?"

She nodded, glad he was leaving her alone but at the same time terrified that he was leaving her alone. "Can you show me how to lock up?"

He half chuckled but it wasn't a nice laugh full of humour like the old days. "There's no one out here, Audrey, you don't have to lock anything."

She lifted her chin. "I would just feel better locking up. You know, strange bed, strange house, that kind of stuff." Did she sound convincing? She hoped so.

He narrowed his eyes like he saw straight through her but then he shrugged. "Fair enough. But leave the back door open just in case I need to come in, okay?"

Her tongue stuck to the roof of her mouth and her heart kicked up a beat as she attempted to swallow, stay calm and casual. "Sure," she managed.

Callum showed her the hook where the front door key sat and she wasted no time fitting the key and turning the lock.

She'd been holding her breath and let it out with a bit of a whoosh. "Thanks."

He gave her that weird look again, the one where he didn't know how to take her and her particular brand of crazy. "Well, good night," he muttered. When he got to the back door, he looked at her again. "If you need anything, come get me, okay?"

"Okay." She repeated the word but her mind had already drifted to the long night ahead.

"Night."

"Good night." And then she was on her own. Again.

The clock on the wall ticked but it was the only sound other than the ones outside. Bugs called to each other but it had been so long, she couldn't pick out which were which. As long as they stayed outside, it didn't matter if they were crickets or cicadas. She wandered back to Mavis's bedroom and stared at the bed. She was exhausted but could she actually lie down and close her eyes?

Not yet. Her phone. She had to charge her phone. She hadn't checked her emails or Facebook in more than 24 hours. Then again, she wasn't meant to. Tinka had said to avoid social media altogether and that her agent would monitor her emails. Most of them would be news outlets and gossips magazine editors anyway. They all wanted to know what had gone so terribly wrong for Audrey Hobson.

Audrey had wanted to tell all but her career might not survive the truth so she couldn't breathe a word. What would they do if they knew what the last year had done to her? The break-in? The break-down?

She rummaged her case and came up with her charger but she had no power adapter for her US plugs. Damn.

Jetlag weighed heavy as well as her trip to hospital and everything else that had happened that day, and the ones before. Flicking her gaze from the bed to her carry-on case, her mouth watered for the vodka she'd bought duty free at the airport. Audrey shook her head and swore softly. She didn't need it anymore. She was home. At peace. No schedule, no demands on her time for work or social engagements. She didn't have to drink to escape. She'd done that just by boarding the plane.

She kept muttering to herself under her breath as she pulled out her toothbrush and went back to the bathroom to wash up for bed. As she was returning, passing the open back door, she pushed it closed. Just to keep the bugs out, she told herself.

She flicked lights off as she went but then as darkness descended, she turned one back on. The kitchen light. Just for Callum if he came back in. He'd need to see where he was going.

Back in Mavis's bedroom she rearranged the pillows and lifted the bedspread to make sure nothing had crawled in. Every night she'd done that in this house after finding a huge spider between her sheets one night. She'd screamed her head off and Mavis had laughed and saved the 'poor creature' taking it outside. She'd have rather killed it so it didn't come back later.

She switched off the light and curled into a ball beneath the covers, facing the door. With a wide yawn, she was absolutely sure she would fall asleep straight away without needing the booze.

She almost did. Her eyelids grew heavy and the heat of the bed that still smelled like her mum wrapped around her. But then a rattling sound thundered across the roof and she sat bolt upright, her breath coming in raspy, short pants, her gaze wild as she checked the shadows, the corners, anything she might be able to see.

Over the sound of her heart galloping in her ears, it came again followed the vicious squeals of fighting animals. Even though she knew it wasn't a person on her roof or at her door, she couldn't help the fear or the panic as it set in and burned a trail up her spine. She was never bothered by the dark until she woke one night to a stranger in her bedroom. Now every bump and sound meant a would-be intruder and she couldn't turn it off in her mind.

She flicked the lamp on and got up and closed the door. It didn't help. The piercing squawk of a bird had her jumping under the covers and pulling the blanket over her head.

"They're outside, you're inside. Animals, not people," she muttered to herself, even her own voice sounding loud. She needed music but then she wouldn't hear if there really was someone in the house with her.

After about ten silent minutes that felt more like two hours had passed, her lids began to droop and she snoozed for a little while but then the screeching animals were back and even louder than before.

She was never going to get any sleep and she needed it so bad. How could she be expected to rest and recover and think about her future if she had matchsticks holding her eyes open come morning? She should have checked into a hotel for a night or two before heading to Jupiter Creek. She would have been safe and looked after. A working telly, room service, double locks on the doors and cameras in the halls. A fully stocked mini bar.

One more time Audrey got out of the bed. She checked the window was securely closed and then pulled the drapes shut. She couldn't lock the door in her mother's room but she could push something in front of it. It took a lot of swearing and a graze to her knuckle before she managed to drag the dressing table halfway in front of the door so there was no getting in without waking her up by either smashing glass or scraping furniture.

The bloody bird squawked again and in that moment she would have paid money to be in a double-glazed lockable room in the twenty-fifth floor of a five-star establishment in New York. Even in her LA apartment the only noise was from street traffic and then only if she cracked a window. But she'd gotten used to that. Well, so she'd thought. Familiarity and a sense of security had left her vulnerable and before she knew it- *No*. She was safe here and she would never let her guard down again.

The only sure-fire way to make sure she slept like the dead was in the bottle in her bag. She unzipped the top and reached in, her hand closing over the cool glass neck of the familiar sleeping aid, the familiar forgetting aid. This is all the comfort she needed. A couple of sips and she could ignore everything else around her.

A tiny voice in the back of her mind roared that she didn't need it. Audrey pretended not to hear.

An old CD player alarm clock sat on the nightstand so she pressed play, uncaring what music it was as long as it silenced the voice of reason. Patsy Cline and her country twang filled the room. Audrey turned it up. "I do need it," she told Patsy with a lot more conviction than she probably needed as she stared at the label on the front of the bottle.

As soon as she'd caught up on her sleep and got used to the wildlife around her then she'd stop. Once this bottle was gone, she'd stop. She'd already promised herself that much. Having barricaded the door, she had no glass and she didn't want to move the dresser again. Unscrewing the top, her mouth watered. *Just thirsty*, she thought. *It's been a long day.*

The crack of the seal had her adrenaline pumping just that little bit harder and when she tipped the bottle up and drank straight from the neck, she sighed. But only a little bit. She kept trying to tell herself it wasn't that good, that it actually tasted awful, but as the heat of the vodka settled in her stomach and radiated from her chest to her arms, calming her like nothing else could, Audrey knew how good it was. After a couple more mouthfuls exhaustion caught up.

By the time she put the cap back on the bottle, there was less than half left and as she tried to put it on the floor next to her, the whole room swayed as though someone had tilted the mattress beneath her. She didn't want to have the alcohol too far away so she tucked it in next to her but on top of the blankets. When her head next hit the pillow, all the sounds that had worried her, the shadows, the memories, blurred away and she fell asleep.

The only thing Callum wanted as he woke up after a hot and fitful night was a hard shower and a big breakfast. He'd spent half the night thinking this whole scenario was bad news and worrying about all the ways it could go badly.

He couldn't spend days with Audrey making small talk and bumming around.

Sure, he didn't have anywhere else to be or anything else to do, but that wasn't the point.

She'd come all this way to spend time on her own anyway. He was seriously thinking about throwing the ropes off and drifting downriver as he tapped one arm then the other, one leg and then the other. There were plenty of places he could pull up, maybe drop a fishing line in or go for a hike. He squeezed his hands into fists and flexed his fingers as he shook out his muscles and rolled his head on his neck until it made a satisfying crack.

She'd probably thank him for it. She could use the ute if she had to go into town or to Adelaide. He'd leave her the keys and maybe get the neighbour, Mrs Bradshaw, to look in on her occasionally.

He whistled as he filled the percolator, trying to instil in himself a sense of fun and anticipation. When he was a kid he'd loved fishing with his mates. His dad spent a few years in a country town as a family solicitor when he and his brother had only been about seven and ten. Only three years after their mother had died in a head on car crash on one of Adelaide's notorious stretches of highway. Erin had been a midwife and would get called away in the early hours of the morning. She'd assisted with a delivery in Tailem Bend, a long way from the city, and then had been killed by an out-of-control truck when the other driver had fallen asleep at the wheel.

So at the age of about ten, Callum's father had fallen in love with wife number two (his version of love anyway) and had moved his boys to the middle of nowhere to chase a skirt. Sally was a school teacher. A really lovely lady but with no idea of the arsehole his dad could be when it came to just about everything. Mick was an arrogant son-of-a-bitch who always had to be right. Even when he was wrong.

That's when Callum had started fishing on his own. That's when Callum had started avoiding his father altogether. If you were in his line of vision, he'd pick a fight with you. Nothing anyone did was ever good enough for his dad.

Callum never liked killing the fish so whenever he could, he'd throw them back and smile as they swam off, imagining them flipping him the bird with their tail fins.

Yep, he thought, that's what he'd do. He'd spend a week fishing, maybe two. Hopefully by then Audrey would be ready to head back to the States and her life. The only date he had on his calendar was his dad's seventieth birthday, a huge affair, one he intended to miss and not feel a drop of guilt over. He'd only pencilled it in so he could remember not to turn his phone on or check his messages for a week or so before or after.

His invite had come via his Facebook account, the one he never used for anything except occasionally seeing what others were up to. What his old army buddies were doing and if they were happy and had adjusted. His brother sent him messages sometimes about this lunch or that weekend away and sometimes he answered with a no thanks, other times he'd just ignore everything and everyone altogether and leave them on open.

He didn't want to live as a hermit really but after spending all those years bunking with others, joined at the hip with his comrades and then seeing those same friends get killed or eat lead when it became too much, it had done something to him inside. How could it not? As a doctor you were trained to distance yourself emotionally from the situation and the sufferer so you didn't go insane, so you didn't get emotionally invested. Nothing had prepared him for the army. Nothing had prepared him for the conflict they'd faced or the endless sand, heat and blood.

He'd seen a psychiatrist after returning home, after he'd snapped and tried to dull the pain with an entire bottle of Valium. She was a pretty little thing, smiley and saying all the right things, but even she hadn't been prepared for his stories.

She'd tried to keep her mask in place but the horrors he relayed had got to her too. That's when he decided no one wanted to hear what was in his head, what he'd seen and done. His ex, Alison, asked at first, glorifying war and him, introducing him as her hero. She hadn't gotten it either. He kept reminding her he hadn't saved *her* so he wasn't her own personal hero. He wasn't anyone's hero.

He sipped his strong coffee and went out onto the deck to stand in the sun. There was nothing heroic about war. Both sides lost. Both sides died by the dozens. Innocent civilians either got in the way or got involved. They died too. He'd thought he was used to death after his residency and time in the emergency department but it turned out he was about as wrong as he could be.

Why couldn't he have just one fucking day where he didn't have to think? About anything? Just turn his brain off and just be? He really did need to find that hobby Mavis had bugged him about.

Thinking of Mavis had him thinking about Audrey. It was only eight o'clock so she'd probably be asleep still but he needed a shower and he needed food, more than he had on his houseboat. If he was going to push off for a few days, he'd need a trip to Mannum too. He'd probably have to make sure she had a few supplies as well. He couldn't very well leave her to fend for herself completely.

He rinsed his coffee mug and left it upside down to drain, grabbed a fresh pair of shorts, a clean shirt and a pair of boxer jocks and headed for the house. There was no way he was nervous. No way he was the intruder here as he faltered by the closed door. Maybe he should have made sure Audrey was happy for him to keep using the facilities in the house? Too late now.

When he pushed on the back door, he heard noise. Music? Or what might have passed for music fifty years ago. It wasn't very loud but he recognised it as one of the only CD's Mavis had owned. Patsy Cline and John Williamson were the only singers she would buy. A country girl through and through was Mavis.

"Audrey?" he called, wanting to let her know he was there just in case she was in her underwear again.

No response. He walked through the kitchen, dumped his gear on the bench and stood in the hall outside her room. He knocked softly and called again, "Auds? You up?"

Still no response. Maybe she was meditating or some other new age bullshit? She had to have heard him over the music. He turned the door handle and it gave way easily but only an inch later, it knocked hard against something. He tried to push but whatever the obstacle was, it was stubborn.

"Audrey?" he called louder, a little impatience edging his voice. Callum put his shoulder against the door and gave it a shove. Wood scraped against wood until he could poke his head through the gap.

His heart stopped for a split second and then ramped up with a thud-thud-thud. She was splayed over the bed, her head to the side, drool on the pillow, an empty bottle nestled in close.

One more hard push and the dresser she'd used to hold the door shut slid across the floor. He was on his knees in another heavy heartbeat, his finger at her throat to check her pulse. There it was, strong, steady.

"Damn it, Audrey," he said, shaking her shoulders. "Wake up."

He had to shake her again but then one eye cracked as she regained consciousness. When both eyes opened, her mouth did too. She let out an ear-piercing scream and tried to push him away, fighting his hands, his presence, fighting him.

Her fists flailed and he couldn't catch them as he said, "Audrey, it's me, it's Callum."

"No, no, no, get away from me, I don't want you here, get away," she screamed, trying to scratch and claw at him. He nearly didn't see the bottle as it swung for his head.

He dodged backwards but then she was on her knees on the mattress, still swinging, still fighting. He caught both of her wrists in one hand and squeeze until she dropped the weapon, easier still to snake his arm around her waist and hold her against his stomach. "Cut it out," he roared into her ear when she attempted to head-butt him in the chin. "Audrey, it's Callum, damn it. I'm not going to hurt you."

Finally, his words penetrated and she went limp, a sob wrenched from somewhere deep inside her as she collapsed over his arm.

Six

She couldn't keep doing this to herself and she knew it. Audrey woke up like that a lot, scared out of her wits that she wasn't alone, that she was in danger. *A random home invasion,* the cops had told her. *Nothing to worry about,* they'd typed on the report. *Increase your security if you want,* the super had said when she'd asked how anyone could have got past the front gates of the complex she lived in.

It's not that they hadn't believed her fear genuine when she'd woken to find a man in her bedroom, a knife pressed to her throat, a rough hand on her breast, but they all seemed to downplay the actual danger Audrey might have been in. So many thoughts had gone through her mind in those seconds, and they were only seconds, then she'd started screaming despite the threats from the blade-wielder. A neighbour had come to check on her and the intruder had jumped out the window, her purse in his hands and her sanity in his back pocket. What if she hadn't been able to scream? What if the guy was stalking her and had just been really good at it so far? What if he'd stabbed her first and she'd bled out in her own bed? The question that plagued her nightmares the worst was, what if he came back to finish what he started?

That one awful moment of her otherwise pretty rocking life had led to her overreaction now and every event in between. It had led to her nervous breakdown and played every action after that like she was a puppet on someone else's very long strings. God, how desperately she wanted to cut the strings and forget it, take her life back into her own hands and own it again.

But it wasn't that easy.

"Are you done?" came from over her shoulder.

She nodded and Callum let her go although he bent to collect the bottle from the floor and took a large step towards the door.

"Want to tell me what happened just now, Auds?"

No one called her that anymore. She was Audrey. She was a star. She shook her head, unable to meet his gaze, to see the condemnation or the pity reflected there. She didn't feel like Audrey. She felt like a child, scared, confused, at the end of her rope. She was just so tired. A tear rolled down her cheek.

"All right then," he said as though he was speaking to a kid. He held the bottle up and leaned against the doorframe. "Want to talk about this? You told me yesterday it was too much booze to help you get through a flight. Just how bad is it?"

Audrey groaned and sagged onto the edge of the bed, some of the panic receding leaving her cold and shivery. Leaving her defeated and deflated. Again. "It's not bad. I have trouble sleeping sometimes." She gestured to the room, to all of her mum's stuff. "It was strange being here and with the time difference and all, I just couldn't nod off."

Callum half grunted and she wondered if he'd buy the crap she was selling. "Auds, this shit is toxic, you know that." It looked as though he wanted to add something else but then he pressed his lips together and turned to leave.

"Why did you wake me up?" she lifted her chin and asked his back, taking in the lopsided dresser, the new scratch on the timber floor.

"I thought you were up already. I'm going into town. I heard the music..." He trailed off, his sentences short and sort of hollow.

She hadn't heard it until he pointed it out. Patsy was singing about a honky-tonk merry-go-round and Audrey felt like she was along for the ride. Her stomach pitched slightly but nothing like the morning before. The anxious, cold sweat on her fingertip pads began to dry and she felt like such an idiot. "I'm fine, Callum. Thanks for checking on me. Sorry I worried you."

He frowned but then just gave her a little nod and left. She'd wanted to start off fresh with Callum that morning. He was obviously hating the fact she was there but why? It was her house. If she told him to piss off, he'd have to leave. Not that she would. She wasn't staying long. Her visit would be even shorter if she couldn't get it together while he was in the same room. She didn't want him to think she was an alcoholic because she wasn't. The nurse at the hospital had whispered the words but she'd heard them as though coming from a fog horn. She wasn't an alcoholic. She wondered if she should say it out loud? Follow Callum down the hall and tell him plain and simple that she was in control. It was about the only thing in her life right then that she had a choice about. But she'd seen the look on his face. He wouldn't believe her.

If sleep had come easily the night before, then the vodka would have stayed safely nestled away in her bag. It wasn't her fault the animals were so loud or that the silence in between the fights seemed so...so...final. In the back of her mind she knew she was perfectly safe in Jupiter Creek. She wouldn't have gone there if it was a risk. But her apartment hadn't been a risk either. Until it was.

She shook her head. She had to stop thinking about the intruder following her. Maybe it was random?

It was early still but now as the rest of the day stretched ahead of her, she wondered what she was going to do. The telly was ancient and wouldn't pick up a channel, there was no DVD player or movies to watch and she was pretty sure if the pizza didn't get delivered neither would the internet or a decent pop radio station. It was if she'd never left.

After Mavis moved them out to Jupiter Creek, Audrey had discovered what it was truly like to be bored. To not have another soul around except for a handful of elderly neighbours. All the kids she went to school with lived in Mannum or closer to the town than she did. She'd made friends on the school bus but she had no one to hang out with. Callum came to visit a few times with his mates, wanting to be close to the water so they could ski and drink. She'd sulked in her room most of the time over the excessive amount of beers and bad language and the fact they all ignored her attempts at joining in.

He'd always been there, she remembered that. Audrey wasn't even born yet when Callum's mum died but she loved to listen to Mavis telling him stories about their teenage years. It was as if Erin came to life in the tales and it was little wonder Callum liked to hang around in the school holidays and after he'd got his driver's licence. His relationship with his father went from bad to worse and never improved.

Audrey still didn't know what the draw was other than stories about his mum. Mavis had the ability to destroy anything good. Her marriages, her relationships, including with her daughter. Her life. Any time Mavis started to feel content, she did something to blow it, self-sabotage was her greatest skill. But never with Callum. He was the only constant male connection Audrey had from her childhood. She'd said goodbye to that kind of existence when she'd fled to America with her biological father but now, back in Jupiter Creek, in this house, in this bed, she wondered if she hadn't been running full circle this whole time.

Happiness had been her middle name up until the break in. She'd been virtually carefree. Her agent, Tinka, handled her career and Audrey just had to show up and bring her A game. Then a thief had stolen her easy-going nature, her naivety and her contentedness. Now she jumped at shadows. Now she was a shell of a person. Now she was lost. Just like her mum had been.

No. Scrap that. Audrey was nothing like Mavis. She was going to find herself again. Inside somewhere was still the strong, independent woman she grew to be. The problem was, at that moment, it felt like that part of her was a dream. If she reached out, she could just brush the notion with her fingertips but then it danced away and she couldn't find it again. Each time she suffered a setback, pieces of her *self* floated away.

How was she going to chase down the missing pieces and put them all back together when she didn't even know who she was supposed to be anymore...

Callum couldn't do it. He wouldn't do it. Audrey needed a therapist and a babysitter and he wasn't either of those things.

What are you then? His subconscious asked, but he pushed the thought away, waving it like it was one of the billion annoying flies plaguing his peace as he paced the back lawn.

Maybe if he could get her to calm down for five minutes and stop jumping like someone was about to murder her, he could talk her into a rehab facility or a hospital. Anywhere but Jupiter Creek. Her name might be on the deed but it was his place. He did not want to share it with anyone.

A four-letter word dropped from his lips as he came to a stop, his toes sinking into the grass. His chin dropped against his chest. He couldn't leave her there alone.

Either she had to leave or he had to stay. His plans for a quiet fishing trip whistled away on the breeze with the screeching corellas flying overhead. She had denial practically tattooed on her forehead and there was an even bigger part of her story she wasn't telling him. No one woke up like she did, ready to fight, ready to scratch the eyes out of a bloke who hadn't done anything wrong.

His blood chilled and his skin goosebumped despite the heat of the morning.

Had Audrey been attacked? She'd had the haunted eyes of a woman who'd been raped and had fought every second of the assault. He'd seen the aftermath of sexual attacks from his time in the ER. Was that why she'd had to get away? Callum curled his fingers into tight fists against his palms and resisted the urge to swear long and loud across the broad, muddy river.

"Shit," he settled for. There was no way he could leave her alone. But there was no way she could stay either. She needed help. Professional help. Did she still have injuries? She definitely had the kind that couldn't be seen. He hadn't glimpsed any bruises the day before when she'd stood in her underwear, but he hadn't exactly been looking for any.

He was a piece of shit for remembering her in her undies after what he'd just seen, her reaction to him standing over her. Audrey definitely had some serious baggage dragging along with her and he still wanted nothing to do with it or her. There was a time in his life where being in the same room with her scared the crap out of him, when he'd started seeing her as more than Mavis's little girl. She'd kissed him once. He'd kissed her back.

Some things obviously just never changed. He was still intimidated by her cool composure even though it was a little cracked now. She'd always been so in control of herself and any situation, give or take a couple of bad judgment calls the year she turned sixteen. What the hell happened to her?

How did he even bring it up? He couldn't very well just ask. He still had some tact when it came to talking to others. He hadn't been on his own that long. Curling his feet into the grass one more time, he shook his head and headed back into the house. He'd have his shower and then work out the rest.

Through the dusty windowpane of her mum's bedroom, Audrey watched him pace. Watched the play of his calf muscles as he walked back and forth over the same invisible trail in the grass, his shorts faded and well-worn. Watched him squint up at the sun as his lips moved. He was angry again.

But she couldn't help it.

Had she remembered Callum was around, she might have woken up differently but then again, she may not have. She hadn't intended to drink quite so much. She never did. Audrey had only got to black-out drunk a few times. The first was when she split open her skull. The second, she'd woken up on the roof-top of her apartment complex wrapped in a blanket and on the edge of hypothermia with no recollection of how she'd gotten there or if she'd been with someone. The third and last time was the worst by far. At a party for the cast and crew of her latest movie, the champagne had flowed and the company had been frivolous and fun. She didn't remember anything after that. Not until she'd woken in Fabien's bed. Naked. Bruised. Completely clueless about the hours before.

Fabien convinced her she was a willing party and asked for it rough even though she liked her sex on her terms and he was married with a kid on the way. Without the booze, she never would have found herself in a position like that. As soon as she started to panic and throw accusations at the producer, he taunted her, told her no one would believe she hadn't screwed him for another part in a bigger movie. Even her agent said the lines were blurred and in a country like America, there was rarely justice for the victim. Unless she pressed charges and proved she'd said no, asked him to stop, there was nothing to be done. Even if she did report him, it was her word against his. A scandal she might not emerge from cleanly right on top of the one already brewing. Alcohol had been her escape, but that night, it turned into her enemy and she'd had enough.

Audrey was mentally and physically exhausted, emotionally drained, tired of fighting herself and the night. The only obstacle standing in the way of her and her old life was this helplessness and fear. This feeling that she had no idea where to start to drag herself out of the hole she'd dug. And could she do it even if she tried?

Was she too far gone?

A Mavis in the making?

If she talked to a therapist there was the doctor/patient privilege but she just didn't trust it. Didn't trust the details not to be leaked. She had no one and nothing now. As she dropped back down onto the edge of the bed, she wondered what to do next. Her biggest problem wasn't the alcohol though it was holding her back. Without the alcohol she couldn't fall asleep. She kept imagining the home invader coming back for more. To really hurt her this time. It was a vicious cycle and her shoulders sagged in defeat. She was totally screwed.

Seven

♥

"Right, get dressed. We're going to town." Callum watched as Audrey's mouth fell open so he got in before she could protest and added, "For supplies. We need food and a few other things."

"Can't I just stay here?"

"Do you like beer and steak?"

She gave him a weird look and shook her head. "Not for every meal."

"That's what I'm buying, so if you're not eating what comes off the barbie, then you're going to be hungry, Princess."

"Okay, I'll come with you. But only if you don't call me Princess again."

Callum shrugged. When he'd had to push his way into Mavis's bedroom that morning, he'd called her Auds. Just like the old days. But that's not who she was now. Even calling her Audrey felt weird. Foreign on his tongue. He wanted to call her wildcat after the beating she'd tried to inflict on him but she probably wouldn't like that much either. "Whatever you want."

"I want a DVD player and a couple of movies? A television that was made this century maybe?"

Callum groaned. "You know we can't get all of that in Mannum."

"What about Murray Bridge?"

He supposed it couldn't hurt. He'd planned to drive over to the next major town the day before anyway. Before she'd interrupted his peace. If she got what she wanted, maybe she'd be happy to entertain herself so he didn't feel the need to hover. God, why did he feel the need to hover? "You've got ten minutes."

Thirty-three minutes later Callum was in the ute waiting, his short fingernails tapping against the steering wheel, when finally she appeared, a big, ridiculous floppy hat on her head, a hoodie ten sizes too big covering her from chin to...where were her shorts? Her legs were bare and went on forever. He swore and climbed out of the driver's seat, calling to her over the roof, "What the hell are you wearing?"

"I can't have anyone recognise me."

"That getup might work in the big cities, but no one is going to ignore you in that here." Callum slammed his door shut and walked towards her.

Audrey frowned and put on a massive pair of sunglasses. "What about now?"

Callum would have laughed had he been the laughing type. "Take that off. And your jumper too. It's going to hit forty degrees this afternoon. All you need is a t-shirt and a cap."

"Spend much time in disguise do you, Callum?"

"I don't exactly have the paparazzi knocking my door down, Princess."

She whipped off the glasses and gave him a sharp-edged glare. "You said you'd stop calling me that."

"You are being a princess, Audrey. No one around here gives a damn who you are."

When she stepped back as though he'd slapped her, the familiar guilt set in. This is why he shouldn't be around people. "I didn't mean it like that. I just meant, if you don't want to be noticed, then you only have to fit in. T-shirt and cap, thongs and shorts. Look, maybe I should go on my own. I'll get you the things you want. Tofu, lentils, tic tacs, whatever."

Then she looked scared. No, not scared, terrified. He was doing a great job considering she was the first person he'd spoken to other than the hospital and post office staff in almost a month. If Mavis had been there, she would have kicked him in the arse.

"Give me a sec, I'll change."

"Take your time," he called after her with a sigh, before mumbling under his breath, "I've got all day."

When Audrey finally came back, she was wearing another one of those figure-hugging tank tops with a pair of shorts, small white shoes and her ponytail poking through one of his own baseball type caps, an army emblem faded on the front. No one was *not* going to look at her. She might as well have *rich and famous* stamped on her forehead. Maybe the hoodie had been a better idea.

"What's wrong now?" she asked with a huff, her voice breaking halfway through the words.

"Nothing. Nothing, you look fine." He wasn't used to dealing with anyone else's ego but his own and she had more than enough insecurities without him being overly critical. What did he care if she was recognised anyway? Maybe that would make her leave quicker? But that scene from her bedroom this morning kept intruding on his thoughts. Kept coming back to niggle at him until he wanted to slap it away like an annoying mosquito. Before she went anywhere, Audrey was going to tell him what that was all about.

They climbed into the cab and put their seatbelts on, Callum deliberately ignoring the way the black webbing sat right between her... *Shit.* He should have let her wear the hoodie. Every man and his dog would stare at her and their jealous girlfriends were going to notice her Barbie doll appearance. He should have conceded she knew what she was doing and he clearly didn't. Apart from his size, he was mostly forgettable. He didn't have to do much to get lost in a crowd.

He attempted to break the silence hoping she'd talk first like any normal female would. "Do you have to wear a disguise every time you leave the house?"

She shrugged and replied, "Depends on what I'm doing. If I'm going to work I don't bother but if I'm trying to have some downtime I do."

"What does downtime involve for a big celebrity?"

She turned in her seat and pinned him with a weird look. "You keep saying big celebrity like there's something wrong with what I do."

Callum deliberately kept his eyes forward, his jaw clenched, his fists tight on the steering wheel as they approached the outskirts of Mannum where they'd get the ferry over the Murray River and head towards what locals called 'The Bridge'.

Finally he answered but it wasn't well thought out. At all. "I guess I just don't understand what you're doing here. You're rich and famous, and obviously in some kind of trouble, yet you came here? To the middle of nowhere really, and for what, Auds? Mavis is gone. The house can't be anywhere near the digs you've been hanging out in..." He trailed off. *Too many words.*

"Maybe that's the point? No one here knows me or what I've been through. I can relax and try to pull my shit back together."

"Yeah, well, Mavis's place is good for that, I'll give it to you, but if someone's coming after you, there's nothing out here to help. We can't even get an ambulance real quick and the police are spread thin as it is. Wouldn't you be better off somewhere like a hotel? Chalet? Something like that? With your mates?"

Audrey turned back to lose herself in the scenery flashing by. "I had to be alone and no one's coming after me. Only my agent knows where I am. And you. There is no one else."

She'd learned the hard way who her friends were. Too late she'd realised acquaintances just weren't the same. The women she hung out with were actresses or the wives of and they all partied hard in a take-no-prisoners kind of way. She was probably closer to her gay stylist than anyone else in LA and even he was too busy to watch bad movies and eat popcorn all night with her. Audrey's reaction to the home invasion and her alcohol abuse after had been too real for those around her and the distance was now too big to get past. Real friends would have stuck by her.

It's something no amount of talent school tutorials or drama college semesters could teach her. People who lived their lives in the LA LA Land of acting tended to remove themselves from reality either a little bit or a lot. She'd begun to think of herself with such a high celebrity status that nothing bad could happen. She could click her heels together three times and shout, *'Don't you know who I am'* and the world would bend to her wishes. Just by being who she was, she could have anything and anyone she wanted. Materialistic needs rose above all else until she was just as fake as the rest of them.

Until reality reared its ugly head in the form of a thief. Until her drunken blackouts had landed her in the bed of a married man. Audrey still wasn't sure if it had been either man's intention to hurt her, really hurt her, or not. If the home invader had been a simple burglar he wouldn't have woken her. He would have taken some stuff and left the way he'd come. Even the police had told her if he'd meant serious business, she'd be dead. A warming thought now she could look back on it. As for Fabien, she had to believe he was just an asshole who thought he'd get away with taking advantage of a woman who couldn't defend herself or say no because she was too drunk.

Once again, Audrey's pity party played out to a soundtrack of the Jaws theme song in her head until they'd reached Murray Bridge. A lot had changed and she took in the sights, noting a new housing development here, a new bank of shops there. But the same old bridge and the same old murky brown surface of the river reflecting the sun off the wake of a speed boat came into view soon enough. The country city was clearly still a hotbed of summer water sports and it made her smile. Ordinary people enjoying an ordinary day. She wished she was one of them.

"Do you think I'd remember how to ski?" she questioned in the awkward silence.

Callum pulled the ute into a carpark and killed the engine. He shook his head. "You couldn't ski then so I doubt you'd be able to now."

It wasn't a criticism, she didn't think. "I could get up on the knee board," she reminded him.

He half snorted and said, "For about three seconds before you got the wobbles and came off. That one time you face-planted the water so hard, you had a black eye for a week."

"Three seconds still counts," she said, remembering exactly the time he referred to. "Do you ever get out on the water?"

"I don't have a ski boat. Only the houseboat and it's not towing much behind it."

Before she could make any more small talk, Callum was out of the car and waiting for her to do the same. Only he wasn't paying any attention to her at all. He looked left and right, back across the street, towards the entrance to what appeared to be a shiny new mall. It was sweet that he was looking out for her but she was pretty sure her hat and glasses and lack of makeup would blend her in to the crowd. Not that this was a crowd. Pedestrians made their way from all over, haphazardly tripping across the wide road from every direction regardless of horns honking and middle fingers up from impatient drivers. Most of them were set for a hot day in bikinis, dresses and board shorts. Just a laid back...Saturday? Sunday?

She didn't even know what day it was anymore.

Callum walked ahead a pace and threw over his shoulder, "Let's just get what we need and get out, okay?"

Fine by her. It occurred to Audrey she'd been using that word a lot. Fine. I'm *fine*. It's *fine*. It's going to be *fine*. She couldn't wait for a day when she could be something else other than the lie that was *fine*.

Like any normal, sane woman, Audrey liked to shop. She enjoyed checking out the bargains even though she had money in the bank. Despite her status, she didn't buy everything she looked at. Her apartment wasn't big enough for a start. But she wanted a few items for her mother's house to make it more comfortable for her stay.

"What size is Mavis's bed?" she asked Callum, while running her fingertips over a plush fleece throw. "Queen or more like a double?"

"We have blankets already. And sheets." He pointed to the plastic wrapped bundle under Audrey's arm and shook his head.

They weren't Egyptian cotton but as least they'd smell fresh and new. Unlike the ones Callum had put on the bed yesterday. They just smelled like Mavis. And dust. Audrey didn't need more reminders of what she no longer had. What she'd missed out on while her head was in the clouds. Her mum was the most painful.

"I bet you don't have sheets like these ones. Or a blanket just like this? How long has it been since Mavis bought anything new?" The pillow had been musty and lumpy so she scanned the overhead signs proclaiming the different store departments until she was almost sure she headed in the right direction.

"You're not staying long enough to get this comfortable."

Nothing like that kind of statement to make her feel wanted. "Uh, it's my house and I'll stay as long as I want." Rewind a decade and she'd said almost those same words to Callum after he'd told her to rack off while he boozed it up with his hyena cackling buddies. What did she care that it sounded childish? She'd never listened to him then, why would she now?

His lips thinned to a line just above his chin and she wondered how many hours of the day he spent with his teeth clenched together. Another thought came to mind. "Why do you not want me hanging around, Callum? Got some big deal in the pipeline? Renting my house out to one of your mates behind my back?"

He shook his head but didn't respond.

"It's a girl isn't it? Well, don't worry about me. I'll buy a dozen movies and spend all my time in the house. It'll be like I'm not even there."

Callum couldn't imagine a scenario where he could forget she was there.

Despite his anxiety over public places and crowds and the possibility of bumping into someone he knew, Audrey was actually a nice distraction. She babbled a bit, her accent slipping from American to Australian and back until she was somewhere in the middle of the two, just hanging over the Pacific.

He hadn't meant to make it sound as though he didn't want her around but really, he didn't want her around. While she looked like a nice distraction, with her perky boobs and tight little body, she was going to be a really difficult complication. He had enough of those already. He didn't bother answering, refuting or flat out denying her stupid question. Let her think what she would.

He didn't believe for one minute that Audrey wasn't hooked on alcohol, only she hadn't had a drink that morning. She hadn't gone looking for a bar or bottle shop yet. Granted, it was only nearly lunch time, but she appeared to be in complete control, shopping, thinking, probably scheming. Maybe he really was conclusion jumping because of Mavis's history and Audrey had just had a rough couple of days?

He'd had a comrade go down the dark path of alcoholism and by the time anyone knew just how bad it had become, it was too late to bring him back. He'd drank from the time he woke up in the morning all the way until bed-time, or pass-out-time. Whichever came first. The fact he was drinking homemade booze a couple clicks off base in Afghanistan killed him quicker than if he'd been stateside getting hammered on good vodka or aged whiskey.

Callum stayed close behind Audrey, attempting to ignore the sway of her hips as she walked, as they picked their way from sheets to towels to pillows to electronics. He'd had just about enough in the DVD section so he went off to find a trolley big enough to carry half the shop in. Lucky he had a ute to cart it all home. They hadn't even gone to the grocery store yet and he was keen to finish up.

Did she really need all that crap? Or was she being snobby and only wanted the finer things in life now? Not that this department store had any of the finer things life had to offer. He didn't question her again because, one, he didn't actually give a damn, and two, it was her money, she could do with it what she wanted.

"Is this the biggest television you have?" she asked the girl behind the games counter when he returned pushing the trolley.

"It's the only telly we have," came the reply.

He watched as Audrey tapped her finger against her bottom lip, deep in thought or hoping the counter girl would change her mind and magically whip out a hundred-inch 3D with all the bells and whistles.

Callum still watched as the pad of her finger touched her bottom lip again and he wondered how soft the skin would be. She wore gloss, he'd noticed that. Would it be sticky maybe? Taste like cherries or strawberries?

"What's wrong now?" Audrey asked him, her hand dropping away to come to her hip as she swung her head in his direction, eyes wide, ponytail swinging.

Shit. How long had he stared at her? He'd forgotten everything else for a minute. "Can we hurry this up?" Sure, the words came out snappier than they probably should have given he had nowhere to be and nothing to do but he was cranky. Cranky with her for all the bullshit. Cranky with himself for thinking about Audrey as a woman and not as a spoilt celebrity first and Mavis's daughter second.

As if reading his mind, she retorted, "Going to be late for your date?"

"Just get the telly and let's go."

"But I need some DVDs and a player too."

He wanted to give her more than a glare. He wanted to say, *'Oh my God, woman, hurry the fuck up'*, but he didn't. He kept his cool. He wasn't that much of a dick that he'd swear at her in front of other people and he would not make a scene.

Eventually he said, "I'll get a player, you grab your movies." And then he realised the words he'd used. "Well, not *your* movies, *the* movies. Whatever."

From behind Callum's back he heard a voice. A male voice. "You're not Audrey Hobson are you? I loved that movie when you played a nurse in that war and fell in love with that guy who was Chinese or something."

Vague much? Callum thought. He waited for Audrey to say something. Deny who she was. Pull her cap down lower. Tell the guy to piss off. But she didn't. She was like a stunned kangaroo in the headlights of a B-double.

Callum took the TV from the stack and put it in the trolley. He looked at the guy who'd spoken and gave him a cold stare. "What would a movie star be doing at The Bridge?"

"Beats me," the guy replied but he hadn't taken his eyes off Audrey, or more specifically, her chest.

Callum did something then that he very definitely should never have done. He slung his arm over Audrey's shoulders, noting the way she immediately stiffened, ignored how soft she was beneath his bicep, her cleavage under his wrist, and said, "Trust me, if my girlfriend was a star, we wouldn't be standing here talking to you."

The guy finally got the clue, shrugged and left. He'd barely cleared the same aisle before Audrey was wriggling out of his embrace and ducking to stand behind Callum.

"Why did you say that?" she hissed.

He turned to her, ready for an argument in the TV Drama aisle. "Did you want to sign your autograph for him?"

"No, why did you tell him I was your girlfriend?"

She'd completely frozen and hadn't said anything, otherwise he wouldn't have uttered a bloody word. "What's the problem? He left didn't he?"

"Yeah but if anyone gets a hold of this, there'll be too many questions."

"Anyone as in who?" She was so paranoid. Beyond paranoid almost. "You said it yourself, no one knows you're here. What's the big deal?"

"The big deal," she said, pointing a finger against his chest. "Is that the press would have a field day if they knew I was here and if they thought I'd disappeared off the face of the planet for a guy, they'd never leave you alone. Or me."

Just when Callum had thought Audrey was the last person in the world he'd wanted shattering his peace, she dropped that gem onto his lap. If reporters descended on Jupiter Creek, his hiding spot would be revealed and he'd be contactable, approachable, in the open. He couldn't be any of those things. The Army would want him back. His comrades would want to know why he'd gone the way he had.

He wasn't exactly AWOL but he wasn't right out either. He'd made some promises that he just needed time away, time to gather his head and put his life into perspective. Time to figure out what the future held for an ex-soldier who'd nearly had a break down over the things he'd seen and done.

But time was an indefinite thing to Callum. He wasn't ready to face the world yet. He wasn't ready to face the wives or girlfriends of the guys he'd failed to save...

Eight

Audrey didn't have to be right on the ball to know something with Callum was off. He was jumpy and edgy and everything else that wasn't settled. His arm had been like a lump of steel on her back and over her shoulder and the sudden contact had shocked her. No one touched Audrey Hobson unless she told them they could. It was her one diva demand. She only air-kissed unless she was in bed. She never hugged and she never touched unnecessarily. Probably a side effect of her childhood with a woman who couldn't get emotionally attached to anyone or anything. Her therapist agreed.

"Let's just do what we need to do," Audrey said, trying to forget how close his hand had been to her breast, but she didn't wait for an answer. She dumped her arm load of items into the trolley and picked two handfuls of DVDs in record time, barely taking more than a glance at the front or back cover. She looked around for a DVD player but Callum beat her to it, putting it on top of the chevron towels she'd picked up.

"Anything else?" he grunted.

She wanted to give him a smart-ass answer but instead shook her head. If she told him she'd need more clothes suitable for the forty-degree heat, he'd probably burst something. She wasn't going anywhere or meeting with anyone, she'd make do.

Another 'wasn't' to add to her list was touching Callum West. She wasn't going to do that again. Her finger throbbed where she'd poked him, her sanity gone for more than a second. He must have been shot in the chest and had a steel plate surgically fitted. Maybe that's why his arm was so hard too? Why did she keep seeing him naked in her mind? The picture was a little blurry but it was there. He had a few old tattoos on his chest and stomach right next to the scars she assumed were from his time in the army. He had on a shirt and shorts now but he might as well have left them at home.

"Can we go then?" Callum bit out.

She got the distinct feeling he hated her now. Funny, because he didn't used to. The way he called her Princess irked also. She'd worked damn hard for the money in her bank account and her expensive things. Callum would never know what it was like to go without as a child. To watch everyone else in their brand name outfits and shoes while she looked like the poster girl for the local thrift shop.

She remembered the weekend Callum got his provisional licence. He'd towed his dad's boat up to Mavis's behind his almost new ute, dirt bike on the back, new ski gear in the tray. Birthday presents from his dad's newest wife. Even then Audrey could have pointed out that they were attempting to buy Callum's acceptance of their relationship. Not that he seemed to give a shit. She'd been so wild with him that weekend. Mavis had revelled in the night, a couple of young lads to drink with. Everyone had a great time. Except for Audrey.

When they hit the checkout, Callum's mood was even fouler. When she pulled a stack of cash from her purse he flexed his fingers into fists and lowered his head. She hadn't been able to see the look on his face but she could guess.

A second trolley was added while they walked the supermarket aisles. Callum dropped in boxes of prepared curries, cans of meat, soups, more bread flour. Not a salad leaf in the lot. She wasn't a vegetarian by any stretch but she liked her food clean and light, her meat lean and her vegies plentiful. "Do you mind if we visit the fresh food section?" she asked.

"Whatever you want," he said, his lips still tight, his entire body tense.

What the hell was his problem now?

In record time he'd pushed the trolley through meat then veg then salad then straight onto the checkout queue. Audrey bit her tongue so hard it hurt. When she tried to pay for the groceries he gave her a look so filthy she shrugged and let him get it. Was he angry that he hadn't been able to play the gentleman? God, she was so confused. Would it kill him to smile? Play nice?

If she hadn't been so terrified about being recognised, she would have made a scene. She wasn't afraid of confrontation and her and Callum were due judging by his more than icy demeanour. How could she relax and refresh if she was constantly surrounded by his frowning face and clipped responses?

She'd give up her new chevron towels if he'd just come straight out and tell her what the issue was.

If it came to it, she might have to ask him to leave the house for a bit. Take that houseboat of his to another location where he could share his negativity and glares with someone else.

Callum's head throbbed along to the erratic beating of his heart as he took in shallow breath after shallow breath. His entire body seemed to reverberate with every mistimed thump-thump. Sweat beaded his forehead and fingertips and his stomach pitched uncomfortably. He knew he wasn't going to vomit but as heat roared around his nervous system, he had to clutch the handles of the trolley tighter and keep his focus on the doors at the end of the mall. Doors meant open air. Doors meant freedom. Doors meant an end to the crushing, darkness descending.

He might not be going to vomit but fainting wasn't out of the question.

"Hey, can we stop for something to eat?" Miss I-Get-Everything-I-Want complained from somewhere behind him.

He knew bringing her with him would bite him on the arse. He should have been straight in and straight out of the shopping centre. He should have been on his way home already. Back to the silence, the peace, the known.

"Do whatever you want," he mumbled, still fixated on the doors, on the sunshine, the fresh air.

His vision started to blur, the colours fading to black and white until he had to squeeze his eyes shut and work on every breath in and out of his chest. Callum missed the metal and glossed glass frame by only a millimetre as he burst outside, his trolley nearly tipping over. *Fuck.*

Breathe in. Breathe out. *Just fucking breathe.*

Regardless of the movie star behind him or the grannies smoking by the entrance, Callum leaned over the green supermarket handles and heaved in the humid heat of the day. The sun warmed his neck but not in the same way as the hand that came to rest gently on his back.

"Are you okay?" Audrey whispered, that hand sliding up and then down over the cotton of his shirt, her other hand holding his arm as though he might fall to the ground like a frightened toddler. Perhaps that's what he was now?

He should have pushed her away. Told her to mind her own business and leave him alone. He would have, only... Her comfort didn't feel like pity. Mavis had rubbed his back once. She'd shushed him and whispered that it was okay to let it all out. Just like his mum would have if she was still there.

But she wasn't. His mum was long dead. And Audrey wasn't Mavis.

"I'm fine. Just...had a moment. Let's get going." He didn't bother meeting her worried gaze. From the corner of his eye he saw the concern and he didn't want it. He was fine. He just didn't like enclosed spaces or crowds. He didn't like noise or the constant worry that he'd bump into someone who'd known him before he was so many types of fucked up.

The Callum West he'd been in university wasn't here anymore. Back then all he'd wanted to do was save lives. Lives like his mum's. Maybe if he'd been in the ER when her broken body was airlifted, or in the helicopter from the crash scene, he could have saved her. In his mind it had been that easy. Until he'd joined the army and even being right there in the chopper wasn't enough to make a difference.

Audrey bit her tongue while Callum tossed her purchases into the back of his dusty pick-up. She bit her lip when the groceries went in, the small amount of meat they'd bought crammed into an esky in the corner of the tray, the rest of the bags thunked in without ceremony or care. She still didn't say anything when he flipped the cover over it all and pulled the elastic thingies tight, stretching the surface until you could bounce a coin right off it.

Her stomach growled and the tension inside her warred with the anxiety rolling off Callum in thick waves of anger and frustration. She wondered again if she was the cause of his behaviour. But she hadn't done anything to warrant the kind of reaction he displayed now.

It was another thirty minutes before they were back on the open stretch of road to Mannum and then onto Jupiter Creek. From the corner of her eye, Audrey saw how tight Callum held onto the steering wheel. She could almost hear his teeth grinding together. Her conscience pricked and she tried to swat it away.

She should have given more thought to her words but the silence got the better of her. She turned in her seat to square off against one very angry male. "Want to tell me what that was back there?"

Unsure of what to expect, she didn't think he'd emphatically drop a *'nope'* to bounce against the bug-gut speckled windscreen. But he did.

"Was it me?"

"Nope."

She wanted to ask if this was who he was now. She wanted to say she didn't care because she'd go back to her real life soon and leave him far behind just like he'd done to her when she'd kissed him that day all those years ago. He'd jumped away from her like she carried the plague and then found every excuse under the sun to not be alone with her again. It was only two short months after that, Audrey was boarding a plane to Los Angeles to move in with her biological father and his young wife.

She'd said goodbye to Jupiter Creek. Her mum. Her dreary life in the sticks.

Audrey did not have time for deep and meaningful conversations with her tenant. Because that's who Callum was to her. He looked after her mum's house and lived out the back. Without paying rent, if she recalled. There'd never been a cent paid to her at all.

It was probably easier to imagine she was indeed the source of his bad mood. Or that he was just permanently sour with the world. Callum West was not her problem and his problems weren't hers. Whatever was ticking him off, she just did not have the energy to deal with so she'd clamp her mouth shut all the way back to the house.

Her stomach still growled away quietly and a part of her, a teeny-tiny part, was curious to know what his deal was. Why a man who'd so desperately wanted to help the world was now shut off from it.

Just what had happened to him in the last twelve years?

Nine

♥

It was unfair to give her the silent treatment and Callum knew it. But he wasn't ready to talk. He was angry with himself that he'd lost the thread of his control and only barely stopped himself from snapping and snarling like an animal who'd escaped his cage.

Someone needed to put him back in that cage.

Preferably with Audrey.

Callum bit back a groan and wiped a hand over his face, his other hand still clutching the steering wheel for dear life. He pressed the button to put his window all the way down, the wind hot on his face when all he wanted was icy cold to chill him.

Why did she have to go and touch him? Why'd he have to go and touch her?

Banging around in his head was the knowledge that her hand on his back had been enough to stop the anxiety attack cold. Usually he panicked and the memories started coming back. Usually, if the attack was bad enough, he'd see their faces in his mind and forget where he was, that he was back on Aussie soil and not in a war zone half-way around the world, surrounded by sand, filth and blood.

But her voice had somehow...grounded him. He didn't want to attribute that much power to a virtual stranger but when she'd whispered her concern, he'd heard her, felt her touch, worried that he was worrying her.

Weird. Stupid. Maybe.

Callum lifted his foot from the accelerator as he approached Mannum, slowing to a respectable crawl. "Do you need anything else before we head back?"

Shock registered on her pretty features and he mentally kicked himself. He was an arsehole.

"I'm pretty hungry but I can wait."

"We can stop at the pub for a counter meal of you want?"

Audrey licked her lips and Callum had to switch his gaze back to the road and the tourists, their unpredictable walking patterns a welcome distraction for the moment.

A few shopfronts whizzed by before she replied, "Sure, that'd be nice."

Almost unbelievably, he found a parking space right out the front of one of the two pubs on the main street of town. He preferred this one because it had an outside balcony overlooking the river. He could sit on the deck and feel the sun and the breeze and feel...safe, at home. Kids would laugh while they chased each other and the quiet hum of conversation would remind him of where he was and why he was there. No sand. No filth. No blood. A free country where you didn't have to worry about being blown up at lunch. He tried to remember it as the main reason he'd joined the army in the first place. To help. To keep his country the land of the free and unoppressed. Jesus, in his mind it sounded so idealistic. So lame. How had he ever been that naive and young and dumb?

He pulled the keys from the ignition but truth be told, he wasn't even hungry, especially after a panic attack. They were few and far between these days but he'd normally take an anti-nausea tablet with a sedative and doze for the afternoon. This was why he didn't spend time around people. It was too hard to try to explain his weaknesses. It had taken long enough to even admit to himself that he suffered.

He used to think panic attacks were for weaklings and attention seekers. He used to think a lot of things before war had damaged him in more ways than the half-dozen scars marring his skin.

When Audrey made to enter via the front doors, Callum put his hand to the small of her back and steered her down the side of the building to the open deck out back. He wasn't ready to go in. It was dark inside, the ceiling a little too low, the room too echoey and too loud. The faces too inquisitive.

Damn it. He'd touched her again.

He dropped his hand and quickened his pace. She must be thinking him completely insane. She'd be half right. Choosing a table right off to the side of the deck where Audrey would have her back to the rest of the diners was a stroke of genius except that left the two of them alone and almost isolated. It was nearly 2:30 so most of the lunch crowd had already gone back to their water sports and walks along the green grass on the river's edge. Sounds drifted from the playground and were only drowned out by seagulls on the lawn and corellas flying from tree to tree to strip the bark and leaves from the branches, not eating it, just dropping it to the ground.

A perfectly normal summer's day for Mannum. Not a normal day for Callum. What if someone saw him? Or recognised her? They should have gone back to the house and fired up the barbecue.

A waiter approached with menus and it was too late to chicken out and run back to the ute. "Can I get you guys drinks to start?" he asked. He looked way too young to be serving drinks at a pub but was friendly and didn't pay much attention to who they were.

Callum breathed a sigh of relief. Until Audrey ordered a glass of wine.

"And for you, sir?" the waiter asked.

Callum sent a glare in Audrey's direction but she was pondering main courses, with a ridiculous amount of concentration.

"I'll just have a coke," he told the waiter.

After the kid left, Audrey finally lifted her eyes from the cardboard in her hands. "You could have a beer," she said. "It's hotter than hell and it's after twelve."

Mavis had a saying. *It's midday somewhere in the world.'* Then she'd crack a beer or open a bottle of wine or a can to mix with her vodka. Eight in the morning. Nine. It didn't matter to Mavis. If she wanted a drink, she'd have one.

It wasn't as if Callum didn't drink. He just didn't make a habit of it and not if he was driving. He'd witnessed a lot of accidents and words like, *'I only had one beer,'* followed with a sickening consistency. Then there was the fact he'd watched the woman who was his second mother waste away with a glass in her hand and a bottle on her table.

"I don't drink if I have to drive."

"One beer won't kill you."

"You never know." And then it was his turn to drop his attention to what he'd have to eat when his stomach was unsettled and his nerves on edge.

The seconds passed and he wondered how many were left until they could leave. Figuring there were at least four thousand, he thought he better say something. Smooth things over a bit.

"So..." Then there were only three thousand nine hundred and ninety seconds to endure. Approximately.

"Why don't you tell me what you've been doing these last twelve years or so?" Callum said.

Audrey had to fight to keep her jaw from the tabletop. After a morning of almost complete silence, now he wanted to talk? The awkwardness was ridiculous. They knew each other. She'd spent her childhood growing up alongside him. She would have called him brother at one stage of her life. Before that stupid kiss. Before she'd seen him naked and fresh out of the shower. She could never un-see that.

"There's not much to tell, really." Usually she loved to regale people with stories about her humble beginnings and where she'd landed now. Although now that she was no longer on her feet, the story felt hollow and empty. The view from her bum on the ground didn't sparkle or look bright.

"According to Anita, you're quite the star. Was she right about that?"

Audrey nodded but couldn't force a smile to her face. "I was."

Instead of asking her why she said was, he surprised her with, "Can you get back? To being a star, I mean?"

Their eyes met and held. His were so dark and broody. She wondered what he saw in hers. "I hope so." She broke the contact when goosebumps formed on the surface of her skin despite it being a million and one degrees out. "I'm keen to return but I guess I'm just tired from playing the games."

"Games?"

"When you're at home watching celebrities on the TV and in the movies, you think it would be so awesome to be them. All that money and fame. Everyone knows who you are. In reality, you have to check your every move. Am I drinking my coffee right or do I have froth on my lip? Do I buy a Pepsi instead of a Coke because of the endorsement for this movie or that? If I leave a yoga session, am I looking my best or am I a sweaty mess likely to have my picture splashed all over the next gossip magazine cover... "It's harder than it looks."

When Callum half-smiled, there was no warmth in it. It was dry and a little condescending. "Not what I'd call hard work. Why don't you just stop?"

"Not hard work? Because my eighteen-hour days aren't spent in an operating theatre? Would you stop being a doctor because it became tough or hard? You do it because you love it, right? Because there's nothing else you'd want to do." *Or can do*, she added in her mind. When she'd arrived in The States to live with her dad, she was enrolled in the best school money can buy. Right after graduation she was head-hunted for her first role. She'd completely ignored any sort of higher education because she'd made it already. The money she had rolling into her bank account meant she could live very comfortably and she hadn't seen an end to that payday.

What would she do if she couldn't perform? She'd never worked in a burger joint or at a retail store. She had no qualifications to speak of. There was nothing else for her.

"Acting is my life."

He shrugged. She wanted to reach across the table and hit him. Here she was pouring her heart out and he didn't take it seriously at all.

"You never did tell me what you're doing out here, Callum. Do you work at the hospital in Mannum? Does your girlfriend live near here too?" She said the last part with so much nonchalance, she mentally high-fived herself. As if she cared anyway.

He looked as though he wouldn't answer but then finally give something away. "No girlfriend. No job."

That was it? "What do you do then?"

"Nothing. I don't really do anything."

"Everyone does something. Don't you get bored? What about an income?" Maybe his dad helped him out with money? Every time she asked him one question, another fifty popped up. Why wouldn't he tell her anything about himself? "Are you hiding from someone?"

The look he gave her this time had edges. Sharp ones. "Who would I be hiding from, Audrey?"

"The government? Aliens? How the hell should I know?"

"I'm not hiding out. I just wanted to be alone for a while. I like the peace." He might as well have added, *before you came along*.

"It's kind of weird." There, she said it. And it was.

"What's weird is rocking up in the middle of the night out of nowhere. Can you explain that?"

"I can, but I don't want to."

"Stalemate then."

Was he getting worse at human interaction or was it just that Audrey brought out the worst in him? Callum wasn't sure but was leaning more towards option one.

His thoughts centred on one of her questions slash statements. *Would you quit being a doctor because it became too hard?* Once upon a time he would have scoffed and told her it would never happen. Years spent at school and then doing his residency and then army training after that. He'd never thought he would waste any of it. Give away any of it. But he had. The sight of blood now made him kind of...freak out. He tried not to think about the exact incident where his life had lost all meaning, where his training had let him down and his morals and principles did him no good in a bloody battle in a sand hell. During his initial training, they kept telling the new recruits they'd probably never see actual battle. They'd probably never fire the pistol they carried on their hip. Training prepared them for the worst outcome, words made them think they'd never have to shoot at anyone or anything that wasn't cardboard with a bullseye painted on it. They were doctors and officers, for fuck's sake.

They'd been so, so wrong.

He used to feel sorry for the empty shells the doctors signed onto a plane and sent home. Guys who used to be men who laughed and played and lived. Some of the casualties did keep their sense of humour. Some of them went home, recouped and then went back. Some were even on multiple tours. Callum was unlucky enough to see all the action he was assured would never happen only eight months into his deployment. Only eight months patching up the unlucky ones and he'd fallen victim to war, to the depravity and horror he should have been able to harden his heart to.

Eight months was all it took to change him from a hardworking, save-every-soul kind of doctor and turn him into a mean arsehole who didn't want to have any contact with anyone.

"Let's talk about something else?" Audrey said, her voice breaking through the darkness and bringing in some of the light.

Callum lifted his gaze and forced what felt like a smile to his lips. "If you think it's safe?"

"We could talk about the weather? The river looks a little low. Muddier than I remember."

Talk about the weather? Like strangers? "The water's low because of the locks upstream. It's also been a few years of hot and dry but this isn't even the worse it's been."

Small talk resumed on neutral ground and he almost thanked her for it. They chatted about nothing of any consequence right through a schnitzel, chips and gravy for Callum and a Caesar salad for Audrey. She offered to go inside and pay for lunch. He didn't stop her.

The quiet between them on the drive back to Jupiter Creek was a little more settled and not so awkward. Audrey once again lost herself in her thoughts and the scenery floating by and Callum left her to it. He tried not to look at her from the corner of his eye. Tried not to let his gaze roam her curves while he was meant to be watching the road. She was just so beautiful. If he hadn't seen her reactions with his own eyes he'd think she was held together well, grown into an attractive young woman, serene and sophisticated.

Mavis would have been proud of the way her girl had matured. Hell, the woman had been proud anyway. Every time Audrey made the gossip pages of the Adelaide newspaper, Mavis clipped the article and tucked it away in a photo album. Maybe Callum would show Audrey how much her mum loved her even though she'd run away the moment she'd had the opportunity.

Audrey wasn't serene or sophisticated or well held together. She was still the confused, messed up girl she was when she'd left over ten years before and it would pay for Callum to keep it in mind. Crazy came in all kinds of packages. Even stunning ones like her.

Ten

♥

The sometimes awkward common ground was a place Audrey was quite comfortable with. It happened all the time on set. You wanted to get just close enough to be able to work with someone but not close enough that you became besties. They were all there because they were career driven workaholics. There were no illusions. Occasionally an actor might meet a kindred spirit and a solid friendship would form but Audrey didn't have the time nor the inclination. Being stabbed in the back once was enough for her, she wouldn't relish it happening again.

With every day you got closer to someone, it was another day they could use against you. Cynical but the truth. Standing on that awkward common ground with Callum wasn't as bad as she'd thought it would be. If they didn't ask any hard-hitting questions, they couldn't fall into the trap of getting close or knowing too much about one another, enough to cause a fallout later down the track.

They worked side by side putting away the groceries, Audrey placing something on a shelf, Callum moving it where he wanted it. After ten frustrating minutes, she left him to it and began unpacking the television and dvd boxes. It would be nice to catch up on a few movies. She rarely had the time to just sit and do nothing, to tune out completely.

But the common ground element didn't make allowances for physical attraction. When Callum passed her a water bottle, his thumb brushed her finger. When she skirted around him in the confines of the kitchen, her hair floated over his shoulder. When she was on the loungeroom floor reading the instructions for setting up the TV, he came to read over her shoulder, his chest almost touching her back. Common ground was about not getting close. So why did she suddenly want to get too close?

Not in a mental kind of way, two minds finding topics to talk about. She'd be happy if they didn't talk at all. It must be the heat getting to her. She got to her feet and mumbled, "It's bloody hot in here."

When she pressed the on button for the air-conditioner, she expected a rush of cool to slow her down but it seemed like it was broken too. How did her mom live like this? Nothing working around her. Everything old and dated and dusty?

Callum stepped in behind her, his height and width making her feel so small and vulnerable. "You have to hit the reset first." He pressed something on the outlet and the machine roared to life. "But it won't cool the whole house down. It's too ancient."

He stepped back as though nothing had happened and went back to the kitchen where he downed half his bottle of water in a few long, loud gulps.

It had to be the heat making her crazy. Together they carried the old brown timber grain television to the shed and tucked it into a corner to be dumped later. Audrey was sweating like she'd run a marathon and was sure there were patches on her tank top.

"I think I need a cold shower," she said before really thinking about her words.

Callum's eyes slowly travelled the length of her but then he snapped his attention away, his body following like the regimental soldier he was supposed to be. "Let's get this thing set up," he grunted.

Oh god, she thought. She didn't want angry Callum to come back. She liked common ground Callum well enough. "I can work it out myself if you have something else to do," she said to his broad back, as he stomped back into the house.

"I doubt it," he threw over his shoulder.

"Because I'm a girl or a princess?"

He shrugged. "Take your pick."

She wanted to throw something hard at him. She settled for jamming her hands onto her hips. "Are you always an ass or did it take a little while to perfect the art?" Just when she thought they could co-exist, he turned into Mr Cranky Pants.

She was definitely not attracted to Mr Cranky Pants. Not in the least. It probably wasn't a bad thing that he swore under his breath and then stormed off to his houseboat with only one petulant glance over his shoulder.

But Callum wasn't being petulant. He found he was thinking about self-preservation more than ever and decided the best way to keep his sanity was to distance himself from the smokin' hot firecracker that was Audrey.

Forty degrees Celsius had come and was making itself known. He didn't think Audrey knew her tank top was wet right beneath her breasts, which meant she was sweating. Right between her breasts. It made him think of her in her bra. It made him think of her out of her bra.

He should have been concentrating on the DVD instructions or making sure the eggs went into their little plastic moulds in the top of the door in the fridge. Or that the flour went in the corner cupboard under the microwave not in the overhead cupboard next to the coffee granules. Instead he constantly found himself staring at Audrey's arse as she bent down to the lowest shelves or reached up, the fabric of her top lifting to show flawless, smooth skin a man could rub his cheeks on before biting-

And this was the problem. He looked down at the tent that was his shorts and willed the blood back to his brain. Audrey was off limits. She had stuff going on he didn't want to know about but knew wasn't good. He wasn't good either. Two wrongs never made anything right, ever.

When she stood there with her hands on her hips, her honey eyes flashing to the rhythm of her temper, he'd been more turned on than he should be. He should have laughed and accused her of being immature. Instead, he wanted to back her up against the wall and-

Fuck. He was in trouble.

Eleven

♥

There was nothing worse than waking nightmares, where you didn't know what was real or if you still dreamed. Sometimes a pinch to the soft skin on the back of her hand woke her. Sometimes it didn't.

Audrey came to with a fright in blinking, artificial half-light. Moaning met her ears, desperate, lonely, stark, followed by an earthmoving thunk. She'd had this nightmare. The one where she couldn't call for help or defend herself. The one where she was always helpless and alone.

The television cast a faded light around the otherwise darkened room and slowly she remembered where she was. She must have fallen asleep on the couch while she and Callum watched TV. They'd eaten a tense dinner with zero conversation and she thought once she put a movie on, he'd go back to his boat for the night. Wrong. He'd stayed. She shouldn't have fallen asleep. It can't have even been all that late.

She stilled her entire body and tried not to breathe too deeply, listening for what had made the sound that woke her. Her heartbeat so fast and so loud, she wouldn't hear a truck if it was next to her.

To the left, there was movement and quicker than lightening, she was on her feet, her fingers extended like claws. She didn't know how to fight but she would if she had to. She wasn't defenceless. She wasn't helpless.

Now that she was fully awake, she noticed the blanket that usually sat on the back of the sofa was on the floor. When the blanket moved, she nearly screamed. Until she realised Callum was beneath it. He must have fallen off the couch. He shifted and writhed and moaned again but she couldn't tell if he was having a nightmare or if he was just dreaming, the blanket covering his face.

"Callum?" she called softly. He didn't answer.

Audrey rounded the back of the couch and carefully lifted the edge of the blanket from his face, calling his name again.

Callum's eyes snapped open and his lips twisted into a feral snarl. Before Audrey could step back both of his hands shot out and gripped her arms.

"What are you- Oomph." The breath was knocked from her lungs when he flipped her onto her back and rose above her. Pain rocketed through her shoulder as the coffee table was shoved across the old carpeting.

"You won't take me alive," he grunted, lifting her a little only to push her back down, hard.

Fear froze her until Audrey felt as though she was paralysed. Memories replayed in her mind, the sharp bite of a knife against her throat, the heavy weight of a stranger lying across her, pinning her down. Just like then, a lump formed in her throat and for a moment she wondered if she could even breathe. When she finally had to suck air in past the fear, she let out an almighty scream, pushing all the way up from her belly and out through her mouth.

Adrenaline finally began to roar in her bloodstream but all she could do was scream. She squeezed her eyes shut and kept screaming until a hand clamped down on her mouth. She thrashed her head but the hand held tight.

"God, Audrey, stop screaming, it's me, I'm sorry."

But she couldn't stop. His weight still pressed, heavy and threatening, and her fear had taken over completely.

"Fuck," was the first word to fall from Callum's mouth. What the fuck had he done? How had they gotten there? On the threadbare carpet? The blanket from the back of the couch twisted around his legs and torso.

The screams got to him first. It wasn't the fact that he was at Mavis's house, in the lounge room, safe from harm because if that had registered, he wouldn't have woken up the way he did. It wasn't the warm body he pressed into the carpet that told him he wasn't back in Afghanistan or stuck in a nightmare. It was her screams. Audrey ripped the air like she was scared for her life.

Like she'd been in this exact position before.

She trembled and shook but Callum couldn't lift himself from her until she calmed down a bit more. Until he was sure she wouldn't get up and try to brain him. Or keep screaming. He might not have many neighbours but the ones he did have would come running if they heard the type of noise coming from Audrey.

Finally screams were replaced with gasping breaths and sobs, not that he liked them any better.

"If I take my hand away, will you scream again?" he asked her. Not words he thought he'd ever say to any woman let alone this one.

Audrey shook her head, tears rolling down the sides of her face and into her mussed hair.

Carefully and slowly he lifted his hand. "You okay?"

A nod, hesitant at first, but then he began to see sanity returning to her water rimmed eyes.

"I'm going to get up now okay?"

Another nod.

Again, he moved carefully, slowly, deliberately, until he stood on his own two feet, trying not to loom over her but entirely unsure what to do next. Had he hurt her? How the hell had she gotten so close anyway? Callum thought Audrey was asleep on the couch and after the night before and that morning, he hadn't wanted to leave her. Not that she was his problem. No way.

He must have fallen asleep too. The hum of the air-conditioner and the boring movie must have put him to sleep. Bloody figures. Every other night that week he'd had to take the devil tablets just to sink into a doze.

"Do you need me to help you up?" Why didn't she do something? She hadn't moved at all, other than the shaking and sobbing. Callum raked two hands through his hair in frustration and she flinched like he was going to jump on her.

"You're not okay at all," he growled. Who had done this to her and how soon could he lay fists on the fucker?

"Go away," she whispered and rolled onto her stomach on the floor, her sobs leaving him feeling more helpless than he ever had in a warzone. He didn't think that was even possible.

Her tiny little tank top barely covered her back and shoulders and already bruising started to show across one side of her smooth skin. He had hurt her.

Someone else had too.

She was never going to talk about it while she was so worked up and he knew it. Callum stalked to the freezer and took out an ice pack and a glossed glass bottle, the light from inside blinding until he used his elbow to slam the door shut.

He yanked open a drawer to take out a clean towel to wrap around the ice pack and then opened a cupboard and removed two scotch glasses. He definitely shouldn't be feeding her booze but it was the only way to numb the shock and try to calm her down.

Audrey had done all right up until that point. She hadn't even really thought about having a drink. She hadn't been scared when darkness began to turn everything around her into shadows hiding secrets. She'd slipped into sleep somewhere around the second act of the movie and hadn't dreamed, she'd just been sleeping. Until he'd woken her up with his own nightmare.

Her heart thumped so hard against her ribcage, it hurt. Had he left? She attempted to breathe deep, to contain the fear, to remember that she was alright and it was only Callum. She'd startled him. He couldn't have known how unhinged she'd become after being pinned down in the dark.

When eventually she knew she wasn't going to lose it again or throw up or cry more useless tears, Audrey rose to her hands and knees and then sank back, her bottom on her heels.

Those few seconds had cost her at least a year off her life, she was sure.

A shadow moved and her pulse galloped a little faster, a little harder. But it was only Callum. He hadn't left.

"You should go back to your boat," she told him, her wet cheeks burning and her body tingling with fear and humiliation.

"I'm not going anywhere until you explain to me what the hell just happened."

"It was nothing. You gave me a fright."

"I gave you a fright? Jesus, Audrey, normal people do not react like that," he threw at her.

"Who ever said I was normal?" she tossed back.

"You're evading the subject again. You can trust me."

She sighed. No she couldn't. She couldn't trust anyone. "I told you, I'm fine."

Callum poured clear liquid into two glasses and nudged one over to her on the scarred surface of the coffee table, now all wonky and no longer squared to the couches since he'd thrown her into it.

She wanted to say, *'no thanks, I don't need that,'* but who was she kidding? She needed it bad. Tipping the glass to her dry lips, she gulped the contents in one hit, only gasping a little at the heat and pressure on her throat.

"If I hear you say you're fine one more time, I'll probably start throwing things," Callum muttered. Instead he handed her the icepack, careful not to touch her fingers with his.

"Well, what about you? You're the one who was having a nightmare, I was just trying to wake you up, make sure you were okay. You didn't have to attack me."

More vodka went into her glass. Maybe it was his apology? She took it, gulped it down again. The tingling in her limbs went away and her heart rate slowed back to some semblance of normal. Audrey was a train wreck, at least she felt as though she'd been through one. Her back hurt, her shoulder ached and her face was dry and scratchy from the tears.

"Seriously though, Auds, don't do that again."

"Do what?" *Lose my shit? Go raving shrew on your ass? Act like a complete dumbass?*

"Don't wake me up. I sometimes forget where I am and... Just don't do it again, okay?"

"What were you dreaming about?" she asked, rising from the floor to the couch.

"It's not important."

But it was. She wanted to know what haunted his night times just so she didn't have to feel as though she was the only one who couldn't cope with the dark, with the isolation, with the awful memories.

"Was it your time in the army? I can't even imagine what you must have seen over there."

Only his glass was topped up this time and she watched as he poured the liquid into his mouth, a little drop running down the side of his chin stubble only to be captured by the back of his hand as he wiped his lips. He stood up so abruptly, she couldn't contain another flinch. Her body reacted with a mind of its own and she was sick of appearing so vulnerable.

"I'm going to leave you to it," he said.

Audrey jumped up and put her hand on his arm. "Please don't go just yet. I promise I won't ask you questions about your time away."

He hesitated, she could feel the tension in the play beneath her palm, hear it in the sigh he breathed. "What do you want to talk about?"

Good question. She actually didn't want to talk about anything but she didn't want to be alone in the dark either. "What would you change? If you could go back and do it all again, where would you start?"

Just when she thought he wouldn't answer that either, that he'd storm off and leave her be, he sat down on the couch and pulled her hand until she was there with him. Both glasses were topped up and he replied, "I'd try to stop mum from going on the call out." He drank a shot. "Your turn."

"I'd try harder to find out why mum was the way she was." She drank a shot.

"I would get a cushy job in a hospital rather than sign up for the army." Another shot.

"I'd lock the window."

Callum lifted his eyes in her direction but thankfully didn't ask what she meant. He only said, "I'd have kissed you back like I wasn't terrified of Mavis throwing me out of both your lives."

Audrey couldn't stop the embarrassed chuckle before it fell out between them. "I was hoping you'd forgotten about that bloody kiss."

A warm hand cupped her cheek and she held her breath as she met Callum's suddenly serious gaze.

"I thought about it for months after you left."

"You did?"

"I kept waiting for Mavis to say she'd seen us, to tell me never to come back."

"She didn't see," Audrey assured him. "And it was my fault anyway. I kissed you, not the other way around."

Callum's interest shifted from her face to her lips. "I think I wanted it just as much as you did."

His thumb slid across her bottom lip in a caress she felt all the way to her toes.

"You did?" Audrey couldn't think, couldn't coordinate her body to do much at all, just repeat his words and sit there like an idiot. "What about now?"

"Now?"

Now he was doing it. "Do you want to kiss me now?"

"I shouldn't."

"I didn't ask if you should." And then Audrey did it again, closed the gap between them and kissed Callum.

This time was different.

This time she wasn't the awkward sixteen-year-old virgin she had been then, throwing herself at the forbidden. Her lips moved over his, her mouth opening his mouth, her tongue dipping in to test and taste. Heat drove out panic, vodka blurred the lines until she was sure she could easily step over it and into his lap.

But Callum stopped her, pushed her gently back even though she hadn't realised she'd leaned in so far.

"We can't do this," he murmured.

"No one's here to see."

"Mavis will haunt me."

Only a cold bucket of water would have had the same effect as those four words. One in particular. Mavis. Audrey sat right back as fury coursed through her veins and lodged under her skin. "Why did my mother have such a hold over you?"

"There were no holds, Audrey. You're so caught up in the *me, I*, pity party, I don't think you ever stopped to think about why Mavis was as fucked up as she was."

She'd said as much only minutes before. "It wasn't my job to look after her, it was her job to look after me and she did so well, don't you think?" The sarcasm emerged in a rain of pain and anger but she didn't take any of it back.

Callum ran his hands through his hair. "You just don't get it."

"And you do? What do you know that I don't?" There was something there. Some days she thought she'd imagined Callum being closer to her own mother than she ever had been, call it teenage spite, but with the wisdom of a few more years under her belt, Audrey realised he *was* closer to Mavis, it wasn't just her imagination. He knew things and now she wanted to know too. Wanted to finally understand.

"I don't know anything," Callum lied.

"Why did you really come out here to live?" Maybe if he answered that question, it might have shone a light on the rest of the confusing story.

"That's still none of your business," he said. And then he was gone.

In his eyes had been a sadness Audrey saw reflected in the mirror every day. Never in a thousand years would she have imagined Callum to be living the same crappy existence she did. He was so big and in control. She'd assumed he was just into hermit living nowadays, not actually serious when she'd asked him if he was hiding from someone.

Like her, he wasn't necessarily hiding, but he was running. He might be in the same place every day but he was very definitely running, maybe not from someone, but from something.

As the hot emotions cooled in her veins, Audrey took very little comfort in knowing they had something more in common after all.

Twelve

♥

T he last two days felt like an eternity and Callum didn't know how the next few weeks would pan out. Audrey was going to get under his skin and he didn't have a clue how to harden himself to her. They'd known each other for too long to be strangers but had been estranged too long to be friends.

As dawn inched over the clifftops across the still, muddy river, Callum didn't feel the sense of ease and calm he should have. He breathed in the already humid morning air to try to clear his mind as he paid homage to his limbs, left arm, right arm, left leg, right leg. But in his mind he kept seeing Audrey, her body rigid, her terror rendering her useless and unable to fight. That Audrey was a damn sight different than the one he'd woken earlier in the day. She'd fought like a hellcat on crack that time. If he didn't already know her family, he'd wonder if she had a history of bipolar running down the bloodlines. First she fought, then she screamed and then she kissed.

In their few earlier moments of human contact, he'd thought nothing of touching her, it was clinical, helping. But then she'd gone and changed the game by tempting him, kissing him, complicating things. Not that they hadn't been complicated way before that. Her mouth was so much softer than it looked when she was pulling her lips between her teeth or using the sharp edges of her tongue to carve metaphorical pieces from his hide.

She wanted to know about Mavis and he couldn't tell her. It didn't matter much now anyway, the damage was done and could never be repaired. He doubted Audrey would believe the words coming from him or anyone else so there was no point saying them. They both needed distance while she worked through her personal shit, until she walked out the door for another decade or more, but he still couldn't leave her alone.

Coffee scents filled the little houseboat, his percolator bubbling away on the butane cooker and an idea came to him. In the back of the shed was the gym equipment he'd bought to stay in shape. He hadn't used it in so long it was probably home to a million spiders and a couple of possums by now but maybe he could dig it out and set it up. Maybe he could teach Audrey some self-defence to fight off her demons instead of the method she currently used which had made his ears ring and his conscience burn. He might be able to burn off a little of his own nervous energy in the process.

She had just lay there beneath him and screamed. She hadn't tried to knee him in the balls or scratch his eyes out or pull his hair. Weren't girls supposed to fight nasty? He'd never started with one so was unfamiliar to say the least. There was the time he'd tried to take a bottle from Mavis and she'd thrown a wild punch, clocking him in the nose and turning his eye black for four days, but that didn't count.

And Audrey was nothing like Mavis. Mavis had had dark hair, freckles, saggy skin and average everything else but she was a fighter. There wasn't a cause Mavis wouldn't get behind when someone was down on their luck. Audrey was the opposite. Blonde then, light brown now, her honey gold eyes alluring, she was supermodel thin and out of this world beautiful despite everything that had happened already. As sick as she was that first day, she should have been pale and drawn with dark, puffy eyes. He almost wished she did look sick or even repulsive. He had her pegged as selfish now too. It was the only reason a daughter wouldn't take the first flight home to bury her mother. She'd never even been home to visit.

She'd taken off and never looked back. If the roles had been reversed, Mavis would have moved mountains to help in any way she could. If she hadn't been tanked most of her life, that is. He didn't really blame Audrey for running like she had, not really. If it was his mum though, nothing could have dragged him away.

Callum made himself busy pouring coffee, adding sugar, grabbing a pop-tart from a packet in the little cupboard under the sink. He didn't bother toasting it, he liked them cold and soft, ripe apple and tangy cinnamon setting his tastebuds salivating for another bite. A guilty pleasure after months and years of bland rations and bain-marie living where every mouthful mixed with the never-ending sand of the war-torn desert country. Even a doctor in the army ate with the soldiers in the mess. Sure, there was an officer's tent, but he was no more or less special than any other man serving. When they were corpses in a tent, there was no telling them apart. Blood was blood and it all ran red no matter your rank, colour, sex or age.

God, even pop-tarts made him feel shitty and morose. He needed a hobby. He needed that distraction.

Tipping the dregs of his now cold coffee into the river, he rinsed his cup and headed for the house. Mentally, he prepared for battle. Physically, he prepared to be faced with bare legs, strappy tank tops and soft pink lips.

When he let himself in through the closed back door, his attention fell on the empty vodka bottle. The level had sat at least half when he'd stormed out the night before. Audrey must have finished it.

Gritting his teeth, he was about to rap on her bedroom door but then he stopped, his hand loosely fisted mid-air. What was he doing? She was not his responsibility.

His chin dropped to his chest.

Her screams now mixed with the ones already in his head and it was too late to back away, to distance himself and get rid of her.

"Looking for me?"

He must have jumped ten feet in the air but he tried to hide it as he turned.

Fuck.

"Where are your clothes?" he blurted out. Only a towel around her body stopped her from being naked. Her hair looked even darker as water dripped from the ends to roll down... He snapped his eyes to her face. She looked tired. He'd concentrate on that instead of her milky skin and... *Snap out of it.*

"I rarely wear clothes when I shower." She dropped her gaze down the length of him and then added with a smile, "And I know you don't."

Heat kicked to life inside him and instead of returning her light teasing, he sounded more like a prudish headmaster. "You can't walk around like that."

"I don't intend to but I only have a few items for summer weather and they're all dirty now." Her hand waved flippantly in the air like this was no big deal. "They'll dry in no time in this heat."

She might not see it as a problem but Callum did. Before he could open his mouth and snap something even more puritanical at her—like he was such an angel—she got in first. "Did you want something, Callum?"

Did he want something? From Audrey? He hadn't ten minutes ago but he sure as hell did now. Since she'd seen him naked, he wondered if he could demand she return the favour? Why wasn't she as unsettled as he was? Instead, he shook his head and raked a hand through his hair. "I just wanted to know if you might like to...um..." Was the towel sliding lower?

"Eyes up here, soldier." She snapped her fingers near her face but her lips, those lips, were turned up in that smile and when it reached her eyes, he nearly smiled back.

Except she'd called him soldier. No one called him that anymore. That wasn't who he was. *No, now you're just soft.*

Two perfectly manicured brows lifted above those honey eyes in question and she lifted her hair to her other shoulder with one hand while the other kept hold of her towel. "This is nice and all," she commented with a wave between them. "But I'm kind of naked. Did you just come for a chat or..."

She was waiting for him to fill in the rather large and awkward blank but his mind had completely fogged and he felt hot and stupid. He should just leave her be. He should about face, march out the door and leave her alone. But he waited anyway. For her grip to loosen, for the towel to drop.

His mouth was suddenly dryer than the Registan Desert. "Um, I was just making sure you were, um, okay, you know after last night."

Those hazel depths flashed dark for a second but then she shook her head and broke eye contact. "I'm fine."

"Yep. I can see that." He was an idiot. A dead-set idiot. "I've got stuff to do. I'll catch ya later."

And then he did what he should have as soon as he'd seen her in a towel. He tried to skirt around her but the hall was narrow and he wound up brushing against her, that hand clutching her towel pressing into his right pec. He swore a little and then did the piss-bolt. He slammed through the back screen door, marched in a straight line to the houseboat, stomped down the side access and jumped straight into the cold, refreshing, forget-about-the-heat, forget-about-Audrey, river.

As for Audrey, she was left standing in the hall, a little smile playing on her mouth and a lighter feeling to her shoulders. Yesterday guilt had racked her thinking what a burden she must be to Callum. Now a different emotion took over. Maybe he was going to say something about the kiss? One of them probably should say something about it. But then that would lead to questions about her melt down and she was determined to do anything she could to not to bring it up or discuss it. Even if it meant playing with a little fire.

She was about to rummage through her suitcases to find something half suitable for a stinking hot day when she heard a loud splash. Audrey hitched the towel up higher and raced out onto the back lawn.

"What are you doing?" she called to Callum, his wet head just visible above the water next to his shining houseboat.

He whipped his head around until he found her, droplets spraying from his shaggy locks. His eyes narrowed and his scowl was kind of hilarious. "For fuck's sake, Audrey, go and put some fucking clothes on!"

She didn't try to hide her chuckle, standing in broad daylight in only a towel, the thick blanket of grass cool beneath her bare feet, as she watched a fully grown man throw a tantrum. Was he afraid of naked women?

There was no way he didn't like the fact that she was-

"Are you all right, deary?" a voice asked from a distance away to the left. Two eyes framed by wrinkles and topped with purple hair stared across a dark, dense hedge from the house next door.

"Uh, yes ma'am," she stuttered.

As she fled back to the house, she heard Callum's laughter and decided the morning wasn't going to be nearly as bad as she'd imagined. Laughing was better than yelling.

Drinking the rest of the vodka the night before hadn't been a great decision but she'd finally slept. No nightmares. No waking up in fear either. No possums wreaking havoc on her sanity. Just the best night's sleep she'd had in months. On account of being completely exhausted.

She'd woken slightly refreshed but nauseated beyond belief. Luckily she'd run to the bathroom before Callum had decided to initiate another early morning wake up call. Did the man never sleep in?

After emptying her stomach she'd felt marginally better so had showered and washed out her shorts, tank top and bra beneath the hot water. There was what looked to a brand new washer in the corner of the huge bathroom but she didn't have enough for a full load yet. After she changed the sheets on Mavis's bed, she'd do some washing but then what?

The day stretched and yawned ahead. She could watch a movie? Take a walk? Audrey slipped on a pair of black skinny jeans over her panties and put her head and arms into a soft grey jersey knit. What she was thinking when she packed her cases was a distant memory now. She certainly hadn't remembered the heat or the fact it was summer half-way around the world. She had no bathers, no more shorts, no more tanks. She hadn't even packed enough bras.

She wondered if the supermarket in Mannum still sold clothing and made a mental note to ask Callum if she could borrow his ute, but then she remembered she didn't have an Australian driver's licence. She'd only had her learners permit before going to America and it would have expired years ago.

Pondering her free time saw her carrying her underwear outside to find a clothesline but all she found was six feet of glistening male.

Surprise, surprise, he didn't look happy at all.

Audrey deliberately ignored his frown and his following scowl and went to where she remembered the clothesline pulled out from a wall to attach to a long pole. It wasn't there. As a teenager, Audrey had washed her own clothes and her mother's. Mavis was terrible at anything remotely resembling domestic chores. Audrey had washed, ironed, vacuumed, cooked and cleaned. She'd hated every second of every day at home and at school. Nothing in her life had resembled 'normal' or even routine. Nothing had been constant or steady. Nothing had ever gone to plan.

Where the hell was the clothesline? Audrey walked barefoot back to the other side of the house to see if she'd got her direction mixed up but it wasn't there either. A smirk lit Callum's face as she walked back again. An outdoor table with four chairs set up around it was as good a place as any. She draped her panties, her bra, her shorts and two tank tops over the backs, sides and arms of the chairs.

"You can't just leave them there," he called to her as his feet hit the grass.

He was so prickly all the time. She'd love to see him ruffled in a good way or even caught off guard with his walls and his temper down. "Why not? Last time I checked, this was still my house."

"What if I have a mate over? What if the neighbours drop in for a cup of sugar?"

"Everyone has underwear, Callum. It's no different here than it would be hanging on a line, if there was one to hang clothes from."

"Use the tumble dryer in the bathroom," was his reply.

Audrey picked up her bra and shook it a little. "The wires will bend. You can't put that in the dryer." She grabbed up her panties next and waved them around too. "And these are French silk and lace. Also not for the dryer."

"Whatever," he finally said, after spending a lot of time looking anywhere but at her silk and lace. Or her. "Just don't let them blow away or anything. I'm not chasing your undies down the street."

At that mental image Audrey began to giggle and then she laughed. He was like an eighty-year-old man now. "Who took all the fun out of you?"

His lips narrowed to that thin line he favoured and Audrey tried to shut her big mouth. It was too hard and more giggles escaped. Maybe eighty-five then? Callum used to be practically carefree and always smiled and laughed. It's what had drawn her fifteen-year-old self to him in a way that wound up with her looking like a desperate country kid. He'd survived his mother's death and his father's emotional absence but had still found reason to be happy back then.

Not anymore.

Maybe it had all caught up with him and turned him into this humourless shell?

There was a bounce to her step as she ignored his drill-sergeant stare and re-entered the house in search of something better to do other than annoy Callum. Not that that wasn't fun but she wasn't used to being bored and she didn't like it. It made her...not her herself. God forbid she should actually use her new-found free time to sort out her career and her future, where she was going in the next five years other than the gutter to beg for scraps.

"I was thinking," Callum started as he came in through the screen door behind her. "Maybe you'd let me teach you some moves?"

"Moves?" she repeated as she turned. Her mind went to places since he was still dripping wet, his shirt plastered to his skin, outlining the muscles of his chest and abs. Her stomach flip-flopped.

"You know," he said, awkward and not in a good way. "I could teach you some self-defence moves. To fight back if you're being attacked or something."

Her world tilted and darkened a little at the edges. She'd rather hatch out a fifty-year career plan than dwell on her lack of fight or flight instincts. "Why would someone want to attack me?"

"I'm not as stupid as I look, Auds. Something's happened to you and I don't need the details but you can't just lie there and scream. You have to fight back."

Yes, she could just lie there and scream. She could do exactly that. Even though she'd deny it, she wasn't strong enough to fight. All she had were her lungs. And her ability to pretend nothing was wrong, nothing was happening. She might as well have been an ostrich with her head buried firmly in the sand.

The little scar at the base of her throat throbbed and she put her fingers against her collarbone.

"Auds?"

She flinched and stepped back from his outstretched hand. "I'm fine. I'm fine. Listen, it's nothing and you don't have to do this."

"I've got nothing better to do and I'm pretty sure you've got nowhere else to be. Fine's just not going to cut it anymore."

She knew it was going to end badly but she was left with little choice. Maybe he'd see how uncoordinated and weak she was and take pity on her? Leave her alone for more than five minutes? But was that really better? Alone wasn't good for her. Not anymore.

Thirteen

♥

What kind of fucking idiot was he? Callum might have to have the question tattooed on his forearm. Upside down and back-to-front lettering would top it off. It was how he felt right then. He'd hauled the boxing bag and a few other bits of equipment from the back of the shed and hosed the spider webs off. Then he'd found his gloves and defence pads for training so he'd pulled them out too. He had enough gear to keep himself busy and show Audrey a thing or two along the way.

A large steel S shaped hook suspended the heavy boxing bag off the ground and Audrey gave it a test tap with her left hand. Callum shook his head. This could take a while.

"Why don't you warm up?" he suggested. "While I set up the rest of the gear."

She raised her soft little brows as she looked at all the stuff laid out on the hot concrete under the pergola. "Like go for a jog?"

He threw her a skipping rope. "You must work out sometimes."

"I auditioned for this one movie where they wanted me to play a featherweight or something but my arms were too small and I couldn't put on the weight they needed for the part." She smiled to herself. "I couldn't even lift the bar."

"Do you know your bench press weight?"

She tossed her ponytail off her shoulder and laughed. "I know I don't have one."

Callum picked up a pad and looped his arm through the handles, his other hand at the back for support and stood in front of her. "Push me as hard as you can."

"What?"

"Put your shoulder against the pad and push. Try to knock me over."

"We both know you're a lot stronger than I am," she said, suddenly nervous, or was it hesitant? It could have been fear.

He'd soon change that. Gone was the sure and confident Audrey and back in her place was this child of a girl who jumped at her own shadow. "Audrey, I won't hurt you and you can't hurt me. Just give it a try?"

Her honey eyes met his and after what seemed like an hour, she shrugged and hung the skipping rope over the chair next to her undies. Callum nearly groaned. That was one hell of a distraction right there.

Her first push did nothing more than dent the padded vinyl. "Try harder. I want you to knock me on my arse."

She huffed and waved her hands around. "This is not what I do, Callum. I'm a lover, not a fighter."

As hard as he tried, he could not stop the image of Audrey, all naked and wanting, to pop into his head. He closed his eyes and summoned the hard, dark metal of a ballistic missile into his mind instead. It was a sad day when he had to use war tactics to un-imagine a naked woman.

He felt the pressure against his forearm but was unprepared for the strength behind it and before he knew it, Callum was on his arse on the soft lawn, blinking against the sunshine, wondering what the hell had happened.

"Do I win a prize for that?" Audrey asked, only just stifling giggles.

"That wasn't playing fair," he growled, but he was kind of impressed. "Did you deliberately distract me?"

Holding out her hand to help him up, Audrey laughed. "I didn't plan it but I'll have to remember how well it works. Did I hurt you?" Her laughter died away and she squatted down to his level.

Callum snorted. "Hardly." Quicker than lightning, he took her wrist in his free hand and pulled, twisting a little but not enough to cause pain, until Audrey was on her back next to him. Lucky the grass was as soft as a mattress.

Before she could panic, he added, "Don't ever feel empathy for your enemy. If he's down, you run. Don't ever wait around to see if he's hurt." He jumped to his feet and held his hand out for her this time. "Lesson one has begun, little grasshopper."

"Is this going to be a dirty fight now?" she asked, placing her fragile hand in his.

Callum half lifted her but then dropped her back down. "Might make it more fun?" He stretched his mouth into a smile that didn't feel forced or foreign and waited for her next move. He was enjoying himself already and shouldn't have been. Teaching Audrey to protect herself should be serious business. Putting his hands on her should have been out of the question.

"Jump rope for a bit and then when you're loose, we'll hit it."

He expected more defiance or even another question but she took the skipping rope and began to jump. Big, bouncing, deliberate jumps. "Do it properly, Audrey. You're going to hurt yourself."

"It's been a while since I got to the gym," she confessed, warming up to the rhythm a little more. Was she even wearing a bra?

"You don't have a personal trainer in your Hollywood mansion?"

"I don't have a Hollywood mansion, remember. Just me. No trainer."

"I thought you guys trained all day and night to keep in shape."

"God, stereotype much? I don't have to keep in shape. I don't really put on any weight and since I used to walk a lot, it was enough."

"You don't walk anymore?"

Audrey half shrugged while still swinging the rope. "I got too busy."

Callum didn't really have a reply to that. He wanted to know why she was so jumpy when caught off guard. He wanted to know who had attacked her, why and were they paying for it.

And where was her boyfriend? She was hot and rich, she had to have a boyfriend. Unless he was the one who'd attacked her? Fuck, he hated all the questions.

He hated even more what skipping did to her. He'd bet money she wasn't wearing a bra. Her tiny toes bent as she lifted and landed, her tight pants leaving absolutely zero to the imagination. Especially since he'd seen her in her undies. The bottom of her top bounced in time, flashing a smooth strip of stomach. Shit.

"Oi," she called out to him, dropping the handles to her sides and tilting her head. She was puffing a bit but she still managed to pin him with an amused stare. "I'm not here to give you something to look at."

A witty reply was needed but he searched and couldn't find one. "Are you warmed up?" he went with.

"I'm cooking!"

"Jeans and a jumper aren't really workout clothes."

Rolling her eyes, Audrey came to stand back in the shade next to the boxing bag. "Can I have a go with this? I think I have some pent-up frustration to offload."

"Gloves are over there." They were going to be way too big for her, but she wasn't going to hit hard. He'd seen the tap she'd given the bag earlier and even though she'd succeeded in knocking him on his arse, she didn't have the power to pummel.

He looked away when she bent at the waist to retrieve the purple gloves, the twin globes of her backside outlined perfectly beneath the tight, black fabric.

Audrey pulled her sleeves up and the first glove went on no worries but then she couldn't slide her whole hand into the second one. "Can you tie them please?"

"Sure." But that would mean getting close. Close to Audrey. Close to a woman wearing no bra and no common sense.

Callum stepped in, his eyes on her hands rather than her face, her frizzed out hair, her flushed cheeks, her sweater that was slipping to expose one bare shoulder. He tried not to touch her but his knuckles brushed the softness of her forearm exactly six times. Four times on the right. Two on the left. And why did she have to smell so good? There was only a slight humid breeze but it carried with it a scent that was sexy and inviting.

Just above her raised wrists, her nipples pebbled on the seventh time. The eighth time, she held her breath with a gasp. "Breathe," he said softly into the small space between them.

When she exhaled Callum did too. This wasn't supposed to be a turn on. For either of them. His attention wandered higher and was caught by a scar running from the base of her throat to the outside of her collarbone. It was barely visible at all except he was so close. "What happened there?" he asked, his hand on her shoulder, his thumb sliding softly. Why was he still touching her? Breathing her in?

Two purple gloves came up and shoved him hard in the chest waking him up a bit. "Let's get on with it. I feel like kicking some ass."

It was an unusual place for a surgery site. More unusual was to get a scar that small, the scalpel had to be sharp and razor thin. "What happened to your throat, Audrey?"

"Why do you ask so many questions, *Callum*?" She said his name with the same hardness he'd said hers.

"Because I have a feeling you're running from someone and if I don't know the story then I can't help you."

"I told you before, I'm not running."

"Are you hiding?"

"Give it a rest. I didn't ask for your help, tough guy. You put me in these gloves remember. In fact, last night, it was you who attacked me. You'd scare the shit out of anyone when you're looming over them in the dark, space cadet sickness in your eyes and a temper in your hands!"

Space cadet sickness? What was she talking about? "You startled me." That was the only explanation she was going to get.

"And you scared me so I screamed a bit. Why can't we leave it at that?"

He'd scared her? He didn't doubt it but what the fuck was he supposed to do with the churning feeling in his gut that Audrey was in big trouble? The Australian public had pegged him as a hero but he wasn't. They'd hung a medal on his chest but he was no hero. No one should get a medal for causing the death of another person. The saving should far outweigh the taking but he didn't want to be reminded. He never again wanted to hear words like *hero, sacrifice, great bravery*. He never again wanted to be held accountable or responsible for another person's welfare or their life. Not ever.

Not even when the other person looked like a million bucks and smelled like home.

Why did he have to ask so many damned questions? She couldn't tell him anything because she didn't trust anyone. It was really that simple. If she came right out and told him that, he'd have a million more bloody questions. Callum wanted to know what it was like to be a hotshot actress living in Hollywood? It was lonely. It was isolating. It was hard!

She only had her stepmother to talk to. Audrey had made friends in her new high school but she'd lost them just as quickly when casting had raised her up higher than them. Jealousy destroyed the few relationships she'd wanted to count on. One of the women had led a magazine interviewer to believe Audrey suffered from bulimia when really she'd eaten bad salmon on a canape the night before. In her mind, she knew Callum would never do anything to hurt her like that.

She'd like to think he'd never betray her but not because she was Audrey. He wouldn't hurt Mavis's daughter.

Again the niggling feeling came that if she unburdened a few things, she'd feel better. Freer. Able to get past some of it. Was it fair though to lay that at Callum's feet? He was clearly battling demons of his own. Maybe she could get him to open up too and they could both let go of a few skeletons?

The heavy gloves pulled more than the weight on her shoulders as she exhaled, inhaled, exhaled again. "I... You were right..." How was she meant to start?

"Right about what?"

"I was attacked. The scar..." She pulled at her top's neckline again and ran the top of the boxing glove over the raised skin. "...is from a knife."

"Who was it?"

"It's a really long story."

"Is that why you came here? Someone is after you?"

Audrey shook her head. "I don't want to rehash it all, Callum. I don't like to talk about any of it."

"Audrey." He came back to stand in front of her and took her gloved hands in his bare ones. "If someone is after you, you have to let the cops know. Daniel can help you, protect you."

Her chin lowered to her chest and she shook her head. "No one knows where I am. He's not a threat anymore."

When a calloused palm cupped her cheek and his thumb put pressure on her jaw to lift her face, Audrey went with it, meeting eyes that had hardened to steel. "Did he do anything else to you? Did the police find him? Lock him up?"

"No, no and no. The LAPD said it was a random home invasion. The cut wasn't deep and nothing else happened. I...I started to scream and then he ran off." There was more to the story but he didn't need to hear the awful things that were whispered in her ear or about the press of hardness against her that made her want to vomit. Callum didn't need to hear the words that she was so frightened she'd frozen completely, unable to fight back even if she'd wanted to. It wasn't until the knife had begun to cut across her skin that adrenaline and terror finally turned to screams.

He especially didn't want to know that she'd been all kinds of screwed up ever since.

His thumb floated over the scar again and rather than fear making her heart skip a beat, it was anticipation, it was lust and heat.

"Stop looking at me like that." Callum's growl emerged husky and raw, needy almost.

"Stop touching me like that," came her reply. His hand was hot where it rested on her shoulder, on her warm skin, his fingers huge against her as he continued his caress over her collarbone.

"Like what?" he murmured.

"Like you want run your hands all over me. Everywhere."

"You're getting all that from just this?" He squeezed with his right hand, his left connecting with her hip but not staying there. He pulled her closer, his fingertips drifting lightly up her side, beneath her top and over the outside curve of her ribs.

Audrey shivered and closed her eyes, biting down on her bottom lip as her head lolled to the side, waiting for him to go higher or lower, whatever he wanted.

"We can't do this." But Callum lacked conviction as he lowered his mouth to her shoulder, his lips closing over her skin, suckling, nibbling.

Searing heat travelled along her every nerve ending eventually winding up in her lower abdomen, settling hot and heavy. "I think you already said that last night." She would let him do just about anything he wanted if only he'd touch her already. *Really* touch her.

He kissed a line across her scar and up the side of her neck to her earlobe. "We don't even know each other."

Audrey rested her gloved hands on his wide arms and cursed the laces he'd tied. She wanted to touch him back, to make him want her too. "Do we need to?"

He chuckled against her neck, his wandering hand moving closer, higher, right where she wanted to lean into him. She swayed and his grip against her arm tightened. But suddenly she couldn't stop swaying. Vertigo swept over her and Audrey couldn't stop falling. Fear swamped lust, confusion trumped passion.

The edges of her vision darkened like she was having a panic attack but the familiar nausea was absent. Callum lifted his head and met her eyes but Audrey couldn't speak, couldn't ask for help.

The brightness of the moment, of the day, slipped away into darkness, only this time she didn't give in. This time she tried to fight, tried to bring back the glorious warmth.

It was hopeless.

She was doomed.

Fourteen

♥

One minute he was tossing up the idea of laying a very willing Audrey down on the grass and taking her clothes off and the next he was laying Audrey down on the grass and taking her clothes off. Silly woman was flushed and so hot she'd fainted. He'd like to think it was cause and effect but his dormant ego didn't quite get there.

Callum pulled his shirt over his head and ran to the dip it in the river. He didn't bother wringing out the fabric, just ran back to Audrey and dripped the cool water over her neck and midriff where he'd pulled up the ridiculous jumper. He should have known she'd overheat too quickly dressed as she was but the jumper wasn't even very thick and she didn't look too hot or feel too sweaty. He'd had his hands on her and hadn't noticed anything out of the ordinary.

She moaned and tried to push away his cold t-shirt. He wondered if she'd put up a fight like she had when he'd woken her up. He undid the button on her jeans, unzipped the fly and peeled the fabric from her legs leaving her only in her underwear. He wasn't gentle. He didn't have time to be. Picking her up in his arms, he waded straight into the water. She needed to cool off. He should have made sure she'd had enough water to drink before their 'workout'. She was just so distracting. So confusing. So damned sexy.

When he plunged her into the cool, murky depths, she came alive in his arms, shrieking and attempting to push him away. She even dropped a few f-words of her own. The water wasn't cold enough to put her into shock but she reacted like it was.

Callum held her closer. "Settle down, woman. You need to cool down and calm down."

"What the...? What happened?"

"Are you prone to fainting?" Since this wasn't the first time she'd passed out, he had to ask the question. He surreptitiously went for her wrist to check her pulse but she wriggled and tried to break free. Callum held her tighter.

A soggy purple glove came for his face and he let out an, "oomph" when her wild punch connected with his cheek. "That wasn't nice."

Her struggles died down but then she became unnaturally still. "Where are my pants?"

Callum gestured with his chin. "Up there."

"You took my pants off?"

"You don't have to make it sound that weird. I had my hand up your top two seconds before that and I am a doctor."

"So you took my pants off because you wanted to or because you're a doctor?"

His lips pressed into a thin line and he rolled his eyes to the sky. He needed to buy some time to come up with an answer. Of course he undressed her to cool her down. "Would you believe me if I said it was the doctor thing?"

She shook in his arms and he thought she was finally going into shock but then he realised she was laughing. "It's not funny, Audrey. You could have done some serious damage getting that hot that quick."

"I did get hot," she said, a smirk on those full lips, a wriggle for emphasis.

"Feeling better then?" Callum countered, calling up the ballistic missile again in his mind.

The smirk fell away. "I am actually pretty thirsty. And these gloves are really heavy."

Had they just dodged a major bullet? He unlaced the gloves and threw them back towards the grassy bank. Sex with Audrey would complicate everything. Sex with anyone complicated things. Callum was protective by nature and by being alone, he'd been able to mostly switch it off but then along came Audrey. The problem with protecting was caring. He hated letting down the people he cared about. First his mum, then more than a few of his friends, the casualties of war, and then Mavis who he could only make comfortable after her life of excess caught up with her. That list wasn't even beginning to count the patients he couldn't save and the deaths he'd caused all in the name of war.

He couldn't control life and death but he could sure as hell stay clear of it and the toll it took to watch it play out.

Callum should have been smart enough to know getting into it with Audrey was bad. Really bad.

"You know there are snakes in the river, don't you?" Audrey said, her body stiff, her gaze darting this way and that, presumably checking every willow tree limb around them.

"They don't eat much," Callum said. Now that she was alert and back to herself, he had to let her go. She just felt so good in his arms. It had been years since he'd had more than a motherly hug and only from Mavis. Years since he'd lost himself in a woman. Years since he'd had any human contact. He hadn't craved it at all. Now his mouth watered and his body hungered.

Audrey's hair tickled his nose and he wanted her like she was the only woman on earth.

More than a decade had passed but he still remembered that teenage kiss she'd tried to inflict on him. She'd practically thrown herself into his arms, clumsy, wet lips, an over-eagerness that should have made him laugh. He was nearly a fully-fledged doctor then. Nearly a man who would have made his mother proud. But the young, innocent Audrey didn't make him laugh. She set him on fire. His male mind had leapt to sex, to bed, to fucking Audrey until she didn't know her own name. But then Mavis had turned the porch light on. He'd almost thrown Audrey across the yard. Shame had followed so quickly. Mavis would have flayed him for touching her daughter. She was sixteen for fuck's sake. He'd barely seen her again before she'd fled to America with her dad. His thoughts at that stage had been illegal, immoral and just plain wrong.

Now it wasn't illegal or immoral but it was still wrong. Between them both, the baggage was heavy and it was intense. His problems weren't going to go away at the wave of his dick and neither were hers.

Damn, it'd be fun though.

Callum let her stand on the river's bottom, covered in fine sand and bumpy and sharp with tree roots. She made her way to the banks but then stopped. "I don't have any pants on. Can you grab me a towel or something?"

His lips curved into a half-smile. "It wouldn't be good to leave you alone in the water. What if you faint again and go under?" He raised a brow in challenge. He attempted to keep his gaze on hers despite the fact her jumper had glued to her breasts and left nothing to the imagination.

More than a minute passed, a few emotions flashing in her eyes. She shrugged and emerged from the water, her back to him, her arse cheeks bare. Was that a G-string she was wearing and why hadn't he noticed that before? He was hard in a heartbeat.

"Aren't you coming?" she said over her shoulder, her brow raised the way his had, a sizzle in the air, tension looping around them both.

"Go and put some clothes on, Audrey. And drink some water."

"What are you going to do?" The challenge fell away.

"Swim," he said to her. Long, hard strokes saw him to the other side of the river in no time. Short, hard strokes saw him not quite so stupid he couldn't think straight.

Once again she'd crawled under his skin. This time he wasn't sure he was strong enough to push her away. This time he wasn't sure he wanted to.

Another shower for Audrey and three glasses of water and she was finally feeling that bit better. A small fan from the sewing room was trained on her and a bowl full of ice rested on the coffee table at her feet. Dehydration was a regular occurrence on set, not only in the summer but even in winter. Heaters were turned up and stage lights never lost their burn. If she had to shoot a beach scene in the middle of December, she sure as hell wouldn't do it while icicles formed and snow fell without a damned good heating system.

Audrey was not dehydrated. She was blaming Callum for this fainting spell. She hadn't eaten breakfast and his hands on her body made her all breathy. She probably hyperventilated her way to semi-consciousness. Hitting the water had certainly woken her up but it hadn't extinguished the fire. Wearing one of his old tank tops wasn't helping either. It took a hundred percent of the energy she had left not to lift the collar to her nose and inhale his scent. The scowl on his lips when he'd thrown the shirt at her just made her zero in on his face even more. She wanted more.

She was almost in pain with wanting. How far would Callum have gone? Audrey would have been happy to shed everything and do it on the back lawn.

Anger trickled through the fiery haze as it occurred to her that this wasn't the first time he'd pushed her away after making her think he felt something. Flashbacks to her teenage years made her cheeks burn. She was just as reckless when it came to him now as she had been then. Maybe the only part of Callum that wanted her was his southern brain but when his northern one kicked in, he didn't want her at all. Didn't want her then and didn't want her now.

At least he was good for one thing though. She'd forgotten her miserable life for a good half an hour, forgotten that she'd just told him about the one moment in time that had screwed her up so bad she was terrified she'd never be the same. He hadn't really said much. Hadn't asked any more questions.

Wasn't she supposed to be lighter now after sharing her experience with someone? Shouldn't the weight of the home invasion lift from her shoulders? Audrey snorted and reached for her glass of water, wishing it came with a little umbrella and a kick.

No.

She needed a clear head to figure this shit out. She needed clothes and she needed a phone charger. She needed to check and see if her name was covered in scandal yet. She knew Fabien would want to keep quiet about what had happened just as much as her agent but these things had a way of coming out. The walls had ears, and eyes were everywhere. How long would it be before the world found out she'd fallen into bed with a married producer? Would they believe she was black-out drunk and didn't remember anything?

Did anyone ever believe that old sob story? She probably wouldn't. No one knew about the home invasion therefore no one knew about the start of her decline into a bottle. They would believe what they wanted or what the media told them. That she was sleeping her way into her next role. Her outside scar had healed so well that you could only see it up close as proof of her ordeal.

Her inside scars were gaping holes that needed to be masked, disguised. But try as she might they were never forgotten, never healed, always there.

Lying her head back against her mother's old couch, breathing in the smell that was Mavis ever since she could remember, Audrey closed her eyes and wished for less complications and more hassle-free days...

Fifteen

House guests weren't part of the plan.

Callum scowled.

Anita bounced her way up the front path from the road where she'd parked and tooted her horn to announce her uninvited arrival.

"Hi Anita," Audrey said as she opened the front door. "What can I do for you?"

Anita peered into the room, took in Audrey's oversized army issue top, noticed Callum standing by the kitchen bench, smirked and then pushed her way past the lounge. "Doc Lawson sent me to check on the patient. Seems no one has a phone out here?"

Callum's phone was always charged and ready to use but he generally left it switched off. He didn't want or need to talk to anyone. It hadn't occurred to him to let anyone know Audrey was all right.

"My cell is dead," Audrey told her, making room by stepping back a fraction but not giving off too many hospitable vibes.

"Did he ask or was this your idea?" he said to Anita. Callum saw bullshit when it walked along and knocked on the door.

Anita flashed him a scowl before turning to Audrey and taking her hands. "How are you feeling, honey? Better now?"

Audrey nodded, clearly taken back by the other woman's concern. Was it genuine? Callum would say it was just more bullshit. "Audrey is doing just fine, thanks. She just really needs some rest."

Anita was not going to be turned away that easily. She started for the kitchen. "How about I make us a cup of tea and we can have a chat. You can catch me up on the last ten or so years? I have so many questions about Hollywood."

Manoeuvring his body into her path wasn't hard. "It's a hundred degrees and Audrey is dehydrated. Tea isn't going to help her."

"Dehydrated?" Anita repeated. "Well, that's not doing 'just fine'."

"I'm okay, really," Audrey reiterated. "And tea sounds nice. Callum is just cranky."

"What else is new?" Anita laughed.

It seemed as though he'd been dismissed but before he could fire off a parting shot, another knock at the door sounded.

That favourite four-letter word may have been mumbled beneath his breath as he went to see who else was destroying the peace. Daniel. "What's up, cop?" he said, swinging the screen wide.

"Not much, doc."

They hadn't had time for their customary greeting at the hospital and for once Callum was actually happy–okay, almost happy–to see another man.

A frustrated huff came from the direction of the open plan kitchen and Callum looked around for Audrey. The sound had come from Anita.

"Did you follow me here?" she half accused, half asked the policeman.

"You did leave a trail from your smoking broomstick," Daniel responded.

"It's an Astra, dickhead," Anita fired back.

"And your roadworthy is due in two days, bitch-face."

"Ooh, ouch, like that hurt."

Callum crossed his arms over his chest. "Now, now, children. No need to fight." It was like watching two kids in the playground. So much tension and immaturity.

"You got any beer?" Daniel asked, heading towards the kitchen.

Was it invite yourself over day and he didn't get the memo? "Out back," Callum grunted.

"Nice one, dickhead. Drinking in your uniform again?"

Daniel flipped Anita the middle finger as he followed Callum outside. Over his shoulder he threw, "The uniform is what you love about me."

Callum thought he heard, "You don't even wear it well," from Anita but he wasn't interested in any more name calling. He wanted to know why he was getting a house call from the law.

"Have a seat," Callum told him. "I'll grab you a beer."

There was nothing he'd done lately to warrant a visit from a police officer. Other than speeding down the main street with a comatose actress in his passenger seat. Maybe Daniel had come to break the news to him that he was getting a speeding fine after all. A big one. Or. He'd come to check out Audrey.

He skipped over the plank leading to the houseboat and returned a few seconds later with two cold beers. After the day Callum had had, he needed it.

"I take it this isn't a social call?"

Daniel raised a brow. "What makes you say that?"

"I've lived here a while now and you've never come unannounced before."

The other man chuckled. "You got me."

When his gaze drifted to the top of the chair opposite, Callum jumped up. He snatched Audrey's undies from their drying places but didn't know where to put them after that. "Bloody women," he muttered dropping them all onto the seat and out of sight.

Daniel laughed. "Making herself at home?"

"It is her home."

Twisting the lid off his beer, Daniel took a long mouthful and leaned back against the weathered jarrah chair. "How's it going with our movie star?"

Our movie star? "She's alright, I guess."

"You don't sound very enthusiastic for a man sharing a house with a beautiful, talented, rich, star."

"And you sound a little too enthusiastic. Besides, we're not sharing the house. She's in there." He indicated the dwelling with his beer. "And I'm over there." This time he swung the brown glass bottle to his houseboat. He wouldn't live in the house even if he could. Even if it was his house and not Audrey's. He didn't do enclosed spaces for long periods.

"I'd be spending more time in there if I was you." Daniel's thumb went over his shoulder to where the women were probably bitching in the kitchen.

"You going to clue me in on why you're here?" Callum asked when the silence lengthened. He was curious now. If he'd come to ogle Audrey, he had another thing coming. Not that she was his to protect, but he would. For Mavis. He gave a little nod before taking another swig of beer. Yeah. For Mavis.

"We've had a couple of incidences across the river, over at the campground, of a feral dog killing pets and livestock. Even went after a tourist two weeks ago."

"Ooo-kay." Callum drew out the o. "What has that got to do with me? It's not my dog."

"I know that. We're going out to track it down tomorrow night."

Callum frowned but took another mouthful of his beer before saying anything else. At least this wasn't about Audrey. "You mean hunt it down? You don't sound like you're going to take it to the pound."

"I was thinking you could come with us."

His beer hit the tabletop with a thunk. "Not going to happen. I don't hunt and I don't kill things."

"I'm not asking you to kill anything. Unless you've got a license, you're not getting a gun. I'm worried one of these yahoos is going to shoot a little to the left and take out another hunter. I wanted you there as a doctor, not a killer."

Unless you've got a licence, you're not getting a gun. He fucking wished someone had said that to him in Afghanistan. No. He wasn't going to go there right now. Not with Daniel across from him at the table and Audrey and Anita getting up to God knew what inside. He'd need a tranquiliser if he went there at this time of the day. This was another good reason to tell everyone to piss off.

"Sorry. I'm busy." There was no way he was going anywhere near guns, men with guns, or men accidentally shooting each other at the same time as sneezing. "You should be busy too. Let the campground take care of it."

Daniel shook his head and then drained his beer. "No can do. It's technically public land and the dog could belong to anyone. I have to head it up. I've got my orders."

"Well, you don't have mine."

"I didn't take you for a long-haired hippy, West."

"So, because I don't want to kill a defenceless animal or be around men who would, that makes me a hippy?" Callum didn't know whether to laugh or tell the man to get out.

"Defenceless animal? Some lady's poodle had his head ripped clean off. This thing is dangerous. What if it was a kid out for a piss in the scrub?"

He had a point. Pity it wasn't going to change Callum's mind. "I'm not going out there."

"I heard you were a man with principles, with honour. Guess I heard wrong."

"There's no honour in taking a life."

"There's no honour in sitting back and watching a life get taken either. Eventually you have to stand for what's right."

Callum did stand then. His vision narrowed and his heart thumped wildly against his ribs. "When you can tell me who gets to decide what's right and what isn't, then you can tell me what I should or shouldn't stand for."

Daniel met his gaze and held it for a little too long. Callum wanted to look away but he'd learned a long time ago to look danger in the eye the same way you would a friend or a challenge. Random men carrying shotguns out into the dark to hunt down a dog who was probably hungry, tired, cranky or all of the above, that was dangerous. And stupid. Callum didn't do dangerous anymore and he sure as hell didn't do stupid.

"I guess I better be going," Daniel said. "Thanks for the beer."

Callum nodded but he didn't offer a farewell. He wanted to say, *don't come back*, but he bit down on the end of his tongue. He stood like that for a while, listening to Audrey invite the police officer to stay for a coffee. Anita telling him to piss off back to where he came from. Daniel saying goodbye, adding to Audrey to keep an eye on the cranky arsehole.

Callum wasn't cranky. He was seriously sick of having his peace and lifestyle messed with. He wanted to go back to four days before when it was just him, his memories and the ghosts of his past for company.

Audrey was confused. Why wouldn't Callum go with Daniel? Didn't he care about the victims of the wild dog or the danger the men could face?

"That was weird, right?" she said out loud but not too loud.

"They're both weird. This is nothing new."

Audrey tried to find the meaning of Anita's words and her off the cuff gesture, wading through the childish name-calling and bias the other woman obviously held. "Do you know him very well?" Audrey asked as Callum's long strides ate up the distance to his houseboat. It bobbed slightly on the surface of the water as he vaulted over the plank, slamming the sliding door with a finality that was a little worrying. She shouldn't eavesdrop but Callum's body language through the kitchen window put her on guard.

"Local cop, pain in the ass, always trying to ping me for something or rather."

Ping? Was that code? "I meant Callum."

When Audrey swung her attention back to Anita, the other woman's cheeks were pink and she fidgeted with the handle on her coffee mug. "Um, I don't know much about

Mr Serious. He comes by the hospital now and then to check up on accident victims or whatever. Sometimes he pinches a prescription pad but I don't tell anyone. He's kind of...haunted, if you know what I mean?"

"Does he help out at the hospital?"

Anita shook her head. "Never. He always skips out before the really gross stuff happens."

Interesting. Back when they'd been almost like family, he'd only ever wanted to be a doctor. He used to talk about saving lives and making it up to his mum. What had happened to make him forget all of that? To turn his back? Was it disappointment that drove him to isolation? Had they both failed their mothers? She knew she certainly had. Did they actually have not one but two things in common after all this time?

"What was it like when you moved away?" Anita asked, breaking apart her dark and confusing thoughts.

"It was scary." Audrey didn't even have to think about that answer. Terrified wouldn't even have cut it as a descriptor. Scared shitless came closer.

"I'd love to escape this place. Go further than boring old Adelaide and have some fun for a change."

Audrey pottered around the kitchen putting cold teabags in the trash, the milk back in the fridge, the pieces of her life on the bench to try to fit back together later when she was alone. She shivered. *Alone.*

Curiosity and the need for a distraction made her switch back on to the conversation. "Why did you stay?"

"I left for a bit. To study. But then the government needed nurses to work in country hospitals. I get paid more to live at home. It was a win-win."

"If you hate it so much, why don't you pack up and leave? You could be a nurse anywhere in the world."

"Do you love what you do?"

Audrey nodded. "I do. I don't think anything can make me happier than the diversity of being someone new every time the camera rolls. It's always interesting and fun."

"Then why the boozey after parties? Google just about has you pegged as public enemy number one as well as most of the magazines coming out of The States."

Audrey groaned and plopped down onto a stool. She let her head hit the kitchen bench and mumbled a minor blasphemy under her breath.

"I thought you'd be used to all of that by now."

Another groan. "No one gets used to be being followed around twenty-four-seven. I can't even go to the store for tampons without someone reporting on the state of my fertility or the brand of my pads."

Anita actually laughed and Audrey lifted her head to raise a brow.

The other woman leaned forward like she was about to share a trade secret or something. "Is it true you binge on salt and vinegar chips when you're pms-ing?"

"Oh. My. God. They did not report that."

"They did." Laughter echoed around the room. "And mint ice cream when you're sad. Spicy salsa when you're happy."

Great. The world could work out her emotions based on her grocery list. This is what happened when you listened to your agent when she said, "*Don't google yourself. Ever!*"

"What else does the internet say about me?" She actually shuddered inside to think.

Anita grew strangely quiet after spilling the beans on everything else. "Is it really that bad?" Audrey asked.

"The producer you slept with is being sued by his wife. They had a pre-nup and if he cheated, she got everything."

"Shit." Scandal it was. "I..." How the hell did she explain it? Should she even try?

"Yep." Anita nodded, her hair bobbing about her shoulders. "Is that why you came back? To hide?"

"You haven't told anyone I'm here have you? No one is supposed to know."

Big, wide eyes stared back at her. "I'd never do anything like that. I'd lose my job for starters. What are you going to do?"

Why was it Audrey couldn't talk to the psychologist or the doctors lining up to check her mental state but she could talk to a girl she'd gone to school with for a few months more than ten years before? If Fabien's wife was dragging him to litigation, Audrey's name was going to be linked with it for months, maybe years. She'd never live it down. In her mind the gurgle of a toilet sounded as her career was washed down the drain.

Her next words emerged barely more than a whisper. "I don't know."

Sixteen

♥

At the impressionable young age of three, Audrey Hobson had wanted to be a singer. At age seven, her ambitions changed to scientist after making a homemade volcano and coming first in a school contest. Twelve saw her taking on her classmates in track and field events. Thirteen was a blur of hormones and boys and finally realising why her mum passed out most nights on the couch, at the dining table, in the bathtub.

When Aiden Simmons had taunted her with the news that Mavis was an alcoholic, Audrey had raced to the library to find a dictionary to look up the meaning of the word. Aiden's dad was the local policeman back then and had arrested Mavis for driving under the influence on the way back from dropping Audrey at school. It wasn't the first or the last time Mavis had been pulled over for erratic driving but damn, she had her only daughter fooled.

Audrey thought her mum was tired. Just like most other mums. She had the cooking, the washing, the cleaning to do and the bills to pay. Only, Audrey did the washing, the cleaning and some of the cooking. At nine, she'd fancied herself quite the chef because she could grill cheese on toast without burning the crusts.

Two years later, a few months after her fifteenth birthday, and after another raging blue with Mavis, Audrey had called her dad and asked to move in with him. In America. Los Angeles to be more specific. She had other dads. Mavis had married a few times. She kept in contact occasionally with two of the men. But she couldn't run off and live with them.

At sixteen, she finally convinced her biological father it was the right thing to do. She'd finally convinced herself Mavis could never be helped and was only a toxic influence in her life. Mavis hadn't put up a fight. Her own mother hadn't shed one tear when she'd put her only child on a plane to move half the globe away. Audrey had cried for ten hours straight. Six months passed before she felt as though she'd done the right thing in moving. Done the right thing in leaving her mum and her shitty life behind.

Now that she was the ripe old age of twenty-eight, she should be sure of her decisions in life and back her choices and stick with them because she was an adult and with her years on the planet should come some level of wisdom. Right? Then why did she feel so out of her depth? So out of control?

Callum stomped into the lounge room and stood before her. "You feeling better?"

"Much," she replied. Audrey could feel anxiety rolling off him in waves. He very definitely had something to say.

"Get up then. Back to your lesson."

"I'm not sure that idea is any better than it was three hours ago."

"We'll be right. We just have to stick to the plan. And maybe not touch each other."

Audrey's lips lifted of their own accord and her insides did a little one-two-skip. As she stood, she couldn't help but throw in, "However will you be able to control yourself?"

"We're both adults. We can stand next to each other without touching."

"What if I want to touch?" she asked, taking a step in his direction. She wanted to play with Callum. In more ways than one. Take her mind off the rest of the shit for a few hours.

"Before..." he started, and then snapped his mouth shut and gave his head a shake. "I wasn't...prepared."

"Prepared?" she repeated, her hopes lifting with every stuttered sentence. Audrey had never had to put effort into getting a guy to notice her. Except for Callum West. He had this mental kind of resistance to her and she didn't like it one bit. It wasn't about ego and she didn't think it was about wanting something she couldn't have. She liked Callum even now. Grumpy bum that he was. He was still hot and he still pressed all her buttons.

"Let's just say it won't happen again."

"Let's not and see what happens?"

He started for the door, his mouth in that thin little grim line. "Get your arse out the back, Audrey."

Callum needed to blow off some steam. Cranky didn't even come close to his current mood. Audrey's undies still sat on the chair, Anita's annoying house call and then Daniel's moronic request had gone from little pricks of problems to a mountain of fury. Why did everyone suddenly think it was okay to destroy his peace and quiet?

They'd left him alone after Mavis had died. They'd left him alone until Miss Movie Star had rocked up. It was all Audrey's fault and he needed to get her back on the road and back to her old life. Starting with a power take back. If she could defend herself then maybe she'd be one step closer to pissing off.

"Right. Lesson one. Stop thinking about sex and start getting mad."

"Who said I was thinking about sex?" Audrey asked, one tiny brow high, that little smirk on her lips and her head tilted so the line of her neck was exposed.

This was going to be a lot harder than he thought. *He* was going to be a lot harder than he thought. "Lesson two. Do not let your guard down. If you manage to get me on the ground again, you run into the house. If you can make it into the house at any point. You win."

Her eyes flashed and she perked up a little more. "Win what?"

"Not sex," he growled. She had it written all over her. Her hands rested on her hips and her chest lifted. It was in her smile, her stance, her voice, even the flick of her ponytail was damned sexy.

It wasn't happening.

Audrey tapped her forefinger to her chin for all of three seconds before her gaze shifted from Callum to the houseboat and back. "Will you take me for a cruise down the river? Today?"

It was too late for a good cruise today but then again, the sun would be out until at least seven pm and then they wouldn't have to go far. "If you make it into the house and get the door shut against me, I'll take you out on the boat."

Audrey held her hand out for him to shake. The last time they'd stood like this Callum had been promising not to tell Mavis that Audrey had gotten into trouble in town. She'd called him instead of her mum and he'd come to the rescue despite his better judgement telling him to stay out of it.

"No touching," he said.

"You have to shake on a deal, Callum, otherwise how do I know you'll stick to the bargain. Or are you scared of this too?"

Too? As in her, or scared of other things? He wanted to retort that he wasn't scared of anything but that would have been a big, fat, fucking lie. Right now he was terrified of the heat that swamped him when she bit her lower lip, when she flashed her teeth or poked out her tongue. All three of those he wanted to taste. To nip and bite and suck. Jeez, he was fucked. All he had to do was not let her in the house.

"Deal." He shook her hand once and then let go like she'd dipped her fingers in shit or something.

Audrey just laughed. "Do we have any rules for this game?"

"Yeah, don't treat it like a game. I'll show you some moves first and then see how you go."

Some of the bravado fell from her face and the real Audrey showed up again. Vulnerable and more scared than she wanted to let on. "You're stronger than me. How am I going to beat you?"

His fury melted away and he gave her a smile. "If I think you've given me a good tap, I'll concede a point. Okay?"

She nodded.

"Every man is going to be bigger and stronger than you, Audrey. If they're not then they're relying on their brains to corner you and that can be just as bad. You have to fight strategically if you want to win. No matter what. And try not to let panic in. You have to stay focused."

"That's impossible. How do you keep the panic out?"

If he knew that, he wouldn't be there. But they had different fears driving their different brands of anxiety. He wasn't the least bit worried about predators or being beaten in a fight. He was strong and fit. His fears were in his head and that was so much worse. Or was it?

"How often do you think about your home invasion?" he asked her. He didn't want to push her to talking about it but she had to.

Audrey didn't hesitate. "Every time I'm alone."

"Only at night or during the day too?"

"Mostly at night. I... This is silly. Can we just get on with it?"

"You what? What were you going to say? You're safe here with me, Audrey. Let it out."

"I feel more vulnerable at night. There are less people around, it's dark and I can't see a thing when the lights are out. Noises scare me. The dark scares me. Everything scares me."

"You were always a little afraid of the dark," Callum pointed out gently.

"You remember that?"

Shit. He remembered lots of things. She didn't have to know that though. "Let's start with the easy stuff. Do you know where a man is the most vulnerable?"

Her eyes dropped and he was glad for the dark turn of the conversation. He'd been on his way to an erection earlier. "Good," he said. "Try to kick me."

Audrey shook her head so fast, her hair swung all around her shoulders. "No way. I'll hurt you."

"If you manage it, I'll live."

"You're an idiot," she said.

Callum laughed. "Maybe. You have to do it like you mean it if you want to get anywhere near my balls."

Once again her brows lifted and the smirk was back. Good. Cockiness was going to help him in the long run, not her.

He was completely ready when Audrey swung her bare foot up towards his manhood. There was no way she was ever going to make contact. He grabbed her heel in one hand and reached out for her other arm with his other hand so she didn't tip backwards.

"Not smart. Now what are you going to do?"

She hopped on the spot, her cheeks pink, a four-letter word slipping into the hot air between them. Callum let her go and indicated for her to try again.

She kicked exactly the same as the last time and he grabbed her foot again. This time one of her hands came out and nearly slapped him in the face. He only just managed to lean back in time.

Her smile grew wider.

"This time try to get me with your knee rather than your foot. It will hurt you less and me more."

A bit closer but nowhere near close enough.

"Have a think of some other vulnerable places on the body. There's the neck." Not touching just was not going to work. He put his hand on her throat and pressed against her windpipe until she nodded that she understood. "There's the stomach." He turned and pressed the back of his elbow to her abs. "And the best one after a man's family jewels is the nose. If you hit anyone in the nose hard enough, you'll stun them for long enough to aim for one of the other soft targets."

"I've seen this before," Audrey said. She turned and gave him her back but took his arm and wrapped it around her neck. "Foot, elbow, head-butt." She kicked down hard on his toes, elbowed him in the stomach, blowing the breath from his diaphragm, and then threw her head back. He just missed the knockout blow but just as he loosened his not very tight grip, she shot out of his arms and was nearly at the back door.

Callum caught her around the waist and spun her back towards the grass. "I wasn't ready."

"Did you have to be?" she asked, chuckling but not resisting his embrace.

Lifting a hand, Callum clamped it over her mouth. "What would you do if you couldn't scream for help?"

She stiffened but only slightly. He could just about hear her thoughts as she tried to formulate a move against him. He was nowhere near prepared when her tongue slid along the palm of his hand.

This time it was Callum who stiffened. Everywhere. "You have to do better than that. If I was here to rape you, you just fulfilled fantasy number one."

The graze of her teeth as she tried to bite only messed with him more. "A common fallacy in movies, Auds, you can't bite a flat hand over your mouth." He had one armed pinned but hadn't managed to grab the other one. Her nails raked his hand as she tried to move his fingers one by one.

She was beginning to panic so he let her go. "Next time, try pulling on my ear. You could have reached it. Or try poking me in the eye."

"I couldn't see your eyes or your ears. And why couldn't I bite? That always works on CSI."

"Never try any form of self-defence you've seen on the telly. Hair pulling doesn't hurt as much as you'd think and biting only works if their hand isn't flat. Mine was, so you couldn't get near it."

"This isn't fair. I can't win against you."

"You're not fighting hard enough yet. You're still treating it like a game."

"I am not going to hurt you," she said, adamant and sure.

"Not like that you're not. Licking the hand that's cutting off your oxygen won't do shit, Audrey. Even biting isn't going to do much. You have to want to do some serious damage. You have to want that arsehole not to get back up."

"This isn't going to work."

"It will if you get mad. Are you getting mad yet?"

"Yes," she said with a huff. "You're starting to piss me off."

"Good. That's a start."

"Right, let's go again. I won't hold back."

Callum snorted. "Do your worst."

Thirty minutes into their 'self-defence' lesson, Audrey was no closer to the door. Panic wasn't an issue but frustration was. Everything she threw at him, he dodged. It was so easy because he was bigger and stronger. This was supposed to be making her feel better not weaker.

"This is useless," she cried, throwing her arms in the air and waving them around. "You could have knocked me out and carried me away by now."

Callum shook his head. "Most attackers want you alive and fighting. That's where they get their thrill."

"Guys suck."

"Not just guys but in theory, yes, we suck. When the guy broke into your house, how did he get in? How did he get to you?"

Audrey shuddered but pushed the fear down. She was half a world away and she was with Callum. She was safe and right down to her bones, she felt it. "I left the window open. It was a hot night and I wanted to catch the breeze." Her neighbours had been cooking on the grill that night too and the smell was delicious. It had reminded her of barbecues with her mum.

"So he climbed in through your window and then what?"

"Why do you want to know the details? He broke in, he scared the shit out of me and then he ran off."

"Did he pin you down?" Callum came towards her as he asked.

Audrey backed up a step. "I don't think so. I can't remember."

"Did he touch you?"

"Can we stop now? I'm done with this."

"We can stop, but you're not done. What happens if he does come back? What happens if it's not him but some other guy? I want you to keep going until you can learn to take down an attacker."

They were her biggest fears of all. What if he came back? What if word got out that she was an easy target and they all came? Stupid, irrational fears but she couldn't seem to get rid of them. What if Callum was right and she could learn to be fearless? To fight back?

"Do you really think I can learn?"

"Anyone can learn. Do you want to be able to hurt someone, Audrey?"

"I want to be able to kick that guy's ass if he ever shows up again."

"That's my girl," Callum said with a smile. "You're not going to pick it all up today but we'll practice every day okay? You'll be ass kicking in no time."

A new sense of hope lifted her spirits. "Thanks, Callum." She lifted her arms around his neck and revelled in his heat and strength and surety. When she kissed him softly on his bristled cheek, he froze.

She ran.

And made it to the door. While Callum swore long and loud.

Seventeen

♥

E ven though Mavis and Audrey had lived on the edges of
the Murray River for a couple of years, Audrey had never
seen more than their backyard worth of the glistening surface.
She'd assumed the towering red cliffs on the other side had
been as big as they got. That their view was worth a million
bucks and more.

She was wrong about all of it.

As Callum's houseboat drifted down the river at a slow pace,
Audrey breathed in the fresh hot air and took in all the sights,
trying to imprint them into her memory forever. Nothing was
as beautiful as the birds flying by, the changing landscape of
cliffs on one side and meadows on the other. No man-made
sound outdid the gentle hum of the motor helping them push
against the current and Callum didn't say much.

Occasionally he pointed out the flood markers from the
fifties when the water had risen to an almost impossible to
imagine height. He drew her attention to rickety, timber
makeshift stairs leading from the water's edge right up the cliffs
to holiday homes perched precariously on stumps at the top.
She tried to imagine the kind of carefree lifestyle where you

could enjoy the endless days of summer with no more worry than getting too much sun or burning your steak.

"I never did understand why mum moved us out to the middle of nowhere. She'd had the house for years and never even visited. Then, bam, up and move to the sticks as far away from civilisation as we could go."

For a moment she wondered if she'd talked out loud or only imagined the words but then Callum answered her. "She told me once that she didn't want the house at all. But she didn't want my dad to have it either. I guess all those memories of being on the water as kids were hard to take."

Callum's mum left the house to Mavis in her will. It's where they'd met and formed their friendship. It's where they'd spent summers as kids. Six weeks a year over Christmas and two weeks at Easter. Not much in the bigger scheme of things but when you were best friends, time didn't have the same meaning. Then their mum's had gone onto university together, his a midwife, hers a nurse. But Mavis had dropped out early after meeting husband number one. He'd whisked her away to Italy for six months before she caught him in bed with another woman.

Audrey looked back on her mother's life and wondered if it was easier to fall in love with men than it was to make something of herself. Her mother had always been directionless and unable to be on her own for long. Audrey's own psychiatrist had pondered if Mavis had been unhappy as a child, unloved by her father. But her grandparents had died before she'd been born. She didn't know anything about them and Mavis didn't like to rehash what had already been done. The only bits of her past she talked about were the times spent with Erin. It was like the other woman was the only shining light in Mavis's life.

"Did mum talk about me much after I'd gone?" Audrey asked after Callum had reversed the small houseboat against a scrubby, quiet piece of shoreline.

Callum smiled. "All the time. I got constant updates on your stardom. She was really proud of you." He led her to the front of the boat where there were two chairs and a patio table. In his hand were two bottles of cold water.

"Sometimes I think she liked you better than she liked me." Where that confession came from, Audrey had no idea. The words just kind of spilled out of her. "She was really proud of you too. She never talked about herself in her letters, only her doctor soldier godson."

Callum's cheeks gained some pink but he didn't answer, just tipped his water to his mouth and drained half the bottle.

"Why do you think she didn't tell me you were out of the army and living with her?"

He closed his eyes and Audrey started to get angry. Why wouldn't he just answer her? Was there a secret she didn't know about?

Eventually he said, "I don't know."

"I need you to do better than that. I need to know."

"Why? All I know is I asked her not to tell anyone I was there. I needed some time out and she offered it to me."

It was none of her business, the why's. Mavis did whatever Mavis wanted to do. Regardless of anyone else. She wanted to change the subject. This cruise was meant to be relaxing not morbid.

"Do you think you'll ever go back to the army?"

"Nope."

"What about being a doctor? It's all you ever wanted to do."

He stood, his chair nearly tipping over. "I'm going for a swim."

"You can't change the subject every time I ask you a personal question, Callum."

"Yes I can. Then you'll stop asking personal questions. I don't want to talk about any of it."

Audrey stood as well so he wasn't looming. He was dark and fierce and a little dangerous like this. "Okay, okay. I just thought maybe this was a two-way street where I tell you something deep and then maybe you return the favour so I don't feel like such a messed-up freak."

His chin fell a little from its defiant angle and his eyes softened and Audrey could tell he battled within himself in those seconds. She wanted him to tell her his story. She wanted to know why Mavis had lied to her own daughter to protect a man who wasn't even blood to her. It didn't make sense and now that her mind was free of worry over another home invasion, her thoughts wandered to other things. Like why Callum was hiding because that's definitely what he was doing out there at Jupiter Creek. The other day he'd had a panic attack in a crowded place. He'd flat out denied a policeman his medical services and cracked the temper tantrums after he'd left.

"You're not a freak, Auds."

She turned her back and let her blurred gaze drift across the water. "Just messed up."

"We're all a little messed up."

Strong hands squeezed her shoulders and she couldn't help but melt back into him.

"Do you think you'll ever be able to talk about it?" She didn't want to keep pushing but she didn't like not knowing.

"Probably not," came his soft reply as his chin landed on the curve of her neck and his hands floated down her bare arms. The barely there touch caused a shiver to take hold.

"Distracting me won't work. I want to know why you're hiding away from the world, Callum."

Fingers traced their way from her hands to her stomach until his arms were around her middle. "I'd much rather distract you than tell you."

Audrey smiled. "What happened to no sex?"

"We're not having sex. We're going to go for a swim. Can you still swim?"

"I can but I don't want to. What about the snakes and the dead bodies?"

His caress of her middle halted and he shook behind her. "What dead bodies?"

"There would definitely be bodies under all that murk."

"I seriously doubt that. Bodies don't sink for long anyway. They always pop back up."

"Ew. How do you know that?"

He chuckled and stepped away. "Doctor, remember? We all get to learn about the truly sick shit."

"Yeah, well, you can keep that," she told him.

"Are you going to live a little and come for a swim with me? Or are you going to sit here and sulk away the end of the day?"

"I don't sulk."

"It's all you do."

"Says the man who won't-" She didn't get to finish her sentence. Callum lifted her up and threw her over the railing and into the water.

When she resurfaced, spluttering and coughing, she was going to let him have a few of her favourite swear words but he was stripping his shirt over his head and her mouth went dry. His abs rippled in the afternoon sun and his tattoos distracted her.

He stepped up onto the railing with both feet and then did a bouncing dive into the muddy water next to her, splashing her as she trod water and drooled at the temptation that was Callum. Why couldn't he have gained fifty kilos and lost half his hair? Why did he have to be the kind of brooding bad boy she'd never even been attracted to until now?

When he came up for air and shook his hair free of most of the water, she asked, "What happened to your oxford shirts and loafers?"

He gave a snort. "I was such a pretentious arse then, wasn't I?"

"I liked that look on you."

"I know you did."

"What is that supposed to mean?" She did not like the egotistical tone to his words or the way he smirked as he said them.

"You know exactly what it means. You were so hot for me back then."

He was dead on right but she didn't want him to know that. "As I remember it, you totally kissed me back until mum scared the crap out of you."

"Us. She scared us both. You would have been in so much trouble if we got caught."

"God, that feels like a lifetime ago," she said as she loosened her limbs and floated onto her back, forgetting about snakes and bodies long enough to let the cool water refresh her. This is what holidays were for.

"And yet nothing has changed in that respect," he teased. "You're still hot for me."

Callum knew taunting Audrey was like poking a bear. Why he did it, he didn't want to analyse. Maybe it was the picture of her on her back with only her chin and breasts breaking the river's surface. She didn't have the biggest of boobs but he guessed they'd each be a perfect fit for his hands. More than enough for his mouth to suckle and his teeth to nibble. Anything was preferable to talking about his past.

Her shoulders lifted slightly in a shrug and she moved her hands beneath the water to stay afloat. "I'd do you," she said as though it would mean absolutely nothing. Just sex.

He should have been annoyed at the flippant way she said those three little words but his libido heard them as three shouted, all in caps, neon lights. His dick heard, *let's have sex*, loud and clear.

He had to get some proximity and he had to get it now. He began the short swim back to the houseboat but then she shrieked and he whipped around in the water.

"You can't just leave me out here," she cried, breast stroking her way to his side. "What if I get into trouble?"

"Baby, you are trouble," he muttered under his breath, genuinely woried that she'd found danger, or danger had found her. This is why he didn't get close. He did not want to care.

"I heard that," came her indignant statement but it came with a barely smothered grin.

Callum did the gentlemanly thing and let her get back up on the houseboat deck first. It had nothing to do with seeing her arse in her wet shorts or even giving her little bum a shove to help out. It definitely wasn't so he could get his rampaging lust under control.

But Audrey couldn't boost herself up and even if he had tried to help by catching the twin globes of her backside, she didn't have the strength. She was breathless with laughter by the third try and said, "This isn't working at all."

"Let me go first and I'll pull you up," he offered.

"Okay, but don't leave me down here."

He was up and on his feet in four heartbeats. He kept his back to her for another before squatting down to take her hand. He didn't pull her up straight away. He was enjoying the twinkle in her eye and the sound of her quiet laughter.

"I'm ready. Get me out of here," she demanded, a little diva coming through.

"Say please."

"Please get me out of here."

"I want you to say, Callum, pretty, pretty please get me out of here, with sugar on top."

"This isn't funny."

Callum chuckled. "Those aren't the words."

"Pretty, pretty please with sugar on top, pull me out."

"I think I like it when you're not getting your way." He'd half pulled her out when she poked her tongue out so he dropped her back in.

She came up spluttering but still laughing. "That was so dirty. When I get up there, you're going to pay for that."

"You've got to get up here first, Audrey."

Try as she might, kicking out with her feet and pulling with her arms, she just didn't have the strength to do the job. Eventually he took pity on her struggles and pulled her the rest of the way, landing in a heap on the deck. She was breathing hard, her hand resting on her abdomen. "You are no gentleman, Callum West."

"Did I ever say I was?" He lay on the deck next to her, taking in this Audrey Hobson. At peace. Relaxed. Sexy as hell. He missed this. This human contact that started to break down his walls brick by brick, lulling him into a false sense of security, telling him maybe he overreacted by hiding away from humanity.

Rolling towards him, Audrey punched him in the arm, her aim true but no pain behind the gesture. "I can't believe you did that to me."

"I can't believe you didn't see it coming," he joked sitting up, his arms over his knees while his gaze travelled over her long, long legs.

Then he saw it. And the world around him dipped and then went black.

Eighteen

♥

A udrey thought they were having fun. Finally getting along. She hadn't laughed this much in so long and it was lifting the weight from her shoulders.

Until he went completely lifeless, his eyes an empty shell in his skull.

"Callum?"

He didn't answer.

Audrey went on to her knees and gave him a shake. Still no response but he was there. His shoulders trembled beneath her hands and for a moment she was truly scared. They were in the middle of nowhere and he was the doctor, not her.

"Callum, you're scaring me, what's wrong?"

Audrey took his jaw in her hands and lifted his hollow gaze to hers. "Callum? Callum, come on."

When he blinked, she could have cried. "Callum?" she whispered.

He inhaled deeply but didn't stop looking at her, or rather, through her. "You're bleeding." And then his eyes closed and he covered his face with his hands.

"I am?" Audrey sat back down and looked over her legs. Sure enough there was a long gash down her shin. She must have scraped it when he pulled her up.

"It's nothing," she assured him. "Just a scratch." Because her legs were wet, the blood trickled in a diluted stream down to her ankle. She'd had worse shaving accidents. "I'll be fine."

"You...you have to cover it up," he said, his voice barely audible it was so low and deep, muffled through his hands.

"It'll dry up in a sec," she said, suddenly confused about how they got to that point. "Are you seriously scared of a little blood?" He'd be the worst doctor ever. She remembered the year one of his friends had sliced his hand open on a broken beer bottle and Callum had stitched him up with Mavis's sewing kit before taking him up to the hospital. He hadn't freaked out then.

"I...just...can't." That's all she got from him on a long, drawn out sigh.

Audrey was really beginning to worry. After his panic attack the other day and now this total meltdown, she was beginning to think maybe he was a lot more screwed up than she was after all.

"Where is your first aid kit?"

His large frame was wracked by shudders and for a heartbreaking second, Audrey thought he might be crying.

"Callum," she called sharply. "Medical supplies?"

"In the cupboard. Above the kitchen sink."

"Wait here." But she needn't have bothered, he wasn't going anywhere.

It took only a couple of minutes to clean the cut which wasn't very big. She slapped a bandage on it and went back out to where Callum sat, his toes in the water, his gaze on the darkening horizon.

Sitting close, Audrey bumped her shoulder against his, friendly, non-threatening, quiet. "So," she started, but then didn't know what else to say.

"Are you okay?" he asked her.

"Me? I'm fine. Are you?"

"Why wouldn't I be?"

"Is that the way we're going to play this? You pretend you didn't just totally shut down over a little blood? I have a giggle and we go back to flirting?"

"Can we?" The hope in his voice was forced. The whole situation was forced now.

"Uh uh, no way. You pushed and pushed until I squealed, now it's your turn."

"Mine is so much worse than yours."

"Whoa," she said. "Is it a competition on which one of us is more scarred than the other? I didn't realise." The last was so sarcastic she almost winced herself.

Callum shook his head. "You do not want to hear my shit, Audrey. You think you have trouble sleeping now? I can't go there with you."

"And why not? You think I'd tell anyone? Look at you differently?"

"Not the first, definitely the second though."

"How about I be the judge? If it's too heavy, which it won't be, then I'll ask you to stop speaking, tell you to shut up."

He made a weird noise and said, "You can't handle it, Audrey. No one can."

"So you weather whatever this is alone? How's that working out for you?"

"I was fine until you came along."

Instead of feeling affronted, she smiled at her feet, twirling the water with her toes. "I would say sorry but I'm not. Maybe the universe had a plan for the both of us?"

This time Callum snorted and let out a humourless half-bark of a laugh. "You do not believe in the universe."

Audrey nodded and hope bloomed that they were getting somewhere, anywhere other than the scary, dark stuff. "Of course I do."

"Of course you do," he repeated, softer, so she could barely hear.

Audrey didn't say anything else. She didn't pull her hand away when he reached for it, lacing his fingers into hers and studying the back of her knuckles.

"I don't know why I'm about to tell you this," he began, but then stopped, inhaled deeply, exhaled slowly. "The helicopter I was on was shot down and half of my crew were killed, some on impact."

"The others?" she asked, dread filling her very being.

"Shot."

"Jesus, Callum, that's awful."

He did that half snort again. "Awful was the food, the heat, the conditions. Awful doesn't even begin to cover what we saw out there."

"How did you survive?"

Callum knew that for the rest of life, he would remember the shots ringing out, the smell of blood mixing with fuel, the screams cut short and the moment he realised he'd have to fight for his life. He hadn't ever really thought of blood as having a smell, it was the same as water didn't really have a taste. Unless it went bad. Covered in blood and crawling through fuel-soaked sand, he realised the smells were real and they were sickening. "Just lucky, I guess."

"Don't do that." Her voice demanded he pay attention. Sharp, feminine, grounding.

"Do what?"

"Don't downplay it for me. I'm a big girl. I want to know what happened to you."

"So you can understand me better?" he said, loosening his iron grip around her fingers. "So you can try to fix me?"

Audrey held on tighter, her other hand folding around his. "I'll never understand war, Callum, or what you went through. As to the fixing, how can someone as messed up as me, fix you? And that's if you need to be fixed. Maybe you just need time? A distraction from the day-to-day bullshit?"

"Are you offering?"

"I'm offering to listen first, distract later, maybe."

He liked how she tried to lighten the moment but nothing was going to prepare her for what was in his head. "I was knocked for a six and nearly passed out but I saw them coming, townsfolk, to see what had happened. Or so I thought." Then the close quarter firing had started but not from him or his remaining crew. "They shot at us, three Afghans. Killed two more crew and the soldier we were airlifting. I wasn't the only survivor, there were two others."

"Oh my God, you were lucky to get out of there."

"Was I though, Auds?" He didn't want to do this but she had to see, he wasn't in a good place, he wasn't the person everyone thought he was. Hero. Pfft. He hated the word more than he hated war.

"What do you mean? Of course you were."

"One of the guys I served with, a pilot, his baby was born three days after he died. He never got to meet her." A tiny little ginger version of her daddy, red face all screwed up. The baby cried all the way through the funeral service for her brave father. "Or the nurse about to celebrate her fortieth birthday and her second divorce? Or the soldier who had already been shot in the back by the enemy and was supposed to be airlifted for surgery, not face more crossfire."

"You can't hold yourself responsible for anybody else's life, Callum."

"That's what I do though. I save lives. I don't take them."

"You didn't take them. You didn't pull the trigger."

Not on them, no. He didn't say it out loud. "I would have gladly changed places with any one of them."

"That's not how it works and you know that. If you could swap your life for someone else's, you already would have. I know you better than you think. You have always had this need in you to help people. Look at everything you did for Mavis."

And he couldn't do a damned thing to save her either. What fucking good was he or his years of training? As a man or a doctor, he was as useless as tits on a bull. Worse. Mavis had slurred that very same sentiment to him one night when he wouldn't run up to the bottle shop for her and he'd felt the truth all the way to his bones.

"Your mum was a good woman. She didn't deserve the shitty hand life dealt to her." Callum should have kept his mouth shut but if they were talking about her mum, they weren't talking about him.

"Maybe not," Audrey conceded. "But she didn't do anything to make it better either."

"What would you have had her do?" Callum wondered.

This time it was Audrey who pulled against their clasped hands. He didn't let her go. He did ask again. "What do you think Mavis could have done differently, Audrey?"

"She had a nurse's training. She could have stopped drinking and gone out and got a job, lived a life worth living instead of making it hell on earth for everyone else."

"She was trying to protect you, keep you sheltered." Callum shouldn't have to explain anything to her but he felt he had to point out the obvious. Teenage Audrey hadn't seen it but adult Audrey might.

She didn't have to know how much Mavis hated him towards the end though. How much she hated everyone and everything. The kind of sickness eating away at her body did that. The pain got to her until there wasn't much left but anger and frustration. By the time the end was in sight, she was a shell of a woman and she just wanted to die. That was the hardest part. He'd seen men hold on for every precious second they could in order to say goodbye. He'd seen men fight death so they could go home to their families. Mavis had had enough. She only wanted it all to end.

He understood that better than most. He'd wished it a few times himself.

Callum wasn't really suicidal but it would be nice to have a few days a week where the nightmares didn't wake him up, where he could go to sleep without seeing faces contorted with fury and pain. He would cherish those few days and it would make living that much easier.

But it was impossible.

"Callum?" Audrey prompted with a shove to his shoulder with hers.

"Sorry, vagued out. What did you say?"

"Have you spoken to someone about this?"

Damn, back to him again. "You mean like a shrink?"

"Yeah, like a mental health professional."

Of course he had. "Didn't help."

"Is this why you aren't a doctor anymore? Because of the blood?"

His head shook from side to side. "I don't know what happens to me. I don't like blood and I don't like enclosed places." He was trapped in the helicopter only for about ten minutes but it was dark and crowded with gear, a dead man strapped to a stretcher had pinned him, and the initial sense of helplessness he'd felt stayed long after the ordeal was over. He'd thought he was as good as dead out there in the wreckage.

She said, "Ah," like it explained everything.

"Look, that's enough for one day. We better head back."

Audrey didn't argue, merely jumped to her feet and asked what she could do to help.

Callum shouldn't look but his eyes were drawn to the Band-Aid on her shin. "Is your leg okay? You probably scraped a barnacle trying to get up. You might even need a tetanus shot."

There was a brief hesitation before Audrey came back with, "I had a tetanus a few months ago when I fell and hit my head."

"What happened?"

"I had a few stitches and the tetanus, a couple of days in bed and then I was back to work."

"No. How did you hit your head?"

"Oh, that, I tripped."

She was just evasive enough to spell out that she was drunk at the time. Not smart. Also incredibly dangerous. He'd patched up a woman in the emergency room after passing out standing up and face planting a footpath. She'd broken her nose worse that any footy player or pub brawler he'd seen by that stage.

He dropped the subject. "If you hit the switch by the door inside, it'll turn on the driving lights and we can be on our way."

Callum turned the key to start the engine. He threw it into gear, his hand on the steering wheel but there were no lights. "Audrey, did you hit the switch?"

She was standing with her hand on it and flicked it back and forth. Nothing happened.

He killed the motor and went to check the switch. It was dead. Nothing happened at all. Crossing the small room that served as his dining room, kitchen and bedroom, he flicked the switch for the main interior lights. Nothing happened there either.

"We must have blown a fuse."

"Do you have any spare?" she asked.

Damn it. They blew so far and few that he didn't bother with backups. "Nope."

"Okay, so it's still light enough. We might make it back? It's worth a shot?"

"We won't make it back tonight. It gets dark quick and it's dangerous with no lights, not to mention illegal."

Panic opened Audrey's eyes wide. "We can't be stranded out here."

"It'll only be one night. We can get going first thing." He wasn't ecstatic at the idea but it wasn't anywhere near as bad as she was about to make it out to be.

"I can't stay here. We can't stay here. Let's try to get back okay?"

Callum watched as Audrey went to the steering wheel and turned the key, restarting the engines and trying everything to make the houseboat move.

He used his calm doctor voice on her and it felt foreign all the way to his toes. "Audrey, it's one night. You can take the bed and I'll sleep out on the deck. It's warm enough."

Her hand shot out and practically clawed his wrist. "You are not allowed to leave me alone."

"I'll be here the whole time. We can even leave the door open if you want but the mozzies will eat you alive." He would. If he was mosquito. Her skin was flawless, delicate, with a hint of pink across her cheeks from the sun. But that was the only colour she had left. She had paled and was clammy. Each breath came in a short pant.

"Sit down before you fall down," he told her. "That's it, head down on your knees."

She shuddered, and then fell into a heap at his feet. He sat next to her and rubbed her back. "I won't leave you and you don't have to be afraid of anything out here. We're surrounded by nothing but dense scrub and I'll be here."

"What if another boat comes across us? Can we get a lift back?"

"You'd rather get on a stranger's houseboat for two hours to go god knows where so you don't have to spend the night with me? Nice. Real nice."

For a second he thought she didn't get his teasing but then she relaxed and looked up. "If it was pitch black, I'd take a ride with the grim reaper to get to the light."

Callum chuckled and his chest wasn't so tight anymore. "The grim reaper would take you to hell," he pointed out.

"Where it's warm and there's a glow from the fire."

His chuckle turned to a laugh and he marvelled in the feeling. How long had it been since he'd really laughed? "I can't help you with the fire but I can create a glow. Hop up and I'll show you."

Once again his fingers met hers and wrapped around one another. He had to stop touching her. Eventually. Carefully he pulled until she was standing and then led her to the kitchen. "Mavis used to order stuff in from a catalogue Nancy would give her at the post office. Most of it was just junk but I saved an oil burner for the wet winters when I can't open all the windows."

He had a dozen tea light candles, an oil burner and a bottle of rosehip oil. He didn't even know what to do with the oil.

"Mum always liked a bargain. Even if you could never use it or store it. I remember when they discounted toilet paper at the shop and mum brought a hundred and fifty rolls. It lasted us more than a year and we had to stack it up behind the couch in the lounge room."

"She was one in a million, your mum."

"Maybe," Audrey whispered, completely distracted, rifling drawers.

"What are you looking for?"

"Matches."

And there was the second problem for the evening. He didn't have any.

Nineteen

♥

U seless. Men were absolutely useless. Audrey would never have pegged Callum for the kind of guy who didn't have plans in place. Like matches for lighting candles. His stovetop cooker had an electric starter and had died the same death as the lights so was no help either. Why the hell wouldn't he have a spare fuse somewhere? A tiny part of the irrational side of her wondered if he'd engineered the whole situation on purpose. Lucky the rest of her didn't believe it.

"Could you swap out fuses?" she asked, hoping that was actually a real possibility and not something she'd seen on a TV show. It was getting darker and their window for at least trying to get back had passed really quickly.

"It's only a small houseboat, Auds, there are only two fuses and you need them both to drive at night."

"What about your police buddy? Can he come get us?"

"Come on, don't think of it as dangerous, it's fun. Don't you remember camping out by the riverbank when you were a kid? You'd get eaten by mozzies and you'd wake up wet and cold from the dew. You would have loved it."

Audrey never loved the camping. She'd loved being out of the house and feeling like she was on her own, no embarrassing mother to bring her down or tell her no. "I haven't been camping since then," she pointed out with a sigh. "I'm more of a glamping kind of girl now."

Callum laughed as he continued to rifle drawers around the room, pulling out this and that only to replace it, not finding what he needed. He moved back to the kitchen and began moving things around in the tops of the small cupboards. "Face it, Auds, you're not even a glamping kind of girl. You're a five-star hotel celebrity who likes bright lights and not doing her own washing."

Audrey huffed, fear getting the better of her as she launched into a terror fuelled tirade. "If you're such a friggin' boy scout, where are your matches, a cigarette lighter? You're not exactly living rough."

"Not right now I'm not."

And then she felt like shit for even putting the words out there. Of course he'd lived it rough. No one else in her life had camped out in a desert in the middle of a war zone. "I'm sorry." She reached out a hand and put it on his shoulder, giving a gentle squeeze. "I shouldn't have said that."

He rose to his full height and turned to face her, his palms lifting to cup her jaw so they were eye to eye. "I will not let anything bad happen to you, Audrey. Nothing can hurt you out here."

The looming darkness fell away. The sounds of the dusk bird calls quieted. Her heart raced for a reason other than fear. His hands were so big and sure and capable. Maybe, just maybe, he could protect her from the night. Would she be a fool to let him?

"Is this your promised distraction?" she asked, licking her dry lips, a thrill racing through her at the way his hot gaze dropped to the movement.

His thumb skated over her chin, stroking softly down her neck. "I'm pretty sure you promised to distract me, not the other way 'round."

She vaguely recalled the words but she didn't really care who'd said them. Her fingers found the hem of his shirt. Her hands slid up and over smooth skin and hard muscle. He didn't stop her. Didn't break eye contact with her even once. When she couldn't take the intensity for one more second, Audrey leaned up and touched her lips to his.

The onslaught that was Callum enveloped her in a steel-like cage, his arms sweeping her up, his body pressing her into the kitchen counter at her back while he kissed her and kissed her. His hands shifted from the hard planes of her back right down to her ass and one moment there was houseboat beneath her feet, the next she was in the air, her butt landing on the counter, sliding back, pulled forward. Her still damp tank top was yanked over her head and went flying somewhere into the darkness. His was next to go.

Audrey held a hand to his chest to slow him down, to create distance, to...to.. What was she doing stopping him? "I thought you said this was a bad idea?" Was she insane to put it out in the open? Why didn't she just let him keep going?

"Yep." Only, he didn't stop, just lifted his hands to cup her breasts, tilted his head down to nip her through her bra.

"What happened to no sex?" Her voice came out all husky and she barely recognised the tone. Her hands moving over his chest of their own accord, mesmerised by the sight before her.

"Are you trying to talk me out of it?" He pushed the lace aside and licked her nipple, pulling the taught peak into his mouth to suckle. When he was done he grinned and said, "This was your idea." His grin did things to her insides that made her melt.

Audrey tilted her head back and he licked a path from her collarbone, right up her throat to her jaw. "You could always say no."

"No."

Her heart jumped and her cheeks flushed. Was he going to reject her again? Here? Like this? "No?"

"No to no. I'm tired of imagining what it would be like to have you naked in my arms. Tired of wondering what you taste like here." He kissed one corner of her mouth. "Here." The other corner. "And here."

"Anywhere else?" she asked on a breathy moan that wasn't supposed to sound as desperate as it did.

"Everywhere else." And then his hands closed around her backside and lifted so she had no choice but to wrap her legs around his hips and hold on tight. His biceps were like granite against her sides, his erection grinding against her like steel. Everywhere she was soft, he was hard. Unyielding came to mind but that wasn't what he was at all.

His strength was undeniable, his arms tightening as he lowered her slowly to his bed. When he didn't follow, Audrey reached for him, her brows high, her body tingling. "What are you doing?"

"I just want to know one thing."

The fire in her veins cooled. "Okay?"

"Do I have to take it easy? As in go slow?"

Moisture dampened her panties and the fire roared to life in her abdomen. Her lips stretched into a smile and she relaxed against the pillows. "Are you trying to tell me you're a minute man, Callum?"

Instead of taking a hit to his manhood, his grin lit up the room and his shorts dropped to the floor. "Baby, we have all night long and I intend to use every inch of it."

Every inch? A vision of Callum fresh from the shower flooded her mind but nothing could distract her from this new image. His dick jutted out, proud, hard and standing tall. She couldn't take her eyes from it. Her mouth watered. She wanted.

For once in her life there was no audience. No cameras. No threats and no danger. They were completely alone in what felt like the middle of nowhere and while it had terrified her at first, she was finally seeing the positives rather than all of the negatives. It meant nothing could or would hold her back, not even her fear. He was so sure he could keep her safe, that he would keep her safe.

If ever there was no time like the present, this was it.

"I always wondered what this would be like." Her admission was candid and raw.

Instead of scaring the erection out of him, it fluffed his ego and filled him with a crazy sense of elation. He'd always wondered too. In his dreams. And five minutes ago when he'd found condoms in his bedside drawer instead of matches.

"This is just a distraction, Audrey."

Her eyes said she understood exactly what he wasn't saying. Just sex. That's it. Nothing more. "Then distract me already."

He'd said they had all night but he hadn't been with a woman in years. The way the pressure built inside him already was a little frightening but he wasn't going to admit it or let it show. Probably lucky he'd had to alleviate his own frustrations a few times since Audrey had shown up. She did things to him and he shouldn't enjoy it but he did.

Like the way she eyed his dick off like it was a cupcake and she wanted to lick away the frosting.

They had all night.

Slow it down.

Callum climbed onto the bed between Audrey's knees and flicked the button on her short shorts. "These have been sending me signals since the second you came out wearing them."

She laughed. "They're just shorts."

He ran his finger below the hem, found the edge of her underwear, inched a nail under. "I wondered if I'd be able to..." He trailed off as he found what he was looking for. God, she was so hot and so wet. A moan escaped her and her hips lifted and then wriggled down.

"Not yet," he breathed, rimming the edges of her heat but not delving in just yet. He couldn't go any further while she was clothed. He retreated and shifted his focus. She made a noise of frustration and he hid his smile against the warmth of her stomach as he kissed a trail over her bellybutton.

She tried to unsnap her bra but he wanted to do it. He wanted to undress her. Taste her as he went. "Keep your arms above your head," he instructed, taking charge, daring her to disobey but knowing it would be the beginning of the end if she so much as touched him right then.

She did as he asked, lifting slightly so he could run his hands over her spine, unsnapping her bra, the delicate lace no longer full as he lifted it away to reveal perfection. Despite it being fully dark now the moon cast a glow that was just enough to see shadows, his mind filled in the blanks. He imagined her hardening nipples would be pink rather than dusky. He licked first one and then the other to gauge her taste and her reaction.

Both surpassed even his imagination. At first she gasped and panted. When he wrapped a hand around one breast and sucked hard, her hips lifted off the bed and her hands spiked through his hair.

"Hands," he reminded her. If she pulled any harder on his hair, he'd rip the shorts from her and it'd be over in seconds.

"I can't take much more," she said.

He guided her arms back up, kissing her long and hard on the mouth. "Oh, yes you can."

Dazed and flushed, she nodded but she couldn't seem to lie still. Each time he nibbled or bit or licked, her hips lifted, searched. He worked his way down over her ribs, her abs, her belly button, all the way to the zip on her shorts. There he stopped.

"How do you feel about oral sex?" Callum didn't know why he was asking. Normally he just went down and she either loved it or she told him no as he was heading south. He'd never talked this much during sex. He told himself it was because she was potentially traumatised here too and he was being careful with her.

He didn't wait for an immediate answer, only unzipped the fly and slid denim and lace all the way past her ankles and onto the floor. He could smell her now, sex in the air and on his blankets, on the top of his finger and hopefully soon on his tongue.

"As the giver or the receiver?" came her reply.

"I'm going to say receiver," he said with a long lick, flavour exploding in his mouth, fire burning in his balls, and then added, "we can talk giver after."

Her little hands floated down to his chest and she sat up on the bed, applying a little pressure. "Lie back."

He thought he was the one giving orders but he went with it. Whatever she had in mind, he wasn't going to say no. God, he wished he could look into her eyes, see the mischief that came through in her tone, but it was too dark. A fact she hadn't cottoned on to yet. His distraction was working.

There was no fear here. Just wanting.

When she bent over his dick and her hair brushed his abdomen, he whispered his favourite four letter word.

Twenty

♥

Audrey chuckled and wrapped her fingers around his shaft. "No fucking. Not yet. And I don't think it will be hell."

On a day that was meant to be all about finding herself, Audrey discovered she'd never had sex with someone as strong as Callum. As commanding or...Manly. It wasn't as though she'd only been with younger guys or anything like that, not that her experiences were so high, but Callum was a real man with a real man's wants, a real man's hands, a real man's mouth. He wouldn't concede anything. He wasn't soft or vulnerable anywhere and he was a natural born leader. It came as no surprise when he gripped her hips and repositioned her so they were facing opposite ends of the bed, her mouth poised over his favourite anatomy part and his breath hot on her centre.

She would have normally protested. She'd never found herself in quite this position before. Under the covers was the only way she could ever be sure there were no recording devices hidden around the room ready to capture her bare ass and feed it to the internet one byte at a time. But not here. Here she was free to express and explore. When she went back to The States,

Callum would be left far behind. There'd be no reminders that she let go. No proof either.

He licked her again and thought fled along with sensibility and the fear of getting caught out. When he touched his hands to spread her fully, she was nearly boneless with need.

"Do you want me to stop?" he asked.

"Don't you dare," she said, breath ragged and ready to beg.

Audrey cried out when he plunged a finger into her, moaned when he sucked, tried not to grind against his face when he retreated. She needed him to slow down. She needed him to go faster. She needed to return the favour.

Each time he licked, she licked. When he sucked, she slid her lips over him and sucked. When he tongued her clit, she wound her tongue around and around his shaft. Two fingers drove into her and she bore down, pressure building, light blinding the insides of her eyelids. The rhythm of the play took her and she was mindless. A little shriek was ripped from her when he flipped her onto her back and came right side up, not giving her even a second to get her bearings. He kissed her and kissed her like she had the only breath left on the planet, her own taste on his tongue, his fingers returning to coax her closer to the edge.

When he let her breathe, she whispered, "Now, Callum."

"Tell me what you want, Auds. Do you want me to keep doing this?" He added a third finger and his thumb found her clit. She stretched around him, tight, the need building and building.

Her head thrashed against the sheets and she cried out, hips lifting one more time. Her world exploded and tipped her over the edge on a promise he'd more than fulfilled with only hands and mouth.

Harsh panting drowned out the sounds of the river and beyond as Audrey tried to regain her breath as her insides rippled. Callum wasn't going to give her the time. In the shadows she saw him reach for the nightstand and then he was on his haunches sliding a condom over his hard length. She wasn't even going to protest. She'd come apart, now it was his turn.

"How have you got protection but no matches?"

He fit between her legs like it was where he belonged and then met her gaze. "I'm a guy."

She began to laugh but the breath was pushed from her lungs as he thrust, penetrating deep, forcing a groan that could have come from either of them.

He paused, his chest high, his biceps bulging. "Is this okay?"

"Stop talking, Callum."

"Yes ma'am," he said, withdrawing halfway only to slide home again. On and on, in and out, flesh sliding against flesh, the friction delicious, the kisses drugging, the moment dragging on for what felt like eternity until the urgency reached epic levels and there was only one peak left to climb. Callum jerked and groaned, called out her name like she was the only woman left on the earth, and then they both went over together, falling in a heap of tangled limbs, soft kisses and a silence that was broken only by the rocking of the boat beneath them on the surface of the water.

For the first time in a long time, Audrey was actually glad for the dark. Her cheeks were flushed, her hips ached and deep in her belly, the throbbing had almost quieted.

She hadn't lied when she'd said she'd thought about sex with Callum. At sixteen her imagination had been so vanilla, him on top, with his oxford still on, her on her back in the grass, smiling adoringly up at him while he kissed her with passion. In her teenage daydreams it was light, the middle of the afternoon, they were sheltered beneath the drooping branches of a weeping willow on the banks of the river. Callum was the hero and he treated her like a princess. Of course she'd also been a virgin then, with no idea how sex could all at once be delightful, awful, complicating and all-consuming.

The way Callum kissed had nothing to do with passion. Well, less to do with passion than sheer, unadulterated lust. Her lips were numb from his chin stubble and her tongue felt as if it had danced a marathon. God, the things that man could do with his mouth!

The throbbing began again. Pulsing and vibrating like an actual tangible thing inside of her. She'd come. Orgasmed. Reached a peak. No. Higher than all of that. She was not ready to go again. He couldn't be ready to go again. She clenched her thighs together.

Callum's breath was hot against her ear, his arm adjusting around her waist as he pulled her close, the little spoon to his big. "I can practically hear you thinking."

"Oh yeah?" It was all she could manage.

"You're about to say, 'Sorry for ravaging you, it won't happen again'."

Audrey twisted in his arms until her bare breasts once again pressed against his chest. "I ravaged you?"

His lips were nearly tilted in a grin and the sparkle in his eye was reflected by the thin moonlight. "That's the story I'm going to go with."

Fear rushed in from all angles. Audrey stiffened and her hands curled to fists against his chest. "Story?"

A finger lifted her chin until they were eye to eye again. "Just an expression, Auds. I won't tell anyone you sat on my face or-"

"I did not!"

"I don't mind." His free hand drifted down the length of her torso until his palm rested on her backside, pulling her close and then closer still. "You can sit on my face whenever you like, baby."

"Remember the part where this is just a distraction?" She was an idiot for reminding him but one of them had to put it out there again. Now that the fear of him telling the story of the night dissipated, she was conscious of the fact that they had to look at each other in the real world when they got back. Keep this thing between them a secret. If the media got a hold of their relationship, Callum's self-enforced isolation would be a thing of the past.

"I remember," he said, his voice clear and firm. "That's what I'm doing." His fingers flexed, curved, squeezed. But now he was distracted in a lost cause way. His eyes lost the twinkle and his movements lacked the heat and urgency they had before.

"I might just need a sec," Audrey said, leaning back in the bed until he was forced to let her up.

"Sure."

Audrey sat on the edge of the mattress and looked around for her clothes. Anything to cover up with and regroup. But it was just too dark. She hadn't been in this kind of inky black for months and the missing lump in her throat returned, her pulse kicking up.

When her fingers curled into the sheets next to her hips, two warm hands closed around her shoulders, almost calming her, almost anchoring her. But she said, "It's too dark in here."

"I know." Just two words but she felt them rather than heard them. He went on. "Close your eyes and pretend it's daytime."

Audrey snorted. "That does not work."

"You could sleep? Then you wouldn't know it was dark."

"Still not helping."

Callum was running out of ideas. He wanted to pull her back into bed but the mood had changed. Where he'd been horny and unable to slow it down, no other thoughts had entered his mind, but now, with a little space, he was able to think about what a monumental fuck up this could turn into. Mavis was going to haunt him forever if he hurt her daughter.

But they were both adults. Consenting adults. Messed up adults.

"Wait here a sec."

Audrey shrieked and reached for his hand over her shoulder. "Where are you going?"

"I'll get you a shirt and then we can sit out on the deck for a bit. Once your eyes adjust, you'll see it's not that dark. I promise."

"Don't go far."

He hated the fear she felt and his mind buzzed trying to find solutions to help her through it. But it wasn't up to him. He was just the distraction. She wasn't his to fix and he was in too dark a place for the responsibility.

Just the distraction.

He rummaged in the hall closet he used as his wardrobe and pulled a shirt off the hanger. Chicks liked that, a button down shirt to hide under. His t-shirts would hang right below her arse... He swore under his breath, nearly chucking the collared shirt back in and opting for arse revealing instead.

"Callum? Is everything okay?" Her voice was so strained, so scared, so small.

"I'm still here, Audrey." How could she not see a thing at all? He could make out shapes, her silhouette against the moonlight. The curve of her back was flawless and her breasts were outlined perfectly, her arms crossed beneath.

He wasn't fully sure who was distracting who just then. He faltered and then dropped to his knees on worn the carpet in front of her. "I got you a shirt."

"Thanks," she muttered.

"You'll have to uncross your arms, Auds." He helped her with the shirt, each button-hole an effort when it was on someone else.

"Leave the buttons," she said, the fear still there despite him being so close. "I need the light. I need to see."

Callum pulled on her hands and guided her towards the door, sure she should be able to make out the rectangular shape. He used the excuse to put his hands on her hips and followed her into the night.

Her long exhalation was so full of relief he was almost insulted. Why couldn't she trust that he'd keep her safe out here? That he could protect her in the dark? Her sparked panic when he'd said *story* earlier reminded him he wasn't with Audrey, Mavis's daughter. He was with Audrey the movie star, the anxious, terrified starlet who'd been through something he couldn't possibly identify with. Or could he?

He led her to a plastic lawn chair and then sat on the deck in front of her, remembering he was naked only after his arse rested on the peeling timbers. She did distract him. Or was it just her worries that filled his mind? He didn't need her fears to be his. He couldn't fear *for* her either. He didn't have the room in his head.

"Thank you," Audrey said, her voice back to a semblance of normal. "It's brighter out here than I thought it would be."

"Just doing my duty, ma'am," he joked in an attempt at an American accent.

She chuckled just liked he hoped she would and then spoke. "I've never dated a military man."

This time it was Callum who froze. "We're not dating."

"That's not what I meant. Let me rephrase. I've never gone to bed with a soldier."

"I'm not a soldier," he pointed out, but he didn't want to darken the moment any more than they already had so he added, "So you still haven't."

"Damn. That could have been something to brag about back home," she said as he jumped to his feet and went back into the houseboat only to emerge with two bottles of water and a couple of large rectangle foil shapes.

"You can still tell your friends that I was the best sex you've ever had."

Her laughter bounced off the water and broke the quiet of the night. "Oh, can I?"

Callum grinned and turned to face her but didn't get up again. He rested his back against the railing post and considered her for a full minute before speaking. "What do your friends think about all of this?"

"All of what?" She opened the packet he gave her and smiled at the poptart inside.

"Come on, Auds. What did they say about you leaving to come back here? What advice do they give you about getting over what happened?"

"I... They..." She cleared her throat and her gaze wandered the shadows, looking anywhere but in his direction, taking three bites before answering. "I haven't really told anyone."

"Why not?" Women were not well known for keeping things quiet. He knew that much.

A big sigh let him know she was about to reveal something else she was reluctant to say out loud. "I don't really have many friends."

"Bullshit." The curse fell out by accident, instinct telling him to question her confession because he didn't believe her. She lived and breathed Hollywood. She was a star, rich, famous, amazing. Audrey had the kind of personality that drew people to her rather than what he was lumped with, a scowling personality that repelled.

"You don't know what it's like to be in the public eye. I made the mistake of getting too close to a girlfriend in college and she went on to sell her story after we graduated, complete with embellishments and lies."

His mind was flooded with images of Audrey in bed with another woman, limbs intertwined, making the same moaning noises she had with him, all fingers, lips and teeth. "That's so hot," he breathed, his dick harder than the steel he leaned against.

A delicate, painted toe nudged him in the arm. "Not like that, you perve."

His fantasy bubble burst and he laughed but the images he tucked away into the back of his brain for later. "Damn."

"We were roommates so there were things she knew about me, found out about me, and then shared with the world. It was humiliating."

"Like what?"

"Look it up on Google. I'm not rehashing it all."

He hadn't thought about looking her up. He tucked that away too. "So what happened?"

"Nothing too bad but it taught me the lesson that I was on my own if I wanted my image to stay clean. Too many starlets walk the red carpet to snickers and lewd calls after a sex tape emerges or their nude pics are leaked."

His interest pricked again but so did his anger. "Do you have a sex tape?"

"Absolutely not!"

He relaxed. "How do you know when you're with a guy that he isn't secretly filming you? Or do you not date much?"

"I don't date at all."

"Celibate?" No way.

The hesitation seemed to last forever. "Not quite."

Callum searched her face but she'd built a wall. He didn't press any further. "Well, you can be sure I wasn't recording anything."

"It's too dark anyway," Audrey pointed out with a thumb over her shoulder in the direction of his bed. The action made her shirt shift, slide and then open, her nipple on display.

Callum reached out a hand and snagged the fabric of the other side before she could fix it, tugging gently until her other breast was bared. "I like the light," he said, coming to his knees and stopping in front of her crossed legs.

"The dark was handy," she conceded, breathless, shifting slightly on the white plastic of the chair.

"For?" He was mesmerised, his attention wandering over her body. He pushed on her crossed knee and her legs opened. He pushed again. Wider. He wanted to see.

"Hiding."

He wanted to touch her everywhere. He wanted to see her fracture and fall apart in a good way rather than bad. "You don't have to hide. Not out here and not with me."

Twenty-One

♥

A udrey started a list of all she was grateful for in her mind, but then Callum went to work and it was like her brain emptied everything out through her ear the first time she tilted her head.

When he spoke, she heard but didn't absorb much. "I think I get, what, an A+ for distraction methods?"

His chin and cheek scratched a path of kisses from her shoulder and over her breasts, his tongue soothing everywhere he scraped. His thumbs pressed into her thighs, his fingers wrapped around her legs, inching closer, higher, until her hips nearly met him halfway. When he dragged his teeth over her nipple, her hands threaded through his hair and tugged on the strands until his face was back in front of hers.

"Gold star," she murmured before plastering her lips to his, invading his mouth with her tongue with a desperation she hadn't ever felt. If she'd been able to, she would have climbed right inside him.

Her cry was lost on a breath he inhaled as first one thumb slid between her folds and the other dipped into her heat. Audrey shuffled her hips to the edge of the chair, wanting, no, needing to be closer, begging for more. The plastic scraped on the deck and reminded her where they were and what they were doing. Her hands left his hair to close the shirt over her chest.

Callum read her mind. "No one is here, Auds. It's just you and me. Even if a boat went past right now, they'd only cop an eyeful of my white arse."

He was right. The play of his fingers never ceased nor did the returned sparkle in his eye go away. His hair stood up and out everywhere and for a second she wondered what she herself looked like. Definitely not a Hollywood starlet.

"I'm not going to stop unless you tell me to," he said, gently coaxing her shirt open and her hands to his shoulders.

He licked, sucked and nibbled and he was tense beneath her palms, hard, hot, there, in the moment. Unlike her. She was always worried about what happened next. The dark. The morning after. The shame and burn of humiliation and the worry that the world would find out what she liked and what she didn't. They'd judge her. Think her dirty, slutty even, with all the stigma and condemnation from conservative types. She knew they judged her.

Callum certainly wasn't making her feel any less a woman or dirty though she was using him as a distraction tool. He sure was good at it.

He circled her navel with his tongue and her sex with his thumb and Audrey's head fell back, empty again, to rest on the back of the flimsy plastic lawn chair. When he pulled back she almost whimpered but then, in the light of the moon, he dipped low and replaced his hands with his mouth and she sighed.

One of her thighs was lifted over his shoulder and her senses went into overload. Breathing was hard. Thinking was impossible. Two rhythmic fingers divine.

Her entire body tightened like a bow about to loose an arrow but then she was in the air, in Callum's arms, on her back on the warm timber, laughing, scolding, begging. "You didn't finish."

"I will, I promise." He leapt up and she rolled to see where he was going but it was too dark.

"Callum, what are you doing?"

He appeared through the doorway and Audrey sank back.

"Condom." One word. One grin. One fluid motion and he was back, pressing into her, his erection hot and heavy against her leg and the intensity of his gaze shook her. "As much as I love your taste, your sex on my tongue and in my mouth-" He stopped to kiss her, long, gentle, languid. "I need something else, more."

"What do you need?" she asked, willing to give him anything, hoping she had what he wanted.

He slid into her and she gasped. "I want to see you when you come. I want you let it all go and just feel. Just you and me and no one and nothing else."

She wanted to tell him she couldn't. That she didn't know how. But then he was moving and she was moving and it all just felt so good and right and- Oh god, she cried out, her back arched, her hips lifted, her world fuzzed and blurred into one big, giant knot of anticipation fuelled by friction, tightening, building, until she stopped holding back, stopped thinking, stopped hiding.

Callum's roar drowned out her own noise and somewhere over the river, a flock of birds squawked into the night. Instead of worrying over the who's and what's and where's, she smiled against his shoulder.

For the first time in a very long time, Audrey Hobson was right side up and in a good place. The only problem with that place was that it was beneath the one man who was as inaccessible as she herself was...

Twenty-Two

♥

Warmth against her closed eyelids was Audrey's first indicator she wasn't tucked up safely in her bed back in LA. She'd be thinking about showering and grabbing a quick breakfast before heading out, beating the traffic and the crew to the set.

Her second clue was the immovable heat at her back, under her head, over her ribs and wrapped around her breast. The deck was hard beneath her body but it was nothing compared to the hardness flexing against her butt cheek.

A smile lifted her mouth as an open, wet kiss landed on her shoulder. She giggled. Actually giggled. The last time she'd woken up next to a man she'd been bruised, groggy and confused. This time she was satisfied, wet and wanting.

"Did you sleep well?" a voice asked over her shoulder.

A light blanket had been draped over her sometime during the night and she hadn't woken at all. "I think so." In fact, she felt completely refreshed. Almost giddy, with energy to burn. It had been so long since she'd slept the night through without waking to check the locks and shadows.

When the wandering hand drifted lower, Audrey pushed back into his hardness, half stretching, half challenging, a full smile on her face and a lightness in her chest. "Did you?" she asked, turning and rolling so Callum was on his back and she was inching onto his front.

First he kissed her, all morning breath and sweaty heat, it was nice. It was sexy as hell. And then he answered, "I didn't sleep."

Audrey pulled back. "Why not?"

"It was just better for me not to fall asleep."

"Why didn't you wake me?"

"You were so peaceful and you were exhausted." He tucked a stray piece of her hair behind her left ear. "You sleep so sound. I had to keep making sure you were still breathing."

Ah, the hand on her breast as she woke. "Sure you did."

"It was purely the doctor in me making sure you were okay."

"I'm pretty sure you can't keep relying on that excuse, Callum. If you want to grope me, at least have the decency to call it what it is."

She knew as soon as the teasing words were out, he'd take it as a challenge. In less than a second, she was beneath him, on her back, his palm on her breast, the other trapping her hands above her head as he flashed her another one of his grins. "I'd call it more than a handful." He tested the weight with his palm and then dipped his head to taste. "More than a mouthful too."

Over the top of his unruly hair, a boat came into view and Audrey tensed, torn between running for cover, and begging for more. "We have company," she whispered.

"Let them watch," came Callum's muffled reply around her nipple. "They'll go away."

"What if they recognise me, Callum?" Fear took hold and Audrey bent her head to his chest to hide, thankful for the blanket.

It seemed like forever passed before the sounds of the other houseboat's engines faded down the river, before Audrey was ready to lift her head and look to make sure they were once again alone.

They were alone but Callum wore an expression that was hard to read. He propped his head on his bent elbow and asked, "Why are you so scared of being discovered?"

She blinked once, twice, three times. "Uh, we're kind of naked, kind of out in the open and kind of exposed."

He shrugged. "We're just two people having fun. Trust me when I say no one would recognise you right now."

Callum took in the mussed hair, the whisker graze around her mouth and the hickey on her neck. Audrey looked like a woman who'd been fucked all night long. She didn't look like a princess movie star. He liked her better like this. All out of sorts and naked in his arms. Tousled and natural.

"What do you mean?" she asked.

She did not want to hear that she looked like sex had knocked her door down so he shrugged again and grinned. "Your hair is a little messy is all and no one can see you past me anyway." Lifting the blanket a little to stare down the length of her he said, "This view is just for me this morning."

"You know they know what we were doing."

"I don't really give a flying fuck what they think they do or don't know." God, she was so tight. Muscles across her abdomen were probably taught enough to bounce a coin off and he tested his theory with a finger, gently pressing and then letting go right between her belly button and her... He dipped lower.

Tension seeped away and finally Audrey relaxed. Callum was just happy she didn't push him away or ask him to stop. In the cold light of day, he'd wondered if she would regret what happened between them. He knew he would, later, when he let himself think about the consequences and the repercussions. But not yet. Not now.

"We should probably go back inside," Audrey pointed out just as Callum got to the good stuff. God, she was beyond wet.

He slipped a finger into her, first one, then another. "Why?"

"Because we are not doing it-" A moan cut off her words. Yep, his thumb found her sweetest spot, her hips lifted, her hand reached for his bicep. To hold on? He hoped so.

"Callum," she groaned, her eyes squeezed shut.

"Yes, Audrey?"

"We have to go back-" Another noise, this one more high-pitched, more breathy.

He shuffled lower, filled his mouth with her breast and sucked hard. Now that he wasn't pinning her down with his torso, she inched up onto her elbows. He flashed her another grin. "What were you saying, Auds?"

Her face was serious, flushed and hot, but serious. "Inside. Now."

He wiggled his finger, transferred his mouth to her other breast.

"Callum, I need... I need."

With every pump of his hand against her, the breath was pushed from her lungs until she couldn't even finish her sentence. But he didn't want her to come like this. Not under a blanket where he could only see the colour change in her eyes. He wanted to take in every inch of her beautiful body in the morning sunlight. He had to see her.

"Fuck it," he mumbled. "Quick, get up and get in."

Audrey finally drew a deep breath and then chuckled as she got to her feet and ducked through the door into the bedroom/lounge room. "I was going to say the same thing to you."

The blanket wrapped around her ended up on the floor within one pounding heartbeat and in the next he was pulling a condom, the last condom, over his erection. She was still standing in the middle of the room, looking kind of lost, her arms wrapped around her body.

"What happened to quick, get in?" he joked, stalking towards her, knowing a deer in the headlights when he saw one.

"If you're doing this just to distract me, it's light, I'm not scared anymore."

"Do I look like the martyr type?" He waved in the general direction of his manhood, straining, almost painful despite the action he'd already seen overnight. "Come here, Audrey."

She hesitated. He cursed.

She still wanted him, her nipples were puckered, hard nubs, her cheeks were flushed pink and she was so wet, he imagined he could see moisture on her thighs. "What's wrong?"

"It's going to change everything."

"It already has. But we don't have to let it be a thing. Remember the part where we're two consenting adults out for a little fun to pass the time?"

"Is that it?" she asked.

Any other woman at any other time, Callum might have played the arsehole and promised breakfast and another date, but he knew damn sure she wasn't looking for that. "That's it. Just you and me and hot sex. I want you, Audrey. Do you want me?"

She nodded. He sighed.

"Then stop thinking and get over here."

After another brief hesitation, she skipped the few steps and crashed into him, both of them falling onto the bed, Callum twisting so she lay beneath him once more, exactly where she was supposed to be.

As he eased into her heat, he tried to come up with a comparison for this feeling of being buried deep inside Audrey. A carefree joy he hadn't felt in years filled his chest and lifted his shoulders. She was like cherries at Christmas time. You knew you would enjoy it while it lasted but then it would be gone. Christmas and summer and the cherries would run out and the cold would once again set in...

Instead of being burdened by the knowledge it would all pass, that she would leave and go back to her life, Callum planned to gorge his fill before it all ended, before there was no more Audrey and no more summer.

"What happened here?" Audrey traced the puckered edge of a scar on Callum's stomach with her fingertips. She had been admiring the Southern Cross tattoo when she found it just below. It looked like it hurt. A lot. He didn't have many scars but the ones he did have obviously came with their own stories. The question was, would he share those tales or would he shut down like he usually did when the conversation turned back to him.

"That was my very first bullet wound. A through and through. "

Audrey gasped and swore. "How many times have you been shot?"

"Only twice"

He said it like it was nothing. Like an ankle sprain or a broken nose. "Was it very bad?"

"The first or the second time?"

She heard the smile in his words but she was too busy looking for another bullet hole looking scar. There was a long white line from his hip nearly to his belly button and another just below the rib on the opposite side. She couldn't find it.

"It's on my thigh. I got hit in the leg after the medivac went down."

"How did you make it out?" He'd never answered when she asked the first time.

"We were actually pretty close to base. The missile came up on radar and then we disappeared from view but by then they could see the smoke, hear the gunfire."

"So you didn't have to fight long before you were saved?"

"Something like that."

"Do you ever have to go back?"

He pulled her back in close and Audrey let him. She rested her head on his shoulder, his arms tight. "I'm never going back."

Post-Traumatic Stress Disorder. PTSD for short. Callum knew for sure it would be stamped in big red letters across his deployment file. Unless there was a world war, people like him were no longer fit for active duty. With his skills, he'd probably wind up in Darwin or Queensland in a military hospital. God, he'd been so keen to serve his country in a way that would make a difference. He'd finished medical school and had signed up straight away having already spent a few years as a cadet. His dad had initially enrolled him as a way to find some discipline. Find some purpose. Callum had found a whole lot more than that.

He'd found he hated war. Hated blood. Hated violence. After a little while he'd even begun to hate himself. Nothing he did was ever good enough. For every one person he saved, another ten died. His side, their side, they all died. He was stationed in a hospital that served mostly British, Australian and American troops. He'd patch them up and a week later they'd be back. He'd watched all the war movies and shows, some of them good, some bad. Band of Brothers, Full Metal Jacket, MASH.

"I thought I knew what I was in for," he said out loud, over Audrey's messed up hair, over the curve of her bare back and out the open window. "I honestly didn't think it could ever be as bad as it was."

He didn't think he'd ever be responsible for another man's death. He'd as good as pulled the trigger himself when he'd pushed the nozzle of a soldier's rifle to stop him from killing an insurgent. The spray of bullets had gone wide, missed the man with murder in his eyes, missed the comrades at his back. But bullets were designed to kill and kill they did. Callum had tried to save them. The old woman had only been grazed, she'd live. Her daughter was another matter. Hit in the stomach, bleeding out right there in the sand. Callum reached her side, put his hands over the wound to stem the flow, screamed for his bag, screamed for help, screamed for a ceasefire.

He'd felt a pressure on the side of this leg but he didn't have time to see what it was. A mosquito bite? A bee sting? Maybe a scorpion since he was in the desert and not back home in Australia. Blood seeped through his fingers from her injury, into his eyes from his own head wound from the crash impact, the smell of fuel still heavy in the air despite the burning wreckage of their Blackhawk. He was knocked by something, or someone, and then he'd fallen, right over the innocent woman, already her vacant eyes stared upwards, and then he'd lost consciousness.

"I didn't save her. I didn't save any of them."

Soft lips pressed to his and a palm lay against his cheek, moving his head until he met eyes glistening with unshed tears. "I'm sure you did your best. You're a good man, Callum. A good man who would have tried his best."

He nodded but threw her words away. He wasn't a good man. He'd tried so hard to be but look where it got him. If he was a good man he'd have saved more lives. If he was a good man he wouldn't be lying naked with Audrey, wouldn't have taken advantage of her fear of the dark, the stupid excuse of a distraction.

A good man wouldn't be hiding. He'd face his fears, admit his faults and get on with it.

He'd searched inside himself these past few years and a good man was nowhere to be found.

Twenty-Three

♥

Audrey should have known better than to bring up his past again. Callum completely shut down every time she had questions. The three hours back to Mannum against the current were mostly silent. She sat on the deck in the sun while he steered and frowned and sometimes scowled.

The only real words to escape his mouth were more akin to road rage, or river rage in this case. It was almost a relief to pull up behind Mavis's house and watch him tie the lines off. He'd only put on a pair of shorts and despite the fact he was miserable and she should have her head in her own troubles, she licked her lips and enjoyed the view despite the queasiness in her belly from the lack of good food and the rocking motion of the boat. Her earlier giddiness had long since fizzled but each time she chanced a look in his direction, her insides warmed. She took in his handful of tattoos, his scars and his muscles, and wondered if he'd still be this person in five years, in ten. Would she still be the same? Scared of the dark. Scared of the scandal. Tired of looking over her shoulder. All of it was a part of life. A part of living. But should it be this damned hard?

"You should go on in and have a shower. I'll tidy up here."

"I can help you?" She wasn't ready to say goodbye to flirty, grinning, cheeky Callum. She liked him. A little too much.

"You look beat."

"Says you. Why don't you come in, shower and have a sleep on the couch? I promise not to wake you this time."

She'd meant the words to be light and playful but his eyes darkened and he shook his head. "Off you go, Audrey. I need some time...out."

Her pulse staggered and she felt the blow all the way to her stomach. She was being dismissed. Her mother used those three words on her all the time. "Off you go." She didn't need it spelled out to her.

"Well, thanks for the cruise. And the distraction. I'll see you around." Audrey turned her back, didn't wait to see if he'd come after her, explain why he was pushing her away. Then again, it was just sex. She'd said the words herself. What did she expect now? A cuddle? More spooning? Happily ever after?

Muttering under her breath, Audrey went into the bathroom to get cleaned up, maybe have a shower and wash away some of the memories.

"You could at least put the seat down," she threw over her shoulder to no one in particular since she was once again alone. Seemed to be the story of her life.

She wasn't needy but every now and then she would like to be needed. To be wanted. Relied on. Almost completely independent since age six, Audrey had always done it on her own. The only time she'd ever asked for any help had been from her biological father to take her away from tedium and give her a better chance at being so much more. Look at her now. Back where she started. Feeling just as alone and confused as ever.

Isn't that how you like it though? Her subconscious whispered.

"You can shut up too," she muttered, stripped off her clothes and stepped into the shower. Alone was good for her. Confused wasn't. Alone meant she didn't have to answer to anyone. She didn't have to always be the one to put the pieces back together every time they fell apart. She only had her own shit to deal with and she was normally pretty good at ignoring everything and everyone else. Only, now her shit effected other people.

She didn't want to admit it to herself but Audrey needed someone to come and pick up her broken pieces and put them back together for her. She'd tried but nothing had worked. Not therapy, not self-medication, certainly not booze. Was she going to be like this forever? Scared of the dark? Scared of being alone?

Scared of admitting she needed more?

Whoa. Audrey inhaled the steamy, warm air, shut off the taps and went to stand in front of the mirror. She used her hand to wipe away the fog and stared at her blurred reflection. She had fame, riches, success. Before the attack, she'd had it all. She was in her acting prime, the perfect age for all the right roles, talented and available.

But it wasn't enough, was it? There were no challenges left anymore. No spontaneity. She'd achieved everything she'd set out to achieve and now that she was there, the sparkle had fallen off and only the stark reality remained. Eighteen- hour days recording the same three lines over and over until it was right. The world constantly watching on through the lenses of random cameras waiting for her to stuff up bad enough to make it into the pages of glossy magazines and e-news. TMZ were going to have a field day when they caught a whiff of her most recent behaviour. If Fabien's wife had discovered their one wild, drunken night, then the world was about to catch up. She had to charge her phone and check in with her agent. Instead of reliving the pity party over and over again, she had to figure out her next move and play the hand she'd been dealt. It was time to stop running. She had to go back to LA.

Callum wasn't hers to worry about and she wasn't his. Just sex was all it was and it could never be any more. The fact she stood there worrying was another reason why they shouldn't have gone there in the first place. But, damn, it had been fun.

Callum leaned against the kitchen counter, his arms crossed over his chest and wondered again just why he stood there waiting for Audrey, waiting for a chance to explain his minor freak out just now.

He had no right to hurt her and after a few deep breaths he'd realised how his angry words would be construed. Once his male brain had caught up, she'd started the shower and he wasn't going to barge in on her there. Despite his body's wanting to. He was torn between that wanting and the knowing. Knowing he wasn't in a good place for anyone. Knowing he couldn't protect Audrey from the shit-fight she'd run from or provide any kind of life for her if she decided not to return. He lived on a meagre pension while he waited in limbo to decide if he could ever go back to functioning citizen. He had violent nightmares, perhaps a minor dependency on sleeping pills, baggage he couldn't just drop because he liked her.

He tried to think what kind of advice Mavis would offer him. When she wasn't blind drunk, she was full of advice, of patience and kind words. Any time he stood at a crossroads in his life, he would call on his godmother and ask her what she thought. Sometimes she helped, sometimes she didn't.

He called up her face in his mind. It wasn't hard to picture her. It was impossible to predict what she'd say. *'Keep your dick away from my girl.'* That would be a start.

The bathroom door opened with a cloud of steam and he knew exactly what Mavis would say. He offered Audrey a grim smile. "You didn't turn the fan on."

She didn't smile back, only lifted one hand to her towel wrapped hip. "I thought you wanted some time out?"

"I don't fucking know what I want."

"We all know that, Callum," she huffed.

When she went to go around him towards the bedroom, Callum snagged her arm and turned her so they were inches apart, two faces together, one stubborn, hurt, the other, his, contrite. He shouldn't have dismissed her the way he had. "I'm sorry."

"For what, Callum? Sleeping with me? Pushing me away? Being an ass?"

"For all of it. I don't know how to do this."

"Do what?"

God, she smelled so good. Fresh, soapy, sexy. "Play happy families. I don't know relationships anymore and I don't think I want to. I've been on my own for too long and I like it that way." He said the words because they had to be said but he didn't expect them to come out so empty. He'd wanted this solitary existence. He'd needed it. Until she came along, he hadn't considered any other way.

"We're not in a relationship, remember? Just a distraction. Just sex."

It could never be just sex with her. He should have known that before he kissed her. Before he touched her everywhere. Maybe he had known. Maybe he hadn't cared. He took a deep breath. "If it's just sex, why are you so angry?"

"I'm not angry. We were just two people who needed something more. A connection to feel grounded, intimacy in the moment. I'm a big girl, I'll be fine."

But he didn't want her to be fine. He wanted her to be happy, to smile and laugh. He wanted to look at her and feel...human. It was something he hadn't even realised he'd been missing. Callum cupped Audrey's cheek in his hand and leaned closer. "It wasn't just sex for me."

Her beautiful honey eyes brightened for a just a moment before a shutter came down over her expression. "What was it then?"

How could he explain it? Did he want to? Once the words were said out loud, there'd be no going back. "I don't know."

She started to pull back from his embrace, disappointment in her frown, her bare shoulders sagging, dragged down.

Callum put his arms around her and pulled her back. "I don't know what it is but I know I want it. I want you. I don't care what you call it but I feel lighter when I'm with you. Fuck, that sounded girly." He shook his head. "I can't find the right words but Audrey, it was more than just sex for me."

"What if I can't give you more than that?" It wasn't what he'd thought Audrey would reply with. He was supposed the be the one resisting. They'd had a major role reversal.

"Let's just pretend for a little while that it's just you and me in the world and do what we want for a change. No labels, no strings, but more than just sex."

"I don't think it's possible. You would have to tell me what's on your mind when it's on your mind. Tell me about your nightmares and your time in the army if I ask. You can't just always shut me out."

Jesus, she didn't ask for much. If he could deflect some of the time, then he wouldn't have to share his every thought with her. "Do you want to know what's on my mind right now?"

There was a long pause and then finally a smile ghosted across her lips. She closed the gap between their bodies and with one finger, traced the tattoo on his chest. She peeked up through her lashes. "I bet I can guess."

His mouth pressed against hers and she met him in the middle, tongues duelling. He sucked her bottom lip into his mouth while he loosened the corner of the towel tucked between her breasts. Her hands were on his shoulders, around his neck, in his hair.

When the towel finally dropped to a puddle at her feet, Audrey was panting with need. "Bedroom," she said.

Callum brushed his thumbs over her nipples, kissed her again, and then lifted her onto the kitchen bench. "Right here."

When Audrey giggled, it didn't seem to fit her, he detected the nervousness, the way her eyes darted over his shoulder and around the room. "No one can see us here, Auds. All your important bits are facing me anyway."

"My important bits?" Her giggle turned to that sexy-as-hell chuckle and what blood and sense he had left travelled south.

"Here." He cupped her breasts and flicked his thumbs over her nipples again, soothing the action with his tongue and then following up with a nip of his teeth until she writhed and arched. Lower still, he used his thumbs again, one on the nub in her curls and one sliding along dewy satin until he could penetrate her heat. Her head fell back, her legs opened wider. Callum grinned and murmured, "Jackpot."

"There's a condom in my pocket," he said, watching the play of his fingers in and around her. She wasn't listening, her breath came faster, her body taught.

Callum stilled but didn't withdraw. "Fingers or cock, Audrey?" He was too hot and heavy and to find a better way to get his point across.

He knew he had her when she grinned back at him. "Fingers first and then cock?"

"Condom," he repeated. "In my pocket."

He didn't move until she did, withdrawing his thumb and replacing it with two fingers as she reached into his shorts pocket. When she brushed his erection through the fabric, he grunted, "Wrong pocket."

When she reached inside his shorts, he rocked into her hand. "Still the wrong pocket."

"I like this pocket." Her grip was firm as she wrapped her fingers around his length and pumped.

Callum braced both hands on the bench near her hips, his forehead against hers. "You're killing me, woman."

His shorts were around his ankles in no time and both of her hands were on him, cupping his balls, stroking, pulling, pushing. She used the head of his dick to rub herself and he was kissing her like she really was the only woman on earth.

Foil crinkled and she rolled the rubber over his length. He didn't need a second invitation. Holding onto her hips, he slid into her, all the way, slamming the final distance until he was home.

Home. He'd never imagined it could feel so right.

"We really should get up," Audrey said, her stomach growling and her hip sore from yet another hard floor.

How they'd made it down to the lino, she wasn't even sure. One minute Callum had her in the most delicious position on the kitchen bench and the next, she was being lifted and lowered. She stretched out, her back protesting the movement. The pros to being thoroughly nailed by a guy who was built like a tank were obvious, pleasure, orgasms, a real man. The cons were bruises and not because he was necessarily rough, just big and strong. Audrey smiled and relaxed back against the warm body at her side.

Callum groaned a little. "I don't want to move. Not yet."

"I'm starving and if anyone decides to drop in, we're both naked on the kitchen floor."

"Fuck 'em," he grunted, pulling her closer with a hand to her hip.

Audrey laughed. "I need to get to the shops and I need food, but in the reverse order."

"What do you need from the shops?" he asked.

"I don't have enough summer clothes and I need an international charger for my phone." She should check in with her agent. Since signing with Tinka, not a day had gone by where they hadn't had some kind of contact. Anita's words about Fabien's divorce rattled inside her head too. There was only so long she could bury her head in the sand and not expect something to bite her in the bum while she did it.

"You don't need clothes and you definitely don't need your phone."

The thought of spending all her time with Callum naked was hotter than hot, but not practical. She was about to argue her point when he said, "One more day, Auds. Spend the night with me on the boat and then tomorrow we'll charge your phone and get back to the real world."

"Your boat doesn't have lights or power, remember?"

"I'll fix it all up today. I've got fuses in the shed."

"Why don't you stay inside with me?" *Where we can lock the doors and windows at night.*

"I can't sleep in the house."

"Because of Mavis?" God, her mother would turn a fit over her daughter having sex in her kitchen.

She felt Callum shake his head and roll onto his back. "Nothing to do with Mavis."

Audrey rolled too, until she could rest her chin in the hollow of his shoulder, nearly meet his unreadable gaze. "What is it then?"

"I don't like enclosed spaces."

He'd said that earlier. She'd only really listened to the blood part. She didn't have to ask if it was because of his time in the army. It was obvious in the tone of his voice, in the pain and the shame. "That's why you live on the houseboat?"

"I like the windows and the feeling of the water beneath me. I like to know I can pick up and push off anytime I want."

"Don't you worry about being unreachable? What if there was an emergency and you needed medical help?"

Callum snorted. "I am the medical help and being unreachable is kind of the point."

Looks like Audrey wasn't the only one with her head in the sand. He couldn't cope with the sight of blood, what would happen if he was the one bleeding?

"You don't need to worry about me, Auds. I can take care of myself."

"I know that…but…"

"Your positivity fills me with confidence," he chuckled. "Twenty-four hours just you and me, no outside world."

"And then what?"

He shrugged and her head tilted with the movement. But then his face was in front of hers, only millimetres from being kissable. "Then we go from there."

She wanted to point out again that she would be leaving. That she had to get her shit together and go home.

Home. LA? Jupiter Creek? Or Callum?

Why was it that for the first time in her life, exactly where she was felt more like home than any other place ever had? Instead of being a warming thought, that she'd maybe found a place where she actually fit after all, terror gripped her. This was definitely not part of her plans.

Twenty-Four

♥

"Anita, what are you doing here?" Audrey was confused and pulled the halves of her robe together a little tighter. One cup of tea and a minor bitch session wasn't enough for the nurse to call back again.

The other woman breezed through the front door holding a white plastic shopping bag up high in her hand. "We got your blood test results back and the doc thought you might like some pregnancy vitamins. They might boost your energy a little since you are quite anaemic."

Audrey closed the door and leaned against the panelling. "What?"

"I came past the other day but you weren't here and Callum's boat was gone – hi Callum – and I didn't want to just leave the bag so I came back." Anita began unpacking little bottles onto the kitchen counter but she didn't stop babbling. "Iron, folate, a multi. Do you eat much in the way of green leafy veg? And don't forget a good dose of fibre since you'll be needing two iron tablets a day to start."

Anita hadn't picked up on the tension in the room yet but Audrey felt the icy blast from Callum. His arms crossed over his chest in a stance he favoured, his lips a thin line, his head shaking back and forth just a little while he scowled at the well-meaning nurse. Audrey wondered if it was because they'd been interrupted only thirty-six hours into what was supposed to be twenty-four, or if he always reacted this way to visitors. The loud shaking of a pill bottle snapped her attention back to Anita again.

"Are you listening to me, Audrey? How many fish oils and how many folate? This stuff is important for your growing foetus. You really should have told us you were pregnant when Callum brought you in last week. No wonder you'd been so sick."

A growl sounded from the other side of the room. "You fucking what?" Callum asked, his tone low and dangerous.

Anita held up a hand to dismiss him, "You don't have to go all caveman on me, Callum West. I'm only the messenger. The doc would have come out himself but a speed boat hit a water skier yesterday and the leg had to be set. If you'd stayed around long enough at the hospital or even checked back in like you were supposed to, you could have saved me the trip out here."

Audrey had had just about enough. "Wait a minute," she said between the two, her hands in the air. "Wind it back a few sentences. Pregnant? You must have mixed my blood up with someone else's. I am definitely not pregnant."

"You definitely are," Anita lobbed back. "Judging by your HCG, you're only around eight weeks but you're pregnant all right."

"Bullshit." She borrowed one of Callum's favourite words and adopted an identical stance. "I'm on birth control. I have a shot every three months like clockwork."

"The bloods don't lie, Audrey." Anita looked at her with pity, finally understanding this was all new news to everyone else in the room. "I thought you knew. We thought you knew."

"Who's we?" Callum asked.

"The staff at the hospital. A couple of the nurses and the doc. Then there's the pathology people but no one will say anything to anyone. This isn't the first time we've treated a celebrity or had to keep our mouths' shut. Especially while there's reporters in town."

The room spun a little and Audrey half sat, half fell onto the couch. "Reporters?"

"Seems your limo driver took a few happy snaps of you on your way out here last week and then sold them to the highest bidder. He lost his job but he got paid quite well according to some of the e-news sites. He hasn't given out your exact address yet though, he's probably holding out for more cash."

"Oh my god," she groaned and clutched the sides of her now aching head. Pregnant? Reporters? One was her worst nightmare and the other was unthinkable. There was no way she was pregnant. It couldn't happen. What about the birth control? And she was so much more careful than that. Except for the night with Fabien that she couldn't remember. Had he not used a condom? *Oh fuck.*

Tears burned her eyes, her heartbeat thumped in her head and her chest, while her stomach churned.

What was she going to do now?

Anita crouched in front of her and rubbed her hands over Audrey's arms. "I'm so sorry I sprung it on you like this, honey. Take some time to adjust and then if you want, you can give me a call at the hospital later and we'll chat."

Audrey barely managed a nod as she squeezed her eyelids together. Pregnant was not possible, well not a possibility. She'd never be hired for another role. She wasn't established enough to ask to work her roles around a baby and she wasn't rich enough to hire a nanny to trail her on the movie set.

Another horror thought dawned on her. She was going to have to tell Fabien. It wasn't that she was celibate but every other guy she'd had sex with had worn a condom and there weren't that many guys to start with. And then she'd call her doctor and yell at him for a bit. She knew birth control wasn't 100% guaranteed but maybe she'd been given a defective injection? Saline instead of Depo?

"Did you know?" Callum's voice was filled with anguish, his tone low, his question sounding as if wrenched from his lips without permission.

Audrey looked up, noting Anita had left while she'd gotten lost in her thoughts. She didn't want to meet Callum's eyes and feel the scorn, the pity, the judgement. There was nothing he could say to her that wasn't already running through her head. She wasn't some dumb kid who'd been irresponsible. She wasn't a teenager who'd made a bad decision. Anger began a slow crawl in her veins. This was all Fabien's fault. And the asshole who'd broken into her apartment in the first place. He'd set this whole bad situation into motion when he'd frightened the life out of her all those months ago. If she hadn't started drinking to numb the fear, she would never have been vulnerable enough to be taken advantage of by her producer, a married man who should have known better. She should have pressed charges. She should have fought harder to bring Fabien to some kind of justice. But who was she? She was a wannabe actress who would be accused of sleeping her way to the top. She was a nobody in the Hollywood scheme of things. Not yet. Maybe not ever now.

"Audrey?"

"I didn't know," she whispered. "There was just that one night, with Fabien, I don't remember what happened."

"As in you were too drunk?" Disgust laced the response and Audrey felt it like a slap.

"I...I think he drugged me." Embarrassment burned hot. "I woke up the next morning and didn't know where I was, who I'd been with. He told me I asked for it, was begging for it."

"Did you call the police?"

She shook her head. Fabien was right when he'd sneered and told her no one would believe her. She'd gone home, showered off the evidence and covered the visible bruises with makeup for a few days. Shame had eaten her alive. "I had been drinking heavily, after the break-in, no one would have believed I didn't go with him willingly."

"Who is this guy, Audrey? Why didn't you get yourself to the hospital? Get tested for drugs in your system? Unless you were already on drugs?"

A sob rose up her throat. He must think her the lowest of low. "I don't do drugs." *I just lost my way*, she wanted to add. "If I'd reported him, the scandal would have been huge. I couldn't remember anything." Finally she lifted her gaze and stared at Callum, willed him to be on her side like no one else was, willed him to believe her. "What if I did go with him? What would it look like if I'd gone with him willingly, if there were witnesses to confirm it? I couldn't just cry rape..."

"You can if you didn't consent."

Audrey got to her feet and threw her hands in the air, a tear trickling down her cheek as her frustrations boiled over. "I don't know if I consented! It's all just a black hole. It's like I fell into it before midnight and clawed my way out sometime around lunchtime the next day."

"Would you have slept with this guy if you weren't drunk?"

She shook her head, tucked her hair over her ear. "No way. He was the producer for the movie but that's it."

"Did you ever give him the idea that you might be into him?"

Thinking that over for a moment, she recalled the times they'd been alone together, on set, at parties and functions. "I was always nice, friendly, maybe a little flirty some of the time." Everyone was like that. It was a line you had to walk. Just sexy enough to be thought about and remembered, not so flirty that you sent out the wrong signals. "Do you think I gave him the wrong idea? Is this my fault?"

Callum wanted to march over to Audrey and give her a shake. Or a slap. But he didn't manhandle women and he did not trust himself in those moments to be gentle. Anger raged inside of him to the point he wanted to put his fist through a wall.

"What that arsehole did to you was not your fault. You should have gone straight to the hospital and taken a rape kit and drug test. He took advantage of you, Audrey, and he should be in a fucking jail cell being someone's bitch right now."

"No one would have believed me." Another tear ran down her cheek and he wanted to wipe it away, wipe away the experience and the repercussions for her, protect her. No wonder she was so messed up, so up and down. It wasn't just the break-in dragging her down.

"I knew you were running away from someone when you got here. Why didn't you tell me?"

"I wasn't running from *him*. It was the situation I had to leave. I wouldn't even have been at that party that night if it hadn't been for the attack. I was too scared to go home alone and I drank too much. I was drinking too much. When I woke up in a hotel suite with my married producer, I knew I had to leave, dodge the consequences, dry out."

"You can't outrun a baby, Audrey, or a scandal."

"I know." She turned her back to him, her body wracked with sobs now.

"What are you going to do?"

"I don't know."

His chest ached for her and it was as if he was given a little push from behind as he went to her, folded her into his arms, her head on his chest while she cried. What else was he supposed to say? This was why he didn't do human contact. This was why he didn't get close to anyone anymore. There was nothing he could do for Audrey except hold and comfort her.

"You can say it," she muttered with a sniff.

"Say what?"

"That I'm turning out just like Mavis."

"You haven't had a drink in days, Audrey, and you are nothing like Mavis."

"I hid from my troubles and drank to block it all out. Sounds like mom to me."

Her accent rolled on *mom* and his arms dropped to his sides. "Your mum was a complicated woman but she was essentially good. If you believe nothing else I ever say, believe that."

Another sniffle and Audrey sat back on the couch. "She always had a soft spot for you, Callum, but not for me. I don't think she ever really wanted to have a baby and I won't have a child to wind up resenting it later like she did. She never even asked me to stay or come back. Sometimes I felt like she didn't even like me."

Callum leaned against the kitchen bench where only two days ago he'd had Audrey on the surface, bare-assed and begging. Two days of little to no worry. Two nights of actual sleep and no nightmares. He could get used to having her around. But not after he told her Mavis's biggest secret. She had to know. It wasn't helping to keep Audrey in the dark. "You were a headstrong teenager with a bloody big chip on your shoulder. Would you have stayed if Mavis asked you to?"

Audrey shook her head and Callum let out the breath he'd held onto before hitting her with, "You weren't exactly easy to be around either, you know."

A little smile ghosted her lips rather than the outrage he'd expected.

"You stomped around telling everyone what to do like the fun police."

This time she snapped her gaze to his. "Someone had to be the adult around here."

"But it didn't have to be you."

Audrey lifted her fingers and began counting things off on the pads. "We would have had no clean clothes, no dishes, no food. Mom's favourite dinner was vodka with a citrus chaser. She would say, 'At least it's fruit, baby girl.'"

He remembered. Every now and then he'd drop an orange slice into her drink so she'd actually have something more substantial but Mavis never ate it, just poured more booze in over the top.

"I'd have to go to the ATM and withdraw her welfare money to buy food which meant skipping lessons because I'd have to be ready to get on the school bus otherwise I'd be walking. Mom would just pat me in the back like a good dog and have another drink."

"I didn't say she wasn't messed up but she had good reason, Audrey. She never resented having you, it's not that simple. There's so much more to it, to Mavis."

Callum could still see Mavis's bloodshot eyes boring into his face, seeing him in some kind of strange way, even reaching out a yellowed hand to cradle his cheek before dropping the bombshell that was the missing piece of her puzzling life. It changed everything for him and once Audrey knew the truth, hopefully it would change things for her too. He just didn't know if it would make things better or so much worse.

Audrey inhaled and then exhaled. She gripped her fingers together to stop the trembling and had to pick her jaw up off the floor before saying, "What do you mean?"

"In the last few months of your mum's life, she spent most of her time delirious. Some days she had no idea where she was, even who she was. Jibberish mostly came out but there were moments when she was kind of lucid."

"You should have called me. I would have come home."

Callum shook his head. "She didn't want anyone. Some days she was ashamed, some days she was angry, most days she was just out of it."

"If you're trying to make me feel shittier than I already do, well done."

"There is a point here, Auds. Stay with me. I'm trying to figure out how to say it best."

"Just say it, Callum. If it's about my mom, I want to know."

Callum dropped to the coffee table in front of Audrey and took her hands in his. "You have to listen properly okay? Take it in and see it from Mavis's standing?"

Audrey nodded and with each tilt of her head, the sinking in her stomach became heavier. *This better be good*, she thought. This better explain why her mom drank every day, why her mom was such a shit excuse for a parent and why she was always putting Audrey second whenever Callum was around. God, she looked at him like he was more her son than she was her daughter.

"Here goes," Callum started.

Audrey stopped breathing.

"You know your mum and my mum met here, in this house, when they were only kids, right?"

"Yeah." She wanted to scream at him to get on with it.

He went on. "Then, every summer, their parents would bring them for the holidays and they'd spend every waking hour together?"

"I've heard all of these stories, Callum. They wound up at nursing school together, shared a dorm in the city, shared a dislike of their parents for being rich rather than kind. Mavis went on and on about it all the time."

"What your mum didn't tell you, or anyone, was that she was in love with my mum. She loved Erin."

"By all accounts, everyone loved your mom. I've never heard a bad word about her."

Callum shook his head, his grip tightened on her hands and his eyes darkened with an intensity she hadn't seen many times. "No. She loved loved my mum. Not loved in the way two friends love each other. Mavis was *in* love with Erin."

"But Mavis wasn't a lesbian. She had four husbands."

"What she had was four failed marriages based on lies."

Thoughts raced and tumbled and crashed inside her brain. Erin had left the house to Mavis, the house where they'd met. But it was years before Mavis moved them both out to Jupiter Creek. She'd slept with men, had a baby. "Are you sure?"

Another shake of his head. "I can only tell you what Mavis told me. She never had the courage to tell mum because she met dad right after university. Mavis spent the next few years trying to get on with it, trying to bury it all. Run from it. Mum was happy with dad then. She clearly didn't return the strongest of Mavis's feelings."

"I... I...don't know what to say. It all sounds a bit too far-fetched."

"Mavis began drinking more after my mum died," he explained. "I remember her coming to the house one night and asking dad for some of her belongings. Specific things that seemed weird because I was young, but made sense later. Dad was devastated and wouldn't let her have any of it. Mavis threw a rock through our lounge room window and dad called the cops."

Her mother had a minor criminal record, mostly for driving under the influence, property damage didn't seem out of the question.

"Mavis lost the one true love of her life, Audrey, and it sent her into a spiral."

It only answered a few questions. "Then why did she spend my life taking it out on me?"

"Grief does different things to different people. Mavis never accepted that mum was gone. She was never happy with her lot in life because mum wasn't in it."

"And none of that was my fault."

"No, it wasn't. I don't know why Mavis held you at arm's length. Maybe she didn't want to lose you too and feel that same pain?"

"That is no reason to do the things she did. To act the way she did. I was still here and I needed her." Tears collected on her lashes and spilled down her cheeks but she didn't attempt to wipe them away or hold back. She felt for her mother, she really did, but Erin was gone and Audrey was still there. Audrey had been there every day, her own flesh and blood, being punished, being pushed away. It wasn't fair.

Callum looked away, got up and walked back to the kitchen, his back to her. "Until you've felt that kind of loss, you can't say what is normal, Audrey. Different people react differently."

Through her tears, she stared at his back. "You got over it. You lost her too and you went on to be a doctor, to join the army, to serve your country. You didn't hate the world and everyone in it."

"Not then," he said, still not turning, his chin dropping to his chest. She barely heard his next words. "I thought I could help people like her. It's why I became a doctor. It's why I joined the army. But it turns out I was wrong."

"People like her?" Audrey asked. "Like Mavis or Erin?"

Callum slammed his hands down on the bench and Audrey flinched at the noise, at the violence. She stood and rounded the bench, close but not too close. His eyes were glazed as he stared at his hands. She wondered what he really saw.

"Callum?"

"I was too young to save mum. Not a good enough doctor to save my friends. Not strong enough to save the woman in the sand and her..." He gave his head a shake, his hair tossing about. "I couldn't even convince Mavis to stop drinking."

"Some of those things were out of your hands, Callum. Most of those incidents were beyond anything anyone could say or do, especially Mavis. Unless you can control bullets or booze or make choices for others, you have no control over those things that happened to you."

When he lifted his gaze, Audrey unclenched her fists.

"What was the point of spending all of those years training if nothing I can do is worth a damn?"

Her heart broke a little for him. Gone was the strong, sexy guy she'd been getting to know and in his place stood a scared boy. He probably wore the same look the day the police knocked on his father's door after the accident. "Think about the lives you did save, Callum. Think about how many men and women came home from Afghanistan because of you. You can't always think of the ones you were too late for."

He blinked once, twice, a third time. "I don't want to talk about this anymore."

He might not want to, but Audrey had a feeling he needed to. Pushing him was like poking an already angry bear but push she did. "You agreed not to shut me out."

Twenty-Five

♥

Sure, he'd agreed not to shut her out but he hadn't agreed to pouring his woes out so she could give him that look of pity, so she could rub his back and tell him everything would be okay. What the fuck did she know? She'd walked away and never looked back. Left Mavis behind to face her demons on her own until it consumed her. Callum bit his tongue so he wouldn't say the words out loud.

"You can tell me," Audrey said, her hand reaching out to him.

He sidestepped. "Talking doesn't help."

"How do you know unless you try it?"

Callum saw red. "I do know! I did try. I tried with the army psychologist. I tried with Alison." He even tried to talk to Mavis when he'd first returned. "Nothing anyone can say or do will take the images out of my head, the feeling of the blood from between my fingers, the smells, the tastes, the sounds. Nothing fucking helps."

He hadn't realised he'd rounded the bench and advanced on Audrey until his vision cleared. His hands gripped her upper arms and she'd paled, trying to lean away from him, trying to get away from him.

He snatched his hands back. "Shit, I'm sorry, Auds. God damn it."

"I think that's enough for one day."

How much had he hurt her? Hell, he'd not been so deep in a rage since he'd first returned. So much for getting better when Audrey was around. So much for feeling fucking lighter. He reached for her again, to apologise more, but she shrank back against the sink, holding her arms against her body. He'd not be surprised if he'd bruised her. If she never wanted to talk to him again. If she told him to fuck right off.

This whole conversation was supposed to shed light on Mavis, not bring his baggage to the forefront. It was supposed to be about Audrey and Mavis.

"I have to go," he mumbled, not waiting for her to say a damn thing.

What was there to say?

This was why he kept his distance. He and Mavis had that in common. Don't get involved. He always lost the people he cared about and if he didn't care so much, it wouldn't hurt so bad.

He kept trying to tell himself that all the way out to the boat. He kept repeating the words under his breath as he pulled the old fuses out ready for the new ones.

Only now he had another problem to add to his growing pile. Now he didn't believe any of it...

Audrey spent the night in the house, in her mother's bed but she didn't sleep much. She didn't drink anything. She wanted to. Her mouth watered and her mind wouldn't shut up. Why hadn't Mavis just told her the truth? Was it because she came from the old school of thinking where a woman wasn't allowed to be in love with another woman? Her mother had deliberately never shared her views on homosexuality. They never had in depth discussions about much at all. Audrey learned about the birds and the bees, about periods and loads more, from *Dolly* magazines rather than her own mother.

The birth control discussion with her dad in the States had been particularly sticky since Audrey had never really thought much about it. 'The talk' had been performed over the dining table in her new home by a bright faced, previously absentee father and his new wife.

Too much of her life had been spent thinking about the fact that no one particularly wanted her. Her biological father had walked out before her first birthday and moved to America before her tenth. The husbands after that had accepted her but she was never theirs. Never a factor in the aftermath of another broken relationship. She'd practically guilt tripped her real father into taking her in.

Audrey had been a burden and as she curled her hands around her abdomen, she wondered if that's what this baby would be? A burden? An afterthought to her career, to her success. Would she resent the kid because of the circumstances? Mavis probably saw Erin every time she looked at Callum. Would Audrey see Fabien?

God, she was over-thinking it all. She was exhausted, wrung out and on emotional overload. Callum hadn't come back in from the houseboat which wasn't a good sign but he hadn't left either. Maybe he was giving her space to process. It had been a long day full of revelations.

She dozed but woke at four am when something scared the corellas from their tree roosts. She went for a glass of water and found a universal adapter plug waiting for her on the bench. Callum must have brought it in for her.

Was he helping or leaving a hint? She didn't even try to work it out. For five minutes she stood at the back door, stared at the dark boat on the still water. She'd love to tiptoe out and slide into his bed, lie in the safety of his arms and make sure he was okay. If she took the hint and left, went back to her life, what would happen to Callum?

Leaving him alone won out and she picked up the plug, found her cell and plugged it in.

When Audrey woke again, only an hour had passed. 5:17am read the digital display.

100% battery charged said the screen on her phone.

This was it. Audrey hadn't checked in with the real world in a week but now she had precious little choice. Pressing the button to power up her cell, she winced with every vibration. Messages, emails, notifications. Hundreds of them. Nothing was more important than calling her agent, then her doctor back home and then Fabien. It was early morning in Australia so she should be able to catch them all before they left work for the day.

She scrolled through her contacts until she found *Super Agent*. It only rang twice. "Hi Tinka, It's Audrey."

"Oh my God! Where have you been? I've been trying to get in contact with you for days. Are you all right?"

Tears burned her eyelids again and she breathed deep, swallowed hard. "I'm okay. I think. I've been trying to relax." Living in an alternate reality where pregnancies, reporters and hard decisions didn't exist.

"I want you on the next plane back here, Audrey. So much has happened."

"Tell me about it," Audrey mumbled. She was about to drop her bombshell when her agent beat her to it.

"They caught the guy who broke into your apartment." Truth be told, she'd just about forgotten under the weight of everything else.

Stammering like an idiot, Audrey sputtered a, "W-w-what?"

"He tried to sell your handbag online, along with your credit cards and ID."

Her thoughts hadn't caught up yet. "Who was he?"

"You'd never believe it but it was a guy in your block. 1D I think."

"Bryan? From downstairs?"

"Yeah, that's him. Do you know him?"

They shared a fire escape and had said hello at the mailboxes. "Not really. We spoke a few times."

"Turns out he's sold a few bits and pieces on Ebay that belong to you. He must have been breaking into your apartment for a while."

"Through the window..." How many times had he invaded her privacy? And for what? Her stuff wouldn't sell for much.

"So, it's over now, right?" Tinka said. "You can come home and we can get you back on your feet and into your next role, I've got the perfect..."

Audrey zoned out, her phone hand falling to the mattress for a moment. Over? Was it that simple? If one guy could get into her apartment in the night, what was stopping anyone else? She'd be sure to always double deadbolt every lock from now on but the dark was still the dark and anything could happen in it. Instead of relief, Audrey only felt worse. Sick to her stomach.

"Audrey? Audrey are you still there?"

She pulled the phone back to her ear and shook loose thoughts about home invaders, treacherous neighbours and night-time prowlers. "Sorry. I'm here."

"I would ask where here is but I already found out with a Google alert. You didn't look your finest in that second-to-last photo."

"I haven't seen them yet."

"Let's just say it was lucky you had a bra on..."

Audrey groaned.

"Don't worry, it can't get much worse. Just book your ticket and we'll work on damage control."

Clearing her throat, Audrey jumped right in. "I heard about Fabien's divorce."

"Your hole beneath the rock would have to have been very deep not to hear that one. Don't worry, you're not copping too much heat."

"Yet."

Tinka finally stopped to take a breath. "What do you mean, yet?"

"There's something the reporters don't know."

"And that is?"

"I'm pregnant, Tinka."

Laughter trickled down the line but when Audrey didn't say anything else, like April fool's or gotcha, Tinka grew quiet and said, "Really?"

"It's Fabien's baby," she said before the question came.

"You know that for sure?"

Another groan, another deep breath and hard swallow. The lump in her throat was getting bigger. "It isn't anyone else's."

"Are you going to keep it?"

Audrey had been asking herself the same question over and over and over. It would be so much easier if she were the type of woman who could just take care of it and try not to look back. Could she be that person? It would have been easier for Mavis if she'd been that person. Audrey cringed.

"Audrey?"

"I don't know. I don't know what to do."

"You know a baby would mean the end of your current success, don't you?"

She didn't want to hear the ugly truth even though she already knew. "I think the scandal with Fabien and his wife is probably going to do that."

Tinka tut-tutted. "I doubt that. The public love you. Him, not so much. Without the baby in question, you were just two adults who had consenting sex. He's going to be hated with more passion than you will be since he's the one who cheated."

Audrey still doubted the *consenting* part. "I don't know what to do. You're my agent, you tell me what I should do."

"Honey, I handle your career and run damage control on your publicity but I can't do this for you."

Audrey knew that.

"How far along are you?"

"About eight weeks."

"So you still have time to make your decisions."

Time? That she had. Answers? Those she couldn't find. She was too tired to think about it all. Too emotional to make decisions. Too exhausted to care about the long term affects her choices would have. How did any woman do this? Discover their unwanted pregnancy and then do something. Anything. Keep it. Don't keep it.

Then there was the alcohol. What if she'd done damage to the baby without even knowing it? Tears fell now. Silent, desperate, out of control. She was out of control. The spiral spun around her and Audrey lost sight of everything important and unimportant as she squeezed her eyes shut. It all blended together in a haze of blacks and whatever colour *too hard* looked like.

"I've got another call coming in, Audrey. Keep your phone on and I'll call you if anything else develops. Kisses." And then the line was dead.

And so were Audrey's hopes and dreams.

Twenty-Six

♥

The night was unnaturally still, like the calm before a storm, but Callum didn't find anything useful in the time on his own. He sat in the darkness at the back table at war with his own thoughts. Should he go inside and sit with Audrey? Should he leave her be? He was out of sight from the windows in the house but if she stepped one foot out the door, she would have seen him. Maybe. Maybe not. Not that she'd willingly go out into the dark night, not for him, not for anyone.

An air rifle set on pre-dawn sent sleeping birds squawking, the kitchen light coming on not long after. He didn't move.

He heard her on the phone, only the slightest guilt on his shoulders that he eavesdropped. He had to imagine what the person on the other end was saying but it wasn't hard. It was back to silence for a few minutes but her sniffles were loud enough to wake the dead. She was crying again. He couldn't even begin to conceive how difficult it must be for Audrey. He'd hoped telling her about Mavis would help her to understand her mother better but then the tables had turned back on him with a hell of a thump.

The images in his mind flashed from Audrey to the woman in the sand in the desert like Christmas lights when you selected a preset. Minding her own business in a war zone one moment, the next she was dead. A soldier had taken aim at an insurgent but he was afraid. Too afraid to move. He hadn't fired on them yet. He was still innocent, clean. Callum had shoved the barrel of the gun at the very same time the soldier pulled the trigger on his semi-automatic weapon. Bullets sprayed wild. Instead of helping the situation, prevent it from becoming a blood bath, Callum had made it worse. He was making a habit of making things worse.

A little niggling voice kept calling from the back of his mind that maybe he could make things better for Audrey. This wasn't a war zone. She wasn't the same kind of alcoholic he'd first thought her. She wasn't her mother or his. He had little money to offer her but he had a home, a name, a title and rank for what it was worth. He could offer her and her baby shelter from the scandal. He could protect them both. Maybe. But then again. What if he couldn't?

Callum made a mental list of all he had to lose. There wasn't much left. His sanity was first. His fragile grip on existing was second. It's all he really had. His family didn't register. His brother and father had given up on him and he had nothing in common with them. He'd pushed his friends away long before so he wouldn't have to care or be cared for. He had some material items like the boat, his medals, his car, but the rest was just stuff. Three things on the list of all he had to lose. Pitiful.

Then he turned to the gains. First came Audrey. God, she was so lost right now but she'd find her way. She'd done it before, she could do it again. When she smiled, it literally knocked him for a six. When she laughed, he wanted to laugh too. When she ran her fingers through her hair and bit her bottom lip, he wanted to kiss her until they were both senseless.

Now she was crying. No laughter, no kisses, no silence.

He abandoned his list, went into the house and found her curled up on her mother's bed, her face puffy and swollen, her sobs almost howls. When she cried, he wanted to make it all go away. Protect her. Save her.

He wasn't qualified.

She had no one else.

Even he had to be better than nothing.

"Audrey?" He knocked lightly so he didn't scare her in the lamp light.

Her only response was louder sobbing. Callum sat on the bed and she climbed onto his lap, her face on his chest, her tears soaking his t-shirt. "Ssh, it's going to work out."

She shook her head, her messy hair splaying over her hands where he held her. "It won't. I can't have a baby by myself. I can't see Fabien when I look at her. I can't do to a child what my mother did to me."

He spoke softly close to her ear. "Whether you like it or not, your mother made you into an independent, resilient woman who gets shit done. You don't need anyone to raise your baby with you. Just don't make the same mistakes Mavis did and you'll be fine."

Her crying softened and her muffled voice reached him but only just. "I don't want to be just fine anymore."

"You have to decide what you really want then," he told her. When she took a breath to reply, he cut her off. "But not today. Maybe not even tomorrow."

"My agent wants me back in the States." Audrey sat up a little straighter, pushed her hair back, wiped her cheeks. "They caught the guy who broke into my apartment."

His grip tightened and he had to forcibly relax his hands. "That's great. Isn't it?"

She nodded and used the back of her hand to wipe her nose. A very un-Audrey action. "It is. I know it is..."

"But?"

"I don't think I'm ready to go back."

"You don't have to be scared of this guy anymore."

"You don't get it. It's not *the* guy. It's all guys. It's the next guy and the one after that. It's the whack jobs who think it's okay to come in and take what they want or follow me home at night or hang around the studio in the day. I don't want to be scared anymore, but I am and I don't know how not to be."

Callum had a feeling they'd gone off track somewhere. "Are you still talking about the thief or are you talking about the father of the baby?"

She squeezed her eyes shut and more tears escaped as she bowed her head. "I don't know. I just don't want to do it on my own anymore. I'm so tired of being alone."

His heart did a double thump. This was his chance to admit he was tired of being alone too. The words worked their way up his throat but he gulped them back down at the last minute, instead, stroking her hair and wrapping his arm back around her with a murmur of something incoherent.

Could he make this easier? Could he just say to himself, 'it's time to man up!'? His list making of pros and cons was a stall tactic and he knew it. He wanted Audrey. He wanted to make her happy again. He wanted the fire and sass and venom to come back out again. He wanted to wake up next to her. Hell, a huge part of him even wanted the baby she carried. He'd have a chance to prove he wasn't beyond saving, that he could do something right. That together their wrongs could make a right.

But what if he couldn't? He'd be setting himself up for a sure failure, jumping in with both feet knowing all along it could explode in his face and leave him worse off. But worse off than what? Damn his subconscious. Only booze and drugs could bring him lower. Rock bottom was a shitty, shitty place.

A car engine sounded from the front of the house and then went quiet. Callum heard the slam of a metal door and was loathe to move, to find out who would come this early, it wasn't even seven yet.

"Someone's here," he said into her hair, the ends tickling his nose. She probably needed time to process it all still. He didn't want to leave her. *Ever*, reverberated in his skull. He ignored the add on. She would go back to the States or he'd move on, back into the world or further into isolation. It would never work between them.

"Callum?" was called from the back door, followed by a heavy tread into the house. "Callum, where the fuck are you?"

Audrey scrambled from his lap and pushed him towards the door. She climbed in between the sheets and pulled the Egyptian cotton over her head, facing the wall and giving him her back. She was hiding. He knew a coward when he saw one in front of him. Or in the mirror staring back.

In the hall stood Daniel, out of uniform and out of breath. "That fucking dog mauled two kids from the caravan park. Doc needs your help or he's going to lose one."

Dread trickled from his nape down his spine and around to his yellow belly. "Did he call for the chopper?"

Daniel reached for Callum's arm and pulled hard until his feet moved. "No medivac. They're on a search and rescue down south. They're turning around but it'll take too long."

Digging his heels in, Callum said, "I can't just come and operate on a kid, Daniel. I don't even know if I still have a medical license." That was a lie. He'd done nothing to warrant suspension or termination from the profession.

Swearing again, Daniel pulled harder. "You're all we've got."

Callum shook himself free of the vice grip the other man had on his forearm. "I can't do it."

The disappointment staring back at Callum was nothing new but this time, when it was reflected in another man's eyes rather than the unflawed gleam of the mirror, something sharp stabbed inside his chest and his eyes burned in a way they hadn't in so many years. He repeated on a hopeless whisper, "I can't do it."

Pity replaced the look in Daniel's eyes and Callum was about to tell him to shove it when a soft hand pressed to his shoulder and a gentle voice followed. "This isn't the desert, Callum. You can do this. I know you can."

Squeezing his eyes shut tight, he shook his head. He couldn't. Audrey was wrong. She didn't know. No one did.

"We don't have time for this," Daniel said on a huff. "I feel for ya man but that kid needs someone. Pull your head out of your arse and man up."

Hadn't he already told himself much the same only hours before? To man up? Only, every other time someone had needed him, he'd failed. Be it age, circumstance, skill, he was always on the wrong end to succeed so he'd given up trying. There was only so much failure a guy could take.

"Callum?" Audrey prodded. "You have to do something. What if that was your child? Or my child?"

"I can't just leave you, Auds. You're too..." He couldn't find the words or the excuses.

Audrey came around to stand in front of him, her face swollen and tear-streaked and said with a finger pointed to his chest, "Don't you dare use me as a crutch. I'll be fine here for a few hours." Her voice dropped low as her palms came to rest on his cheeks, to tilt his head towards her. She pressed her forehead to his. "Go. Do some good. Rediscover why you are who you are."

His head moved without his okay and tipped up and then down. "What if I can't?"

"You can. That kid is only better off with you there no matter if you save him or not. Go."

Callum kissed her hard on the mouth and then he followed Daniel out the door and into the police cruiser. *That kid is only better off with you there.*

He sure fucking hoped so.

Twenty-Seven

♥

I t had been hours since Callum had left for the hospital and Audrey was beyond worried about his state of mind, the injured child's wellbeing and basically any part of the future from the next few seconds all the way to the next eighteen or so years. She fell into an exhausted heap and napped on the sofa but by the time she woke, she didn't feel much better. Just more worried.

She tried to ignore the fact it was getting darker by the second, clouds gathering after another humid and hot day. Now that her phone was charged she was able to check the weather and had been glued to the thing since he'd left.

Callum.

No word at all. Not a text or a phone call or even a Facebook message.

Another hour passed and then another.

What if he'd frozen up the way he had when her leg had bled? What if the blood was too much and he had a breakdown or the child died and it pushed him that one more step too far? She should have gone with him. Her strength might be questionable at times but she'd give him what she had. She'd give him everything she had to see the carefree Callum she remembered from her teens instead of this tortured soldier with nowhere to turn and not many places left to hide.

Of course, he wouldn't want much from her now she was pregnant. He'd said all the right things about her being strong enough, about Mavis raising her to be an independent woman who could handle anything, but at the end of the day, they were just words designed to make her feel better about her situation. He'd heard her when she'd said she'd have to go back to the States but he hadn't said anything in reply. He didn't ask her to stay. He still wanted her gone so he could continue to hide in peace.

Her pulse slowed to a crawl as she stared at the ceiling above the sofa, one hand over her head, the other toying with the hem of her tank top. She tried to imagine how the conversation would go if he did ask her to stay. Would he want her to stay to help him? To help her? For the mind-blowing sex? Forever?

When she'd first arrived, he'd been pissed to see her but things had changed. Hadn't they? Would he smile at her, take her hand and thread his fingers through hers? Would he argue that they were going somewhere and should explore it? This hiding place was big enough for the three of them wasn't it? The reporters in town would get bored soon enough or her agent would call in a bogus story that would send the not so smartest of them off on a wild goose chase.

A car pulled up out front, the engine cutting to silence before multiple doors were clicked open and then slammed shut.

Callum's voice sounded. "You don't have to come in."

Daniel's followed. "We'll see you inside."

"I'm not a child and I don't need you to look after me."

Audrey reached the front step just as Callum cut the air with a slash of his hand, his angry words smothered by the oppressive tension of the day, the moods, the anticipation. He looked like his same angry-at-the-world self, his spine straight, his head up, his shoulders stiff like a concrete statue.

She went to him and cupped his cheek with her palm as she stared right into his eyes. "Are you okay?"

His irises flashed and his lips thinned but then he jerked away from her touch and crashed into the house with a muttered curse.

Whirling on Daniel and Anita, Audrey asked, "What happened? Did the child survive?" So many more questions buzzed but those were the two most important.

Daniel raked a hand through his hair with so much frustration, Audrey was sure he pulled some out. "The kid's fine. Both of them are. On their way to Adelaide as we speak."

Confusing. "Why is he so dark still?"

Anita stepped around Audrey on the brick path and headed for the house. "He's Callum," she said with a shrug.

When Daniel went to also side-step her, Audrey held him back with a hand to his chest. "What really happened?"

The police man sighed. "He did good. It took him a few minutes and a kick up the arse but he did really good. I honestly didn't know if he had it in him."

Audrey's chin lowered to her chest and she said a little prayer of thanks to whoever listened. Maybe he was just tired and wanted to be on his own. It would have been hard for him to be surrounded by not only the blood but also the noise and the people.

By the time Audrey reached the kitchen, Anita had made herself at home at the back table and Daniel was climbing off the houseboat with a six pack of beer.

"Is he okay?" Audrey asked.

Daniel shrugged. "He's not on the boat. Must be in the house."

A chill lifted the hairs on her arm despite the sticky weather. "You guys don't have to stay. I can call you if there's any problems?"

Both of their guests shook their heads at once but Anita was first to reply. "We're not going anywhere until Callum comes out here and shows us he's not going to fall apart. Duty of care and all that."

Audrey forced a scoffing noise from her throat but anxiety roiled inside her gut. "He'll be fine. I can take care of him."

Four eyebrows lifted in her direction and not one face looked convinced.

Turning her back, she re-entered the house in search of Callum and heard water running in the bathroom. She knocked lightly but got no answer. She knocked a little harder and still nothing came back but the sound of water. Later she'd say courage made her turn the handle and open the door but she'd be lying. It was good old fashion fear that propelled her now and as she spied Callum leaning against the basin staring at the water overflowing from the sink to the tiled floor, she entered silently and shut them off from the world, preparing herself for what would come next.

"Callum?" Audrey prompted from a safe distance, but he was lost to his thoughts. Remembering how badly he reacted to being woken from sleep, Audrey wondered how he might react now if she startled him. He stood there so still, so sombre, so lost.

"Callum, it's Audrey." Still no response.

She had no courage left. She had no words that would make any of it any better. She did have the tenuous thread they'd already wound back together over the last few days and she hoped like hell it was enough to bring him back from wherever he'd gone.

Blood.

Blood under his fingernails. Dried dark.

Blood clinging to his cuticles and the hair on the back of his wrists.

Blood gushing from a little girl's arms and face. Blood splashed on a mother numb with shock and worried into stunned silence.

He'd never wanted to see that kind of blood again. Dripping onto the floor, making it slippery if you shifted your weight, seeping through fingers and flooding wounds. It felt like an eternity passed by as he surveyed the horror before him but then a sharp nudge in his back brought it all into focus. Anita was yelling his name while she straddled the child lying on the hospital bed, holding a tiny arm in the air. Three more nurses were busy with drips, needles and gauze. All at once the noise hit him and then the nudge in his back came again, more insistent.

The edges of his vision had darkened and the sound dipped in his ears until he heard a sob. So small. So pained. The child moved, cried, whimpered.

Anita looked down at her and smiled. "It's alright honey, the doctor is here now. We're going to make you all better."

All better. All better. All better.

He still wasn't sure what propelled him, held him up, kept him going. Three hours of surgery to repair a torn artery in her arm and sew a face that would never be the same again. She, Matilda Grace, would need hundreds of hours to repair what one dog did to her in only minutes, seconds even, her little friend worse off with damage to hands, a leg, a shoulder. Two mums who would have nightmares about this day for years, one more so than the other, having taken to the dog with a fishing knife in a panicked attempt to save the girls.

Callum just kept thinking what if this was Audrey's baby girl? Audrey's child holidaying by the river only to be ripped apart by a starving, mad dog. Wouldn't he do anything and everything he could to fix her?

As he stared at the blood on his hands, the face of the pregnant mother in the sand looked back at him. He closed his eyes and the image was replaced over and over with the dead and dying until his head hurt.

Time passed but he didn't know how much. Audrey was with him. He heard her call his name. Coldness started to make his toes hurt and distantly he wondered why since the day had started off so hot.

He preferred the cold. Blood was never cold when it poured into his hands.

A small part of his mind savoured the victory. He'd saved her. Matilda Grace. He'd taken her arm from Anita who was literally holding her finger over the tear to a major artery and he'd fixed her. He'd shooed the other doctor away when he'd come to take over the stitching of her poor little face. Callum took his time, did what he had to do, did it well. There were no bullets, no fear of what was over his shoulder, no thought to anything else but the skin beneath his hands and trying to make it right.

Callum opened his eyes to stare once again at his fingers still caked with her blood. Two more hands covered his, clean and fragile, covering the brownish stains and gripping the sudden tremble.

When his name fell from her lips again, he lifted his gaze and met hers. A worry like he'd never seen before lingered in honey depths darker than usual, darker than when she was laughing or happy.

Words tripped along his tongue but his mouth felt glued shut. He wanted to tell her he was okay, that he'd be fine. But Audrey had said it herself. Fine was no longer okay. Fine was no longer safe or secure. Fine was lonely and he didn't want to be just fine anymore.

"Speak to me," she begged, trying to inch her way in front of him so she could steal his attention away.

He shifted and made room but not much. Her body came into contact with his and he knew what he needed, knew what would replace fine and bring him back from wherever it was he hung, suspended, alone. Before he could consciously think about moving to lift her to the basin top, she was already there, her arms around his neck and her legs around his waist, holding him, grounding him.

She whispered the words he never knew he needed to hear. "You're not alone, Callum, I'm here with you."

His head throbbed and his eyes burned like he'd been ambushed by tear gas as he rested his forehead against her shoulder. "You'll leave me."

Hair floated over his collarbone as she shook her answer. "I'm not going anywhere."

The press of her lips to his head was his undoing. His mother used to comfort him with a kiss to his head. Mavis had given the same assurances after the funeral, the same kiss. If he closed his eyes, he could see both of their faces, happy, smiling, alive. The antithesis of his current state. He felt as though he'd died inside when he'd woken up in the base hospital and they'd told him the pregnant woman in the sand had perished along with her unborn baby. He hadn't pulled the trigger that day but he had pushed the tip of the semi-automatic until it had sent a wide spray of bullets in the air. Her death had been the last straw for him, the one to break the camel's back or the soldier doctor's will. It was the last life he'd account for with his own conscience. He'd shut down and refused to get close to anyone after that. Mavis had crept in because she was like a mother to him. But then she'd died too. On his watch. They all died.

"Except for Matilda," he whispered. She was alive. She was broken but she was young and resilient and alive.

"Please talk to me," Audrey pleaded softly. "I need to know you're all right."

Callum pulled her closer still, the cold spreading from his feet to his legs but only the in the places where he didn't touch her. In those places, he burned with a need he'd never fully comprehend.

Twenty-Eight

♥

A udrey contemplated slapping or pinching or pulling hair to get a response from Callum. He held her tight and occasionally whispered against her shoulder though she didn't hear any real words, just sounds filled with despair. The basin bit into her hip and cold water sloshed onto the floor even though she'd turned the tap off. None of it really mattered as long as he showed some sign that he was still in there.

He muttered something that sounded like a question. Audrey pulled back far enough to take his face in her palms. "Talk to me, please."

His eyes stayed closed and moisture wet the lashes on his cheeks. This time his words were clearer. "I need you to make me human again."

"How?" She held her breath. In that moment she would have done anything, given him anything.

"I need you to make me whole again, make me warm, make me feel," he said, the despair turning to anguish as though he begged the impossible.

"How? Tell me what to do and I'll do it." Tears threatened and she kissed his cheek, his nose, his chin. "Tell me how to make it better."

His mouth crashed against hers in a kiss so potent and fuelled by emotion she wanted to pour herself into him so that their two undamaged halves could make a near perfect whole. His teeth grazed her lower lip and his fingers were greedy as they sank into her hips to pull her closer still. Audrey would have stopped to ask if sex would make the situation worse somehow but his desperation was heartbreaking and she gave in, in a fractured heartbeat.

Sliding off the wet basin edge, her shorts and underwear were shoved to the floor where she stepped out of them barely getting the chance to draw a breath as he ripped at the opening of his shorts. Callum lifted her back to the vanity's cold surface but didn't give her a chance to brace or regroup. He entered her in one long, plunging invasion that would have sent her colliding into the wall except that he had hold of her. Waves of pleasure tinged with the beginnings of pain washed over her like a tsunami, wild, dangerous, out of control but ethereal in its beauty as he continued to pull out only to slam back into her. A hysterical sob rose in Audrey's throat as her body tried to deal with the onslaught but Callum swooped in to take that too, his tongue tangling with hers, his mouth stealing her breath to make his own as if trying to suck the life from her.

His movements were a hurried frenzy of hunger and need and she took it all, as much as he wanted to give and as much as he needed. He was both rough and gentle at the same time, passionate but far from disconnected. His eyes were almost hollow as he cried out but it was Audrey's name on his lips, it was Audrey's life in his hands as surely as it was her body and her skyrocketing pleasure.

When he was finished, he stepped away and interlocked his fingers behind his head, seemingly more broken than he had been to start with. She didn't say anything, just pulled her shorts on and waited. Either he'd speak or he'd leave. She hoped he didn't leave. Not like this.

Rubbing his hands over his face, he crumpled to the tiles and Audrey wondered if he really had checked out, if what they'd done was his way of saying goodbye. But then a great sob was wrenched from his chest and her heart broke in two. She couched next to him, wanting to touch him, to comfort him, but terrified he wouldn't let her. He reached for her and she wrapped her arms around his shaking frame, cradled his head against her chest in the same way he'd done for her that morning.

When Callum had spoken of war and of loss, Audrey couldn't fully understand, only empathise, but this she knew. She knew what it was like to break, to feel so hopeless and lost that there might not be a way back other than through human touch, a connection to reality and the security that in that moment that you weren't alone. She also knew there was a chance this day had truly tipped her tortured soldier right over the edge.

She had to hope she was enough to bring him back.

Twenty-Nine

♥

Exhaustion was something a soldier got used to very quickly. The next three steps after that didn't even have a name. It was usually the early hours of the morning where even the strongest of the dirty camp coffee barely gave your senses a flick let alone a kick. He'd once stayed awake for 41 hours straight in the crudest hospital facilities you could even imagine. Five hours were spent operating and the other thirty-six were spent worrying and operating some more. His sugar levels had been depleted, his adrenaline long gone and his bones had physically hurt. His fingers shook until a nurse had to take the pen from his hand and lead him to a cot. She even tucked him in. He'd slept for two days after that nightmare. No sleeping pills, no sedatives and no dreams for two entire days.

Callum didn't get two days to sleep this time. He was no less exhausted than he had been then but now it was mostly emotional fatigue that kept his eyes shut and his body boneless. The events of the past week seemed like a dream he'd lose like a whisper of smoke if he woke and dressed and started the day. Audrey had returned home and upset his world. She'd wriggled into his heart until he'd wanted her and only her.

Until he'd *needed* her. It was scary. If he had to admit it, it was scarier than anything he'd faced overseas.

The object of his thoughts nestled in closer, the little spoon to his big once again. He smiled against her hair as it tickled his nose and caught on his chin whiskers. When he opened his eyes he was surprised to find them on his houseboat, in his bed, the predawn glow lighting up Mavis's house and the gardens that surrounded it.

"How did we get here?" he murmured, not even pretending Audrey might still be asleep.

"Daniel and Anita helped after...after..." Audrey trailed off and Callum sifted through his brain to piece the parts back together.

It was all there. He swore under his breath. "I didn't hurt you did I?"

Her head shook against the pillows and he wondered if she was crying but then she said, "Would it be wrong to say it was the most intense orgasm I've ever had?"

Not wrong, just not right. "You don't have to sugar-coat it for me. I'm sorry you had to see me like that."

Audrey rolled over on the bed until she faced him, her little nose only inches from his and a stern expression on her lips. "I'm not sorry and you shouldn't be either. I think you needed it."

"To break down and cry like a baby?"

"There's no shame in tears, Callum, you know that. It's part of the grieving process."

"I wasn't grieving though," he felt he had to point out. The child survived. He'd survived.

"Maybe," she conceded. "But maybe there's a part of you that couldn't hold on to all of that guilt for another second longer? Do you feel better today? Lighter at least?"

Did he? Could Audrey be right about this too. "When did you get so smart, Auds?"

She play-punched him right in the chest. "I've always been this smart. You just mistook it for seriousness."

He captured her wrist in his hand and brought her fingers up to his mouth to kiss each one. "I must have done something right in this fucked up life."

Did she hold her breath? Had he said it wrong? "Why?" she eventually prodded.

"Because you're still here. I'd have run a mile."

"I know you want me to go and I will, but I wanted to make sure you were okay first."

"I'm fine," he said, and she chuckled when she caught his meaning.

"Maybe I'll hang around until you're a bit better than fine?"

"I thought you were due back in The States?"

When the playfulness dimmed from her eyes, intrigue filled him. Did she not want to go back after all? It was her decision to stay, not his.

"You can stay as long as you want, Auds. It's your house."

"What about you?" she replied.

"What about me? I'll still be here. One minor breakdown does not mean I'm ready to face the world."

Audrey rolled her eyes. "That was not a minor breakdown."

Callum shrugged. It wasn't a major one either. He'd had one of those in the field hospital just before being shipped out. He didn't want to talk about it anymore. He had the perfect conversation changer. He ran his hand beneath the sheet to reach for her. She wasn't wearing shorts. His conscience did prick at him. "Are you sure I didn't hurt you?" Dread fell like stone to the pit of his stomach. "The baby?"

Audrey raised a brow but then rolled over him to sit right where he wanted her. As she rose up and lifted her top over her head, she flashed him a smile and gave her arse a wriggle. "You weren't that rough, soldier."

Heat shot straight to his groin at the sight of her beautiful breasts and her hair sparkling in the morning light like spun gold. He filled both hands and grinned back. "I prefer doctor, rather than soldier, thanks."

"What does the doctor order?"

"How about naked until next week?"

Her head lolled back on her shoulders as he ground his erection into her, the barrier of her underwear the only weak link holding him back.

"I like the sound of that," she breathed, covering his hands with her own, prompting him to squeeze harder, showing him how she liked to be touched.

Callum smiled and said, "I'm beginning to feel better than fine already." He closed his mouth around one pebbled nipple in an attempt to convince himself the bullshit he peddled might actually be true.

For Audrey, the next six days were spent in a cocoon of ignorance and pleasure. While she ignored the outside world, he pleasured her. It was a win-win. They weren't exactly naked all the time but they certainly spent every night like that, wrapped in each other's arms until dawn shoved aside the dark.

Audrey began to come to terms with her pregnancy and Callum seemed to warm up into a semblance of his old self.

He joked and laughed and even became playful with her. They ate simple meals so they wouldn't have to go to town, Audrey washed out her clothes rather than shop, and she switched her phone off and left it dead on the kitchen table. Reality was only a step away but it didn't breathe down her neck like it had before. Until Anita and Daniel came to check on them.

"We thought you two might have killed each other," Anita said with a chuckle. It was a Sunday and she and the police officer had the day off.

Audrey shook her head and said with an answering laugh as she flicked the kettle on, "Not yet."

The other woman slapped a piece of paper down on the kitchen bench alongside the newspaper from Adelaide. "I have your ultrasound form and the gossip column. Your limo driver is holding your drop-off address hostage for another million dollars so you're still safe out here but maybe not for much longer. I'm surprised none of the locals have spilled the beans for their own five seconds of fame."

It hadn't occurred to Audrey that anyone would remember she'd come from Jupiter Creek. Probably because she hadn't been there with Mavis for long before she'd gone to America. She was the quiet kid who didn't make friends because her mother was an embarrassment. Once it was outed that Mavis was a raging alcoholic, no one would have been interested anyway. Their only visitor had been Callum and occasionally his mates. Audrey wondered if her mother had been outed as a lesbian all those years ago, if they would have been run out of town. Probably.

"It doesn't matter," she replied. "I'll have to go back soon." She'd been lying to herself by thinking she could stay in this imperfect bubble with her imperfect soldier for much longer. She had to face the music with Fabien, check in with Tinka and look to what she would do in the coming months. She did have one contract in limbo for a few cameo appearances on a sitcom. They were due to start recording around May.

Her hands flattened across her stomach. Would she be showing by then? She felt fine. Great even. Those few days of her stomach being unsettled probably had more to do with kicking the booze than morning sickness. That was Callum's official diagnosis anyway. Her boobs were a little tender but they were also well loved of late. She hoped they got bigger so she could sport a proper killer cleavage rather than rely on push up bras. She hoped it was a girl. A daughter with her own eyes and nose but without a freckle to her features. At least a dozen more had shown up across Audrey's nose as her skin darkened with a natural tan.

Anita prattled on. "I've booked you in for your ultrasound at the hospital in Murray Bridge tomorrow morning. I hope you don't mind. I thought you'd like a dating scan sooner rather than later and they had a cancellation."

"You mean I'll be able to see the baby?" Hope flared to life in her chest and made her feel as light as a feather.

Anita laughed. "You might be able to make out a jellybean type shape with a heartbeat in the middle?"

"It's that small?"

"Yep. That small."

She was quiet as she made tea, the men already cradling cold beers at the back table. Audrey could see Callum through the kitchen window and while he didn't look happy, he also didn't look murderous. A good start. Daniel said something and then laughed like it was hilarious. The edges of Callum's lips lifted but then he swigged from his bottle to hide it.

"You and Daniel seem to be getting along better," Audrey commented.

"Better than two vipers trying to off each other maybe."

"What's the deal with you two?"

Anita sipped her tea, her cheeks blazing. After putting her cup back down, she said, "We went out, we had sex, he didn't call."

"Did he say he would?" In her LaLa world, one-night stands happened more often than relationships so the after-sex-call rarely ever followed.

Another sip of tea.

"Anita? There has to be more to the story than that?"

The nurse took her tea and fell into a sofa. "There is more but it's so embarrassing."

"I won't tell a soul, I promise. Distract me with the details, please?"

Anita's eyes went wide. "Distract you? You're the one doing the war hero built like a brick shit house and you want the inner workings of my boring life? I was hoping to live vicariously through you since you're having more sex than I ever will."

Audrey didn't bother denying anything. After Callum's minor breakdown, Anita and Daniel had to help her lift him from the bathroom floor wearing only his t-shirt and ripped shorts. Take away the seriousness of that situation and it would have looked like he was the victim and she a man-eater.

She threw the other woman a bone. "Let's just say it's a good thing I'm already pregnant." They hadn't bothered with a condom this last week, giving over instead to a deeper level of pleasure that could only come without the layer of latex between them. Skin to skin had taken it all up a notch. God, it was good. Better than good. Worlds away from just *fine*.

"So, have you decided what you're going to do?"

Audrey dropped her gaze to her hands in her lap. "I want to stay."

Anita clapped. "That's great! What did Callum say?"

"Sshh. I haven't told him because it's not going to happen."

A frown followed. "I don't get it. If you want to stay, then stay."

"It's not that easy." Audrey stood up to pace the room. "I have commitments back home, a baby to consider, a career to put on hold."

"Go clear it all up and then come back. I don't hear where the hard part fits."

Audrey huffed and stared right back at Anita. "He doesn't want me to stay."

A four-letter word fell from Anita's lips. "I've never seen Callum so...so...not unhappy. I don't think he has it in him to look truly ecstatic but with you here, he's almost a little better. More human."

That's what he'd said. *Make me human.* But he'd been hurting, so bad. Audrey remembered his words from earlier that morning a week ago, before the proverbial had well and truly hit the fan. He'd wanted to lock the outside world away and just have fun. They'd done that. It had to come to an end. He was better. He was on his way to being nearly whole. They all knew it.

"Callum needs time on his own to deal with the rest of his demons."

Anita scoffed. "He needs a good woman to bring him around. His demons are all in his head and day by day you're helping him to get rid of them."

This time it was Audrey who scoffed and then muttered a four-letter word. "What about *my* demons? I have to go back and face them too."

"Do you though?" Anita paused for effect. "I've been doing some reading and it seems Hollywood has already painted you as the wronged party. Your publicist must be in damage control because you're the darling and that Fabien arsehole is coming out smelling like a pile of horse shit."

"What does it say exactly?"

"Three days ago a headline appeared on one of those women's mag sites that you're pregnant with his babies."

"Babies? Plural?" She was going to be sick.

"According to that smarmy journo, you're having twins. Twins always heightens the sympathy with an unscheduled pregnancy."

"How much of this crap do you read?" Audrey had to ask.

"As much as I can. Night shift is boring. Most of the time anyway..." Anita trailed off and her cheeks grew red again.

Realisation dawned and the subject changed again. "Surely you and Daniel didn't... At the hospital? While you were working?"

Anita nodded and fell back against the cushions fanning herself with her free hand.

Laughter rang out in a house that was long overdue for some merriment.

Thirty

S tudying the drops of condensation as they rolled from the neck of his brown beer bottle to the edge of the half peeled green sticker was easier than meeting the eyes of the one guy who was sort of his only friend in this world.

The past week had gone from one of the worst of his life to fucking fantastic but with each tick of the clock, he knew it was going to come crashing down. He was holding on, but just barely.

Daniel's quiet voice reached to him across the table. "Are you sure you're okay, man? You're extra broody and while it might turn the chicks on, it's working the opposite for me."

Finally Callum found the words he'd been trying to find. "How do you do deal with the bullshit?"

"What bullshit in particular?" came back.

"I know you've seen some shit, bad shit, how do you sleep at night?"

Daniel shrugged the question off while he drew a long gulp from his bottle. "I don't have trouble sleeping if that's what you're asking. Not from the job anyway."

"Do you just switch it off?" Callum was confused by the nonchalance from the cop. Surely he had to know what it took for Callum to broach the subject? Unless he didn't want to talk about it and was about to tell him to piss off out of it.

"I'll tell you honestly but you can't ever bring it up, not later, not ever." Daniel tipped his beer bottle in Callum's direction as he spoke and then looked around to make sure the women weren't on their way out. "I just make sure I'm never alone at night."

"As in you're scared of the dark?"

"Don't be stupid," Daniel barked a laugh. "If I'm thinking about sex, I'm not thinking about mangled bodies in the wrecks of cars. If I'm holding onto a pair of magnificent tits all night, I sleep like the dead."

Callum stared at him for all of a few seconds and then said, "You're full of shit. If you don't want to talk about it, you don't have to. I just wanted to know... Don't worry about it."

Two hands raised in the sign of surrender across the table. "I'm being serious, man. When I'm on my own, I can't sleep at all. I can barely close my eyes. Our torments might wear different forms but anyone in the line of work we are can't be normal, functioning people. They should tell us that before we sign up, arseholes they are."

"What about when you're between girlfriends?"

"Doesn't happen often."

"You're lucky then." The answer wasn't that simple for Callum. He had nightmares. Sometimes he didn't know whether he was awake or asleep, it was all so real. He hadn't had any this week but he was drained from the episode they referred to as the breakdown. It wasn't even close to that. He thought of it more as opening the lid to the bottle where he'd tried to shovel everything he didn't want to deal with. What had happened was like the hiss of the escaped gases from said bottle. Like fizzy drink when you half opened the lid to make sure the rest didn't bubble up and spill free. The rest was still inside somewhere waiting to come out. Some days he felt like he'd been shaken up, other's he was happy. Audrey was making him happy.

Another question spilled from his mouth. "How dumb would I be to ask Audrey to stay here with me?"

The beer was stuck halfway to Daniel's mouth which was open like a gaping carp. "You fucking what? I knew you two were doing it but I didn't know it was serious. I thought it was like holiday sex. A fling to pass the time."

Not for him. "Do you think that's what it is to her?"

"I don't know her," Daniel replied. "What does your gut tell you?"

"The same as it always has with Audrey. That she's trouble wrapped up with pretty paper and a sexy ribbon. She's just as messed up as I am."

"But she's here isn't she? Letting someone like you screw her brains out?"

He knew what the *someone like you* was for but Callum still growled his next words. "Be careful."

The two hands sprang back into the air. "You know what I mean. She's so far above you in the pecking order. She's rich, she's beautiful, she's successful. What would a rich, beautiful, successful woman do around here? She'd be bored out of her brain in seconds. It's why she left in the first place isn't it?"

"Who told you that?"

Daniel's gaze shifted to a passing boat on the water. "Anita told me a few things after Audrey first got here."

"I thought Anita hated your guts?"

"Some days she hates me, some days she loves me. It's complicated."

Callum's eyebrows rose and his chin dropped. "But she's...she's...always ranting and raving. How did you..? Never mind. I don't want to know."

This time it was Daniel who lifted a brow. "You're always raving too but we don't hold it against you in the long term."

"Can you give me some helpful advice for fucks sake?"

Leaning forward in his chair, he was all seriousness as he said, "Let it go. Have your fun and then say goodbye. You're worlds apart. She lives in LA and you live out the back of nowhere. She has friends in high places, you have no friends apart from me. She'd stay because you're broken and she wants to fix you but then she'd resent you and the small town ways around here. You'd end up worse off. Let her go back to her life."

As much as Callum wanted to get up and punch the man, Daniel was right about most of it. Except that Audrey was broken too. Callum had been forced to face one aspect of his fucked-up existence and with the arrest of her home invader, so had Audrey. But what about the other stuff? Her affair and resulting pregnancy? His nightmares and guilt? It all seemed to melt away when they were together.

How much of it would come rushing back when they parted?

Dinner was made up of sprouting potatoes, five sausages and an onion that Callum fried all together on the barbecue. The flavours brought back so many memories of hot nights on the river when the barbie was the only way to eat, straight off the hot plate so there were no dishes to wash.

But Audrey wasn't eleven anymore. She ate off dishes now and they had to be washed. She stood at the sink where she'd been doing nothing more than washing the same invisible grease mark from the same already sparkling plate. The soap bubbles in her vision blurred until she didn't even know what she was doing anymore. Her mind was a riot of thoughts and as yet unspoken words. After her chat with Anita, Audrey had charged her phone and called her agent. They were in crisis control and the pregnancy had to be leaked in order to make her image shine rather than stick her in the poo with the other marriage destroying wannabes.

They were spinning the 'director seduces young actress with the promise of bigger parts and better money' angle. Making Audrey out to be some airhead who didn't see it coming. She certainly didn't see it coming but knew they couldn't tell the real story. If she started up with stories about being drugged and raped, the media would go into overdrive and the stories would be wild and inaccurate. Only Fabien knew the real truth about that night and she was in no hurry to be set straight on the details. She shuddered.

All Audrey had to worry about was the baby inside her. Over the last few soul-searching days, she'd come to the decision that whatever this baby needed, she was going to give it. If she managed her money well, it would last her years. She had a roof over her head. She only needed a car and food on the table. In her mind it was all so simple. Her career would wait. Hollywood would still be there in a few years and they'd still remember her name.

Footsteps sounded behind her and strong arms crept around her middle, hands resting against the flat of her belly, a heavy chin coming to land on her shoulder. "You've been washing that same plate for ten minutes. You okay?"

Audrey let the porcelain drift to the bottom of the sink and turned in the circle of his arms, her heart in her throat. It was now or never. "We need to talk."

Callum groaned, ignored her, kissed a line down her throat, pushed the strap of her top over her shoulder so he could kiss the skin there too. His voice was muffled when he said, "Tomorrow. I'm busy now."

As hard as it was, Audrey pushed him gently until he was forced to take a step back. "I have an ultrasound tomorrow."

He stopped dead, his arms falling to his sides. "You do?"

"Anita organised it. A dating scan I think she said. I have to go to Murray Bridge."

"I'll drive you," he offered. But there was something off. She didn't have to be an expert at body language to see he'd stiffened and the pulse at his neck flickered an uneven rhythm.

"That's not what I want to talk about."

"Should I sit down?" Callum joked half-heartedly.

"I want to stay," Audrey blurted out. Damn. She was going to prod him on his feelings first, if he still wanted her to go. "It's my house and I want to stay. Here. In my house."

Silence descended for a full minute, only his heavy breath sounded over her much shallower, lighter intakes of air that suddenly seemed too fraught, too tense, too thick.

"For how long?"

"I don't know. A while. A long while maybe."

His jaw ticked, his arms crossed over his chest. "Where does that leave me?"

"I..." she began but then stopped. Audrey had a feeling a line was about to be crossed and she wasn't sure there was any going back if she said what she wanted to. It was crazy. He was going to laugh his ass off and then head back to his houseboat, throw off the lines and leave her there just as she'd come, alone, frightened, scared of her own shadow.

When she didn't say anything at all, just cowered in the corner of the kitchen, he jumped in. "Do you want me to leave? You say the word and I'm gone, Auds. I didn't need pity or charity from Mavis and I don't need it from you."

That spurred her into action, her spine straightening. "I doubt that's why Mavis let you stay all those years, dumb-ass, and it won't be the reason I want you here either."

"Just spit it out, woman. You're killing me."

Now or never. "How would you feel about raising another man's baby as your own? How would you feel about us exploring whatever it is that burns between us? God, that sounds as corny as all hell."

In her peripheral, as she stared at her toes, came her tortured soldier. He did that thing she secretly liked, where he gripped her chin in his oh-so-capable fingers and forced her to meet his gaze.

"Why didn't you fucking say so?" he said. "I thought you were giving me the boot."

Audrey tried to shake her head. "What man in his right mind would take me on let alone a baby too? I was worried *you'd* give *me* the boot."

He cupped both sides of her neck in his palms and kissed her before saying, "Baby, I'm not in my right mind, you should know that by now. I was trying to think of a way to get you to stay but Daniel told me I was out of my mind to even try."

"There's nothing for me in America while I'm pregnant and knee deep in scandal. Besides, I want to raise this baby here in Australia, away from the paparazzi and their cameras. I'm going to shelter her for as long as I can."

"What about your movies?"

Two weeks ago Audrey was desperate to get back to the silver screen, desperate to sort herself out and rise again. But so much had happened. She could never go back to her apartment knowing how easy it was for her privacy to be invaded like it had been. She could never work with Fabien or his network. She would never let that man near her child. Jupiter Creek was about as far away as she could get and it's where she wanted to stay. She'd give her baby a stable life filled with love and laughter. Make right the things her own mother had got so wrong.

Judging by Callum's reaction, this baby might be able to heal them both and give them a new chance at life. It was like the last puzzle piece fitted perfectly and the jumbled picture of her life came into focus. When he kissed her, she kissed him back despite her smile and happy tears.

Callum's fingers drifted to the hem of her shorts as he whispered, "Let's celebrate," in her ear.

The button came off and bounced across the floor causing Audrey to laugh out loud. "Right after the ultrasound I need to shop for clothes."

"That's tomorrow," he told her between open-mouthed kisses. "You won't need clothes tonight."

For the first time in a long time, Audrey looked forward to tomorrow rather than dreading the night and what followed. For the first time in a long time, hope lodged in her chest, warm and full, and refused to be moved...

Thirty-One

A s perfect as Wednesday had been, Thursday was the complete opposite. Callum woke early, wrapped right around Audrey, completely in the moment and not worried he'd woken in a desert hospital with limbs missing. The last week hadn't been a delirious, feverish dream.

By eight am, the temperature was a cooking thirty-four degrees Celsius and the threat of a thunderstorm loomed on the horizon as he ushered Audrey into the shower so they weren't late. There was quite a summer storm brewing and he hoped they could make Murray Bridge and back before it hit. Dry heat he could handle, humidity he hated. Lightning strikes that came before the rain were especially dangerous after drought and heat. One bolt hitting the ground could start a fast-moving grass fire which would be fanned by the strengthening winds and burn through crops almost ready for harvest.

Instead of excitement, Callum was nervous. Nervous about the day, the week, the month. He hadn't had anything to look forward to in so long, it was terrifying. Every time he did try to grasp onto any goodness that came his way, it usually all turned to shit. He wanted to this to be different. So different.

When Audrey emerged from the shower, no steam in her wake, he wondered if she'd just had it cold. Her towel was wrapped tight, another on her head, but it was the brightness of her eyes that told him something was off.

"You okay, Auds?"

Tapping a finger to her bottom lip, she didn't answer right away. "I'm a little nauseous but that's a good thing, right?"

The poptarts he had in the toaster bounced before he could answer. He put them on a plate and rounded the kitchen counter. "Probably just morning sickness. You just need some food in your stomach is all."

Her other hand moved to her belly where she rubbed a palm over the terry towelling. "Probably."

"You want a poptart?" he offered.

"Definitely not," she said with a laugh and then headed for the bedroom.

Half an hour later they were on their way. The silence was almost as heavy as the heat as Callum tried to get the air conditioner to a better temperature in the ute. Small talk came and went in the way of, "Geez, it's hotter than hell." And, "I think we'll take the ferry."

He didn't get much of a reply, but then he didn't expect to. Audrey was off in a world of her own and he didn't blame her. Shit was about to get real. It was one thing to know you were pregnant, probably a whole different matter to actually see it with your own eyes.

He left her to her thoughts and concentrated on the road, the wind whipping up a few small obstacles in the form of tumbleweeds and gum tree leaves hanging on to the tiniest of twigs.

When he pulled into wait for the ferry, flashing red and blue lights stopped him short. He rolled his window down and waited for the officer to let him know what was going on. Daniel beat the other constable to them.

"Good morning beautiful people," he said, his shiny aviators reflecting Audrey's brilliant smile.

"Good morning, Daniel," she bounced back, pushing her own sunglasses to the top of her head.

Callum grunted a greeting. He didn't like the way his supposed friend stared at Audrey like she was a new toy fit for a bored dog. They had to get moving. He nodded towards the river. "What's going on?"

Daniel sighed. "Bloody tourist didn't put his car into park on the other side and rolled right into the drink."

Callum shifted in his seat, went to unbuckle his belt. "Everyone okay?"

"Yeah. His window was down so he just climbed out and walked to shore. Now we have to wait for a crane from Adelaide to come round to the Bridge and then back to get him out. He better bloody hurry too. If the current picks up, the car could drift anywhere."

Callum was about to ask if anyone had tied it off to try to stop that when an attractive blonde stuck her head over Daniel's shoulder and waved. "Hi there," she said, her accent close to Audrey's and definitely not Australian.

Callum grunted the same greeting he'd given Daniel.

The blonde ignored him, ducked around a bewildered Daniel and poked her head into the cabin. "Audrey, you got a minute, I really need to talk to you."

"What the?..."Audrey muttered. "Where's your camera, Barb? Got it behind your back?" There was enough acid in the words to know these two had history.

Callum turned in his seat to see Audrey pull her sunglasses back onto her face, slide down in the seat and put her hands up to protect herself.

The blonde just said, "I really have to talk to you, woman to woman."

"No you don't," Audrey shot back. "You just want your photos so you can make up a headline and rake in the cash. Piss off."

Callum didn't let 'Barb' get another word in. "We'll go around, thanks, Daniel." He didn't even wait for the blonde to step back before he threw the ute into reverse and headed back for the main street with a spray of gravel kicking up behind.

"Reporter friend of yours?" he asked. He'd forgotten about the limo driver selling his story to the media. He guessed they should have been more careful.

"She's no friend of mine. They're like parasites, only worse. They hang around and wait for you to mess up and even if you don't, they still tell the world you did."

He waited a moment before asking another question. "Is this going to be a problem? Them knowing where you are?"

Audrey shrugged but she was tense. "I guess they were going to find out sooner or later. She'll get bored and move on eventually."

"You know this one personally?"

Did she what. Audrey had tangled with the toughest of TMZ's reporters and Barb made all of them look like girl scouts. She was more of a rogue reporter, a freelancer who answered only to herself and made a killing selling to the highest bidder. Which, unfortunately, hadn't been Audrey.

"Auds?" Callum prompted gently.

"Middle of last year I was at this party in New York. The day had been hot and long and I was dehydrated, hadn't eaten in hours, lost my better judgement to a few glasses of champagne and wound up heaving out back of the club." It wasn't the only time the paparazzi had caught her losing her lunch lately though.

"Was this before the home invasion?"

"Yeah. God, I felt so dumb the next morning, worse when Barb emailed me the pictures along with a three-hundred-thousand dollar price tag. When I refused to pay, she sold them to Entertainment News."

From the corner of her eye, she noticed Callum's knuckles turn white on the steering wheel. "That's extortion, Auds. Have her charged."

If only. They'd all be locked up where they couldn't hide behind bushes and in bathroom stalls. "It's more like an auction. It's a fine line between having the pictures for sale and holding them for ransom."

"I wonder why she followed you all the way here?"

Audrey went back to staring out the window, grateful for a ten-minute change of subject, and then muttered, "I don't."

She had so much more to worry about than if Barb had more photos of her throwing up or without her makeup or eating a hot dog. She was about to meet her baby. Nothing else could be more important. Nothing would overshadow that.

Thirty-Two

♥

*S*tupid, stupid, stupid.

What the hell had happened to her, Audrey asked herself an hour later as she stared at a black and white monitor while the carefully constructed puzzle she'd assembled for her life burst to pieces around her.

Callum's grip on her hand turned harsh and unyielding as he asked, "What did you say."

The sonographer had begun her hunt for the baby's heartbeat but after a few moments, said Audrey might have to drink more fluids to get a better picture. She then excused herself from the room only to be replaced by a doctor wearing a white lab coat.

He'd introduced himself but Audrey didn't catch his name. Something was wrong. He placed the ultrasound thingo against her abdomen, clicked a few buttons on a keyboard and then wiped up the gel.

"I'm so sorry to have to tell you this but there's no heartbeat there. I'm sorry."

Audrey unplugged her tongue from the roof of her mouth and said, "Maybe it's too early? I'm only about ten weeks."

The doctor shook his head. The look he gave her was probably meant to placate but the impotence of pity settled behind his thick glasses instead. "It looks like the embryo didn't implant in your uterus the right way. You should have had a period to flush the egg from your system naturally but your HCG is still high and it's holding in there. We'll have to do a D&C to clear your system."

A single tear rolled down her cheek as she closed her eyes, numbness settling in. Why had she let herself get excited? She knew better than to pin everything on hope.

Callum let go of her hand and rose out of the hard, plastic chair. "Check again," he growled.

"It's not going to change anything," the doctor said, his tone finally placating, empathetic. "These things happen and while we don't know why, Audrey's uterus looks healthy and she's young. You'll conceive again."

It's not going to change anything. Wrong. It changed everything.

Words floated around her like a living nightmare but she tuned them out.

In her mind she kept seeing a blonde-haired little girl, curls at the ends of each pigtail, her skin tanned from the Aussie sun and wet from a swim in the river with her daddy. They'd play on the grass until it was time to barbecue fish for dinner. When she was too exhausted to play another minute, Audrey would put her to bed and then spend a night under the stars with Callum at her side.

They were supposed to be happy. A happy family. She'd wanted it so bad.

But now what were they?

"Audrey?" he asked, quiet, contemplative.

"Yeah?"

"You have to sign the surgery release."

Another tear rolled down her cheek and she wiped it away. "Do I have to do this now?"

"It's better done right away," the doctor interjected. He was different than the other guy. She hadn't noticed him enter the room.

Audrey signed her name slowly.

"I'm going to need some health information from you," he said, checking boxes as she gave her monosyllable answers.

She couldn't even meet Callum's eyes. When he tried to take her hand, she squeezed her fists so tight, she must have left half-moons on her palms.

The nurse came to take her to change into a paper gown and get ready for the surgery and Callum was sent to the waiting room.

"I'm a doctor, why can't I be there with her," he pleaded.

The nurse shook her head and tsked. "You're too close to the situation. Family can't come into theatre and you know that."

"I'm not family. We're just...just..." he trailed off and finally Audrey met his gaze, his eyes red, his face pale.

"I'll be fine on my own." She didn't mean the words to come out the way they did, so hollow, so final. More like a goodbye than an assurance.

He gave a little nod and Audrey turned to follow the nurse. She heard his footsteps behind her and wasn't surprised when he took her by the elbow and spun her around. He kissed her hard and Audrey just stood there. So numb. Just kind of dead inside.

He cupped her cheeks in his hands and said, "I'll be here when you're finished."

"I have to go," was her only reply.

This was exactly the reason Callum hated hospitals. Death and despair filled the hallways and spilled out into the carpark. It clung to the patients lucky enough to walk out on their own two feet despite them being alive. Time spent in hospital waiting rooms wore even the strongest of men down to just about nothing. Himself included.

Was it wrong that he wasn't completely sorry she'd lost this one? The tiny life would have forever tied her to the son-of-a-bitch who'd taken advantage of her. He was so sorry she was going through what she was, no woman should have to bear it, but they could start fresh. Just the two of them with nothing to stand in the way of their happiness, their plans. She could have *his* babies and they'd be his and hers and he wouldn't have to share.

But he hadn't missed the devastation in Audrey's eyes just before she'd gone down the long corridor. He'd seen it in men who'd lost their friends, their units, their limbs. She looked just as lost as she had that first day she'd arrived, hungover, sick as a dog and just as scared. But he could turn it all around. He'd give her the time she needed to grieve and then he'd show her how great they could be together. They could throw off the ropes and drift down the river for a few months where the world couldn't find them. He was good at hiding. It would be nice to have a friend and lover by his side.

But would it be enough for Audrey? She'd left this place for America and had never looked back until she needed a place to lie low. She'd hated her mum and the drinking but the isolation had eaten at her as well. It got to most everyone in the end.

Audrey was used to nice things, fancy restaurants, being busy. He was happy to bury his head in the sand when she'd said she wanted to stay, happy to ignore the most obvious reasons why she'd hate it soon enough.

He paced the blue linoleum floors for hours until the same nurse wheeled a very pale, exhausted Audrey towards him. Pale was normal, exhausted too, but the pure defeat on her pretty features made his stomach drop.

"She's going to be a little sore for a few days, there'll be some bleeding and cramping which is normal. She may also be a little lightheaded but we've given her an iron shot so she's good to go providing you're going to be staying with her tonight?"

Callum squatted down in front of Audrey and placed a finger under her chin, tilting her head until she was forced to look right at him rather than anywhere but. "I'm not going anywhere."

Thirty-Three

A udrey had once played a character in a mini-series about a mother whose child had gone missing from a playground. She always tried to put herself into a real person's shoes when rehearsing for a part and she'd thought she'd nailed the right mixture of grief and worry.

Nothing could have been further from the truth.

Reading articles and watching documentaries did not prepare you for the awful days after losing a baby. One minute she'd been pregnant and dreaming about what her daughter would look like and the next she was lying on an operating table having her insides sucked out with a gurgling straw.

All the assurances from the doctor that she could try again didn't amount to shit. Callum said all the right things too but even his advice and assurances echoed in her ears and then fell uselessly to the ground at her feet.

Two days passed in a blur of black and white, like all the colour had been sucked out too. She didn't eat much, didn't drink much, didn't talk much. Callum gave her some space but he was worried, she knew that. She was worried too. Second and third thoughts plagued her hour after hour. She had been prepared to give it all up for another human being. For her baby. Now she didn't have to. Now her decisions were once again hers alone to make.

Alone hadn't even factored in, in the last few days. But what about now? Now she didn't have the next eighteen years to think about, to plan for. Now she was alone again. The second thoughts were for her career, the career she had been trying to build since the day she'd landed in the States. The third thoughts were for Callum. Had he truly wanted her to stay or was she a means to the end of his isolation, his boredom? He hadn't talked about moving to the city or any other changes, just living on his houseboat and playing happy families. He was saving her.

Now that the rose-coloured glasses had been shattered, she wondered if that would have been enough? Had it been more blind optimism than realism keeping her feet moving one step after another or did they truly have something she could get up every morning for?

A knock sounded on the other side of her bedroom door but Audrey didn't move. She didn't want to talk. She didn't want lunch. She didn't even want a drink whether it was a cup of tea or a tall glass of vodka. She only wanted to lie still in her mother's bed until the world faded to black and the pain went away.

"Audrey, are you awake?" Callum had tried a few times to coax her out of her misery but she wasn't interested.

"I have to go into town for supplies, do you need anything?"

Only for the last few weeks never to have happened... If she hadn't hopped the plane to run from her demons, she never would have found happiness in Callum's arms. Her career would still be number one on her list of priorities and she likely would have chosen to abort before losing her baby. No one in her professional network would have convinced her to keep it. Her decisions would have been firmly still in her own hands.

Audrey didn't want the feelings of loss, of hopelessness, of defeat. She could have kept going the way she had for a few more years, she was sure. Minus the alcohol of course. The idea of settling down wouldn't have occurred to her, wouldn't have shown any allure whatsoever, if she had have stayed in America.

"I'll be back in a few hours," Callum called. His footsteps beat a rhythm down the hall, the front door slammed shut, his ute roared to life, and then he was gone.

Not even ten minutes had passed before another knock sounded, this time on the front door of the house. Audrey ignored that too. They'd go away eventually. Only, Audrey really had to go to the toilet. Her body hadn't caught up with the lets-lay-here-till-the-world-fades-to-black idea.

She got to her bare feet slowly, the room no longer spinning thanks to the massive doses of iron the doctor had prescribed. The cramps had lessened, the blood thinned out, her baby completely gone like it had never even happened.

As she crossed the living room, the knock sounded again followed by, "I know you're in there, Audrey!"

Barb? Great. The reporter had found her. Maybe if Audrey gave the woman a piece of her mind, she'd go away and never come back. Fat chance of that happening.

Two more steps and Barb knocked harder, louder, called, "I really need to speak to you, Audrey, I have information you'll really be interested in."

"I doubt it," Audrey called back, still intent on leaving the door shut and the nosey bitch on the other side. Why couldn't they just leave her alone? Why couldn't everyone just leave her alone?

She'd made the bathroom threshold before Barb spoke again. "It has to do with Fabien and the night he drugged you."

Audrey couldn't ignore that. She had only told three people about the fact she suspected her producer of drugging her and not one of them would have told any members of the paparazzi. Changing direction mid-stride, Audrey went to the front door and opened it wide.

"What do you mean?" she asked.

"Jeez, Audrey, you look like shit. Are you sick?"

They weren't friends, her and Barb, and they never would be but the pity in the other woman's eyes pricked at her until Audrey had to blink away more useless tears. "You wanna take a picture?"

Barb raised two hands and from one dangled her long-range Canon. "I don't want to take a picture, I want to show you a few."

"I'm really not in the mood for this today, Barb."

"Do you really think I would have come all this way if it wasn't important? I've been in my car for two days waiting for your boyfriend to leave so I could talk to you alone."

Two days? "Did you follow us when we came back through town?"

Barb nodded and when Audrey went to slam the door in her face, she stuck her foot inside just enough to ruin the effect Audrey was going for. "I have proof that Fabien drugged you." The words tumbled out, shaking up an already shaken up Audrey. "If you didn't go with him to his hotel room willingly, you'll let me in. If you did, I'll go, but before you think of lying, he's done this to other women, other actresses."

Numbness gave way to a spark of anger. If Fabien hadn't attacked her that night, she never would have fallen pregnant. None of this would be happening to her, to Callum. They would have had their holiday fling and Audrey would have gone back to the States all dried out and ready for her next part.

Audrey stepped back and said, "Show me."

The spark of anger roared to life until Audrey was beyond furious. The little screen on Barb's camera showed a movie of its own, each frame more damning than the one before. It showed Audrey at the bar, her little black dress not much more than a strip of fabric around her slender middle. The succession of slides showed her leaning her elbows back on the dark timber bar, flashing Fabien a smile as he'd approached to order two drinks. Audrey turning to greet another cast member, Fabien passing his hand over one of the dark liquid drinks before offering her the glass. She was a vodka girl but took the Jack Daniels and Diet Coke because it was there.

"I didn't see anything," Audrey said, wondering of it was a setup on Barb's behalf to be invited in. "No one is going to care that my producer offered me a drink at a cast party."

Barb rolled her eyes. "Look closer," she said before hitting the zoom button.

And there it was. Closure. Falling from Fabien's hand through the tall, clear glass was a white tablet. The picture was clear enough to see from wherever Barb had taken the shots.

"A split second either side and I would have missed it."

"They'll accuse you of photoshopping this," Audrey told her, not wanting to get her hopes up.

The eyeroll came again. "You can't photoshop something still on the camera. It's why I left it on the card. It's why I flew halfway around the world looking for you."

Her heart did a weird little double thump as a thought came to her. "How much do you want?" She had some money put away but it wasn't much. It might not be enough.

"I'm not going to sell it to you."

"Then why are you showing me? How does this help if I can't take it to the police?"

Barb narrowed her eyes and gave her a strange look. "Do you want to take it to the authorities?"

"What do you mean? Of course I do! I would never have gone with him willingly. This one photo will clear my name." Another thought came. "Why haven't you handed it in? You would have heard the whispers about me being a homewrecker and sleeping with the boss for the parts. You could have already cleared my name."

"Or made it worse."

"What are you talking about? How could it get worse?"

"Just tell me one thing, Audrey. Are you coming back to the States or are you staying here? In Australia?"

Yesterday she was staying in Australia. Today changed everything.

Barb didn't wait for a reply. "You're going to have to testify in court. You'll be in the spotlight for months, maybe even a year and it won't be good publicity. Fabien has friends in high places who will back him, they'll claim he'd never done anything like it before. They'll make stuff up about you and if he wins in court, you'll sink even lower than you have in the last few months. Are you ready for that?"

Nowhere could be lower than her current shitty position. Fabien had to pay for what he'd done, what he'd put her through. He'd drugged her, attacked her, not used a condom and then painted her as prostituting for a movie role.

"I want to make him pay." Audrey's vision blurred as tears filled her eyes again. "I'll do whatever it takes."

"Then you can have the pictures, I'll come with you to the police station."

"What's in it for you?" Audrey asked. Reporters like her didn't do anything like this out of the goodness of their cold, black hearts.

"He's a predator. Imagine how many times he's gotten away with it. I just want to nail the bastard the same as you."

Audrey didn't believe it for a second. There was so much more to Barb's words and actions but there was no way she was going to say no to the opportunity to clear her name and get back to her life.

Barb turned off her camera and said, "There's a flight leaving in five hours if you want to be on it."

"I... I'm not sure..." *Callum.* She couldn't leave things the way they were. Could she? Would it be easier if she just left a note and disappeared? No prolonged goodbyes, no hollow promises or empty pleas.

Would he try to talk her out of it or would he pack for her? He'd hated her for destroying his peace in the beginning. When he'd found out who she was, why she was there, he hadn't been thrilled. It wasn't the easiest way but maybe it was for the best?

"What the fuck am I supposed to do now?" Callum sat at a table at the pub with both Anita and Daniel. His beer sat in a tall glass before him but was untouched.

He'd called them and asked them to meet him. Anita was on her lunch break and Daniel was on the evening shift due to start at six. Callum couldn't remember the last time he'd asked for help and here he was three times in as many weeks.

Anita spoke first. "She'd going to need some time to come 'round."

Daniel sighed and then said, "I told you this was going to be bad."

Anita glared, "That's not helpful. I told you so's can't undo what's been done."

Callum reached for the beer but then pulled his hand back. "Nothing can undo any of this. She wanted to stay and raise the baby here but now... Now I don't know what I'm supposed to do."

The glare softened and Anita fixed her attention back on Callum. "Do you still want her to stay?"

Of course he did. The only thing that had changed for him was that Audrey was no longer pregnant. "It's so complicated now. If there was going to be any resentment, it would have been towards that producer guy who started this in the first place. If I ask her to stay and she's miserable, then it's my fault."

"What makes you think she'd be miserable?" Anita asked.

"This isn't the life she wanted."

"She's not sixteen anymore, Callum," Anita reminded him. "She's been out in the big wide world, maybe she's ready to come home and settle down."

Callum shook his head. "I don't think she is."

Daniel finally decided to throw his two cents into the ring. "Why can't you go with her? To the States? It's not like you're doing anything here."

His stomach pitched. Get on a plane? Not to mention the crowds. No way. "I'm not going anywhere."

Anita put her hand over his on the table and leaned in. "How much do you like her, Callum?"

He didn't even hesitate. "A lot."

"Then ask her to stay," she told him. "If she knows how you feel, it will be easier for her to make a decision."

If he knew exactly how he felt, he'd be able to tell her. Damn, he was so confused. In his mind, he only had two options. Fight for her and hope it all went well or let her go. If he fought for her and it all turned to shit, he'd lose her forever. She wasn't in the right headspace now to make any more big moves. He didn't have to specialise in psychiatry to know it could all backfire on him in a heartbeat.

"She wasn't staying for me," he tried to explain. "She was staying for the baby. I don't think I can ask her to give up everything she's worked so hard for."

"Then let her go, man." Daniel had already told him to let her go. He'd tried to listen to his friend then and he heard the words more clearly now. About the only clear thing in his brain was to let her go. It was selfish to want to keep her all to himself, living the kind of life he'd forged. She thrived on the limelight, on the dazzle of Hollywood and the buzz of fame. Even though he'd glimpsed the old Audrey inside her somewhere, the new Audrey was who she wanted to be.

Two weeks spent with him, a veritable hermit, wasn't going to change her any more than a baby would have. After a few months or years, she would have realised how much she missed her American life and she would want to go back to it. It was a place Callum would never fit. If he let her go, he saved them both the heart break. If they made a clean cut now, it would be better. It would.

The drive back to the house seemed to take forever. He paid no attention to the landscape, the setting sun, the pinks and reds and greens on the horizon. He kept both eyes on the road and one thought in his head.

Twenty-four hours ago the three little words he'd been hoping to find had been in the direction of *I love you*. Now he pushed them back into the box and let his brain repeat a different three-word combo.

Let her go.

After the first fifteen minutes of the drive, he'd decided Audrey should make her mind up. He wouldn't sway her either way. He'd give her some time and respect her wishes. He was in the impossibly crappy situation if he asked her to stay and she did and hated it, it was all his fault. If he told her to go, then she'd think he didn't care and he did. He probably cared too much otherwise he wouldn't feel like he was going to throw up. He'd hardened his heart to caring about anyone for so long and then just when he'd opened up enough to let someone in, it all turned to shit just like it always did.

This was the one time in a long time he'd actually hoped like hell for a different outcome.

Callum pulled into the driveway and waited a few minutes after he'd killed the engine. It was time to start pulling Audrey out of her grief but he didn't relish the job. If she was strong enough to do it for him, then he could definitely man up and do it for her. And then, if she was still there with him, he'd tell her his days were better when she filled them with her brightness, her smiles, her laugh. He'd tell her *he* was better when she was in his life. She made him want to hope there was more to his existence than nightmares and guilt. She made him want to be a better man.

The front door was locked when he tried the handle so he fitted his key and let himself in. No lights were on, no dinner cooking, not telly sounds. Maybe she was still in bed?

He thought about knocking but it hadn't worked earlier so he opened the door and took two steps in. The speech he'd come up with died on his tongue. The room was empty.

No mess.

No expensive suitcases.

No Audrey.

Thirty-Four

"I should have waited for Callum," Audrey said under her breath, more to herself than to anyone else.

"Is he the guy you were staying with?" Barb asked, the greedy glint in her eye flashing at the chance of a useable story after all.

"Just a family friend," Audrey explained, tripping over the half-truth. She'd just left him a note. Didn't he deserve more than that? Her subconscious was awake and in full swing and had been since she'd sat in Barb's hire car.

Back at the house it had been easier just to pack and leave, holding onto a no goodbyes stance. It was easier this way. She'd call him in a few weeks and see how he was going, explain it all, apologise. It was just easier this way. There was an urgency to get back and prove Fabien had drugged her, that she hadn't been making it up.

So why did she have to feel so shitty about it now?

Usually because it was wrong.

How would it have helped though? Staying to say she was leaving? He would have felt obligated to convince her to stay even though he had to know it might not work.

The painted white lines on the road flashed by and minute by minute, Audrey began to question her decision to leave without saying goodbye.

What if did work out? What if, even without the baby holding them precariously together, Callum waded through the chaos that clung to her and they found a way to be happy? He'd already shown her he wouldn't run away at the first sign of trouble. She was nothing but trouble and running was his M-O but he'd wanted her to stay. He'd wanted to give a relationship a go with her. Despite the trouble, someone else's baby, her emotional baggage and his.

Finding out the truth about that night with Fabien was important to her and nailing the son-of-a-bitch to the wall was important, but so was Callum.

And she'd just left him a note.

Audrey groaned and cradled her head in her hands. What was she doing? The last six months had been one terrible decision after another. Was she about to make another one? She had such a bad track record in the choices department that she couldn't figure out what was only a little bit bad and what was train-wreck bad.

She only knew that leaving wasn't good. The awful sinking feeling in her stomach wasn't good either. That feeling had all but disappeared when she was with Callum. Even before news of the baby hit her like a sledgehammer, she had been pondering a future with him, wondering if it could ever come to fruition. And then he'd said he wanted her to stay. Had even asked the advice of another guy. Talked about her with a friend.

Those weren't the actions of a guy who was just being nice and saying all the things just because she might want to hear them. She knew him better than that. They had been healing each other, working out ways to survive in a shitty dog-eat-dog world.

And she'd left him a note.

"Audrey, are you all right?" Barb asked.

Was she? Pain and frustration had made her accept the first offer out of Jupiter Creek at sixteen. Pain made her want to run now too. But how long could she keep running in circles? Her career was her success but it wasn't her happiness. Achievement didn't keep her warm at night or safe or happy.

The interior of the car spun in her vision like she'd already hit a whole bottle of vodka and her insides were in turmoil. "You better pull over," Audrey said with another groan.

Dear Callum,

Something came up and I had to head home. Please know you did everything you could for me. Put me down as a lost cause and forget I ever came back into your life.

I'm sorry.

Audrey.

Callum crushed the envelope in his fist and roared like he'd been shot again. The hastily scrawled note on the back of an electricity bill had been waiting for him on the kitchen bench. She may as well have carved his heart out of his chest and written it in his blood.

Forget I ever came back into your life.

How the fuck was he supposed to do that? Why wasn't he ever good enough? He could have really made her happy, he was so sure of it. Leaving without an explanation was what she had done all those years ago. He hadn't suspected she'd do it again. Not now. Not after everything they'd been through lately. And how did she leave? She didn't have a car and he hadn't passed her on the road.

His heart raced as he flipped open his ancient mobile phone and called Daniel. "Did you see Audrey come through town?" he asked without a greeting.

"Nope. She do a runner did she?"

Callum ignored the smart-arse tone and said, "If you see her, pull her over, arrest her, just don't let her leave."

"Mate, if she wants to leave, you can't stop her."

"But you can. She left a note and she shouldn't be flying, not yet. It's a medical emergency."

"You're reaching," Daniel pointed out.

"Just fucking stop her, okay?"

"I'll see what I can do."

There was no way she was running from this. He hadn't done anything proactive since he'd rocked up on Mavis's doorstep with his duffle in his hand. He'd let life slip him by after she'd died, vowing to stay out of the way of the world and not get involved. He'd lost so much already in such a short space of time.

Fuck not getting involved.

Fuck letting her go.

He wouldn't let her get away with it again. He'd track her down and he'd make her see running was no longer an option.

Thirty-Five

♥

What the hell was she doing? As soon as the rental car came to a pause on the gravel shoulder, Audrey exploded from the door and fell to her knees, rocks biting into her flesh. Her entire adult life had been spent trying to erase the past and make a future for herself, a name and a measure of success that was hers and hers alone.

Damn it, she'd been happy! Before the home invasion, before Fabien's attack, before the drinking, she'd started the day with a smile and ended it with contented exhaustion.

How could two weeks with a traumatised soldier living the life of a hermit throw the confusion into a clearer picture? Callum's baggage should make it worse. Callum's nightmares and violence should have had her running for the airport. The miscarriage gave her the chance to start over, to do it differently this time. The camera footage meant she could start on the right foot and clear her name. She had everything she needed to move on. Closure. An explanation into why her mother had acted the way she had. Nothing holding her back. The past had worked itself out and now the future loomed bright and full of possibilities.

Except. Without Callum it was still colourless and dark. Empty. When he kissed her, the world came back into focus. How many times had she felt alone in a room full of people? She didn't feel lonely when she was with him.

Audrey laid her hands against the warm gravel and breathed deep the dust and lingering scents of another Australian summer day. If she went to the airport right now, if she went home to LA, she'd not only be giving up on her home here, she'd be giving up on Callum. He wouldn't forgive her or forget. She'd likely never see him again. Pain bloomed in her chest at the thought.

"Audrey?" Barb called from the car. "We have to get a move on if we're going to make the flight."

As the last rays of light disappeared behind the trees, Audrey knew she wasn't going to make the plane. The damage had probably already been done if Callum had gone home and found the note but she was going to do what she hadn't done in a long time.

She was going to ignore the what ifs and the scenarios where nothing worked out for her and she was going to fight for what she wanted. She was done running. She'd run from her seemingly uncaring mother as a teen. She'd run into the bottom of a bottle after the home invasion and she'd run to Jupiter Creek after her terrible, foggy night with Fabien.

She was done running. Now was the time to stay and fight.

Thirty-Six

♥

It must have been the shortest day of the year and the longest thirty minutes of his life. Callum had thought the fear of being pinned in a helicopter about to catch fire in the middle of a warzone was the worst it could get. You saw your life flash you by. You wondered how you would do it differently if you had your time again. For a little while, you kind of just waited for it to be over. Then when you knew you weren't dying in that second, the fight roared to life inside and he'd done everything he could to save himself and everyone around him.

Now he didn't feel the fear. His past didn't flash by but his future did. A future in which he and Audrey were happy and whole. She'd offered that to him but then had chickened out and fled. He wouldn't let her take it back. He'd find her and tell her she had to follow through. He'd tell he needed her.

Dust picked up behind him and blew through the shadows of the roadside trees and scrub. It was getting dark, windy, desolate. He had to find her even if he had to pull every car over from here to Adelaide.

He rounded a corner too fast, losing traction for a moment but then correcting the car back onto the gravel. He saw the figure almost too late. He slammed both feet down on the brakes and slid to a stop only inches from a gum tree, his front tyre in a ditch and a cloud of dust drying his mouth and obscuring his view.

He erupted from the car but then stopped still. She stood there with her suitcases at her feet and her sunglasses hiding her expression. Now that he was there, he didn't know what to say. Where to start.

He slammed the ute door shut but didn't cross to the other side of the road. It might be better to keep a safe thinking distance.

"I got your note," he said. Kind of lame but he had nothing else. It occurred to him that she might just want to leave. God, how could it all have got so out of hand? They'd both lived three lifetimes of guilt, shame and emotional tsunamis. So much had happened in such a short time.

"I-" She started to say something but he cut her off. He was tired of waiting to hear what she thought first. It never ended well. He wanted her to be very sure of his feelings and his intentions before she shot him down and went on her merry way.

"Hear me out, Auds. I want to make sure it all comes out right."

"You don't have to-"

He shushed her and decided to close the distance. He jogged across the dirt road and came to a stop a few steps away. "You can't leave."

Her mouth opened and he glared until she closed her lips.

"I know you've got so much going on right now and I'm all fucked up and you're all fucked up but we have something real. It might have started as a distraction or a coping mechanism but then it turned into something else. Maybe it was just me, I don't know, but you can't run from it. You can't leave. You said you wanted to stay and you can't just take the words back and write them on a note." Callum raked a hand through his hair and tried to sift through the rest of the mush in his brain. He had to say all the right things or she'd leave and if he thought he'd felt fear before, the concept of her never coming back was enough to bring him to his knees. "I need you, Auds. I need you to keep me in the land of the living. I need you to kiss me and love me and tell me it's going to be more than fine."

Audrey inhaled, dropped her gaze and then lifted it again. She pushed her designer sunnies onto the top of her head and took a step closer, her suitcase dropping to the ground. Elation filled her and emotion threatened to choke her.

She wanted to say, *'What you need is a punch in the head'*. But she didn't. She was as much to blame for the mess as he was. When she'd left the note, she'd thought it was the right thing to do but she was an idiot if she thought she could just walk away from someone like Callum.

"Can I speak now?" she asked. She had to know he was done before it all tumbled from her. If he could lay his cards out for her, she'd do the same. If they both survived that baring of souls, they could survive just about anything.

Callum gave her a terse nod of his head.

"I've always looked for signs from the universe. Always taken my cue from the people around me. After you left today, Barb came with the evidence we need to have Fabien charged. I thought it was a sign that I could start over. Go home and pretend none of it ever happened. That you'd be better off without me..."

"So you left me a note? You didn't think I'd come after you?"

"Two broken halves don't always make a whole, Callum. Every time it starts looking up for us, something happens to make it all crash down. I tried so hard not to still love you. You're so broken and different, but right down deep inside you're still you and even though all the time had passed, the distance, the crap, I have this spot in my heart for you and it's never gone away. I don't think it ever will."

"Then why did you go?"

She ignored his questions and forged ahead. "What if all we have is the past twelve years of our crappy lives slamming into us head on? You said it yourself, we have so much baggage. What if together, we're just too far gone?"

Callum shook his head and put his hands on her hips, drawing her forward. "The only time I've felt any hope in my life was with you. I was so lost. You don't even know what too far gone is." He nodded to the space between them. "This is different somehow. I feel right when you're in my arms, Audrey. Better. I'm glad you left when you did all those years ago."

She swallowed hard and tried to work him out through her teary gaze. "You're glad?"

"That kiss on the porch might have been innocent for you but it wasn't for me. A few more months of your angst-ridden teenage presence and I would have jumped you the moment Mavis turned her back."

Dumbstruck was how she felt. "You would?"

"I always loved you too. I just didn't know it until now. I didn't exactly grow up thinking about happy endings, Auds. Neither of us did."

She half hiccupped on a sob. "I was coming back. I thought I could leave you far behind but the further I got, the harder it was. I don't want to run anymore. I don't want to spend one more minute of my life like that."

"So spend it with me."

Her heart jumped and raced. "What are you saying?"

"Let's make a life together. We've wasted so much time already. Marry me and stay by my side forever. I'll keep the dark out and you can keep my feet on the ground. I love you, Audrey, and I won't let you walk out of my life again."

She'd made so many crappy choices and they had all led her full-circle back to the one constant in her life. Back to Callum. And just like that, her forever topsy-turvy world tilted back to right side up as he took her in his arms and kissed her like there would never be anything more important than this one moment in time.

Epilogue

♥

The sun was relentless and the humidity stifling. Hot sand burned the pads of Callum's feet as he yelped and hopped his way to the water's edge.

A teasing *I told you* so sounded from behind him. "I told you to grab your thongs."

He should drop the plastic pail and pull Audrey into the waves to teach her I told you so's didn't help anyone. But she was right. And she had her arms full.

Shaded by a huge, silly umbrella stood his wife. In her arms slept their tiny daughter, her lips puckered on a frown identical to her daddy's. Around them families milled, chatted, made the most of the summer get together. Two years ago when they'd sold everything and said goodbye to Jupiter Creek and all that had held them back, he couldn't imagine they'd be here now. In Brisbane, Queensland. Starting fresh.

Callum had finally conceded to needing to work through his PTSD and had found a support group through Mates4Mates, an incredible organisation helping past and current diggers and their families cope with the fallout of war and everything that came after. He was finally seeing the light and it was all thanks to Audrey.

He still imagined that morning when he woke up and found her in the house. He still thought of all the times he wanted to throw off the lines and leave her far behind. But she always had this pull. He hoped it never faded or grew lax. Mavis would have been proud of her girl. He sure was.

The love of a good woman might not be enough for every tortured soul but it was enough for Callum. More than enough.

Now they never had to be alone ever again. Two broken halves coming together to make a whole.

Author's Note

♥

If you or someone you know is struggling with past or present trauma, please reach out for help. You don't have to do it alone. The resources are all around you, you only have to ask...

I first had the idea for this book after attempting to write a Mills and Boon. I was going to call it – A Hero on a Houseboat. Audrey was going to be that washed up actress she is in this version but she was going to hold a shot gun on a well-meaning doctor whose houseboat would break down near her isolated home. She'd be drunker than two skunks and be in desperate need of drying out but it's not enough to just make someone a drinker or an alcoholic. Most people don't just wake up one day and decide they can't stop drinking. It's usually that they don't want to stop drinking and for Audrey, it was numbing the pain and aiding in not having to stand back and really look at her situation. Callum was meant to be a total stranger, stranded and forced by his Hippocratic oath to help someone in need, no backstory, no prior contact between the two.

But then somewhere along the line, the backstory started to weave itself into my head and I started the story anew. Not all parents are angels and not all children are either. What would cause a mother to hold her daughter at arm's length? How much trauma did someone with a 'helper' personality need to experience before he decided nothing was good enough? That everything and everyone was hopeless?

In a world with real life situations and real life post-traumatic-stress-disorder triggers, maybe the happily ever after might never have come for Audrey and Callum, but by the banks of a murky, winding river, beneath towering gums and to the sounds of flocks of corellas, anything can happen if you believe in the magic of new beginnings...